USA TODAY BESTSELLING AUTHOR
MJ FIELDS

Copyright

Copyright © 2024 by MJ Fields
All rights reserved.
Visit my website at
www.mjfieldsbooks.com

No part of this book may be reproduced or transmitted in any form or by any means, electronic or mechanical,
including photocopying, recording, or by any information storage and retrieval system without the written permission of the author, except for the use of brief quotations in a book review.
This book is a work of fiction. Names, characters, places, and incidents either are products of the author's imagination
or are used fictitiously. Any resemblance to actual persons, living or dead, events, or locales is entirely coincidental.

ISBN- 978-1-958804-94-0

Thank You

Thank you to all of these amazing humans
who have helped bring
TAKING FIRST
to life
Photographer- Katie, Cadwallader Photography
Model- Aaron
Cover Designer: Kari March
Editor: Jovana Shirley, Unforeseen Editing
Editor: Kristin, C&D Editing
&
PR: Autumn, Wordsmith Publicity

The Series
EACH BOOK 'FIRMLY' STANDS ALONE

If you love binging a series, this order 'hits it home'

Taking First
Steeling Second
Force at Third
Catching Feels

About Taking First

From USA Today best-selling author MJ Fields, comes a small l town, marriage of convenience, standalone sports romance. This steamy romance will make you blush, *everywhere*.

<u>Whitley</u>

When Pope left our hometown my life changed. When **he came back** and saw his **nemesis' ring on my finger**, I knew he would be angry, but people change, right?
When he found out I had a little girl he demanded I call things off with Kal. He says he refuses to let a man like him raise his child.
I told him she wasn't his, but he still won't back down.

<u>Pope</u>

The last thing I expected when I finally came home was to find out ***my best friend was a single mother*** to a four-year-old little beauty. Especially since that best friend asked me to ***rid her of her virtue*** before I left to play in the minors, nearly five years ago.
She says she's not mine, but I know she belongs to me.

They say all is fair in **love and baseball**, but when **secrets are revealed** and **truths are finally** told, will he fight for a **love he never expected or the game he was born to play?**

Playlist

"In The Stars" by Benson Boone
"How Do I Say Goodbye" by Dean Lewis
"Doxology" by Anthem Lights
"Beautiful Things" by Benson Boone
"Fast Cars" by Tracy Chapman
"Wish You The Best" by Lewis Capaldi
"Have You Ever Seen The Rain" by Creedence Clearwater Revival
"Cop Car" by Sam Hunt

POPE

1

Friday

Exhausted, I step out of the shower, reach for the towel hanging on the hook, run it back and forth over my head a few times to dry off my hair, and realize it needs a good trim. I place the towel back on the hook and head over to the sink to grab my toothbrush.

Glancing down, I notice that my screen is all lit up, no doubt from one of my teammates—probably Tony—who, like me, left the fundraiser a little early, got their date off and out the door, and wants to meet up.

The only place I'm going is to change my sheets and slide in between fresh ones and sleep like a baby.

My phone rings. Toothbrush in my mouth, I blindly hit *accept*.

"Well, shit, rookie, you didn't have to get off her to take my call." Tony chuckles.

I spit the paste into the sink. "What can I do for you?"

"Put your dick away," Turner grumbles.

What the fuck? I think as I look down.

I quickly lift the phone up so they're not eyeballing the goods. "Is there a reason you're video-calling me?"

"Wanted to invite you to Mom's for dinner with some of the team on Sunday. There's going to be a lot of food, man. Homecooked." Tony smiles.

I catch Turner giving a subtle shake of his head, his eyes growing bigger, almost comically, and I remember the last time Tony invited us to his mom's. His entire family was there, like aunts and second cousins, and a huge group of friends. The one o'clock meal ended up being served at four. We sat with them for hours. Any attempt to break away from the onslaught of questions, making the day feel more like an interrogation than a gathering, proved futile. When we finally got called to eat, it was ... not good, and I'm not a picky eater. Obviously, none of us were rude enough to say a damn thing, but you bet your ass that I will never put myself in that situation again without an exit strategy.

"Appreciate the invite, but ..." I pause and try to come up with something—anything—but I can't. I'm a horrible fucking liar.

Turner chimes in, "He's heading home to Texas before the exhibition games in Vegas, remember?"

My stomach knots, and the call ends. The reality is, yeah, I need to head back to Texas soon.

I shoot Turner a text.

ME:
Thank you for the save.

TURNER:
You owe me one.

When I walk out of the bathroom, I see that Mallory hasn't moved an inch. She has her completely bare back facing me, her mass of blonde hair flowing down from the pillow. The woman is gorgeous and knows it. She's also highly career-driven. She's a media specialist who worked for a pro basketball team, the Stallions, before the Mets hired her. Our stance on relationships is the same—neither of us has the time or a desire for a one. We're married to our careers.

The thing about careers is, that you can't fuck them or take them to an event that requires a date. This is exactly why our arrangement has worked. She's aware of the rules—hell, she helped write them six months ago—so the fact that she's still here is disconcerting.

She rolls to her side, facing me, props her head on her hand, and says those four words that can fuck up a good thing. "We need to talk."

I know what's coming, so I cut her to the quick. "Respectfully, please remember that we agreed this wasn't ever going to be more than—"

Laughing, she sits up. "Are you kidding me?"

"You're a great woman, but—"

"Pope." She slides off the bed and walks over to my closet, pulling out one of my jerseys and sliding it over her head.

No. No. Hell no. She's not doing this.

She laughs as she clearly reads my face. "You're settled here, and you have this great home with rooms to fill—"

"Mallory—"

She holds up her hand. "I watched you with those kids at the fundraiser tonight, and it was so obvious you were in your element. You're going to make one hell of a father." I open my mouth to object, but she cuts me off with a quick, "I'm not offering my uterus. I'm trying to tell you that we're both heading to the same place in life, but not together. I'm moving Upstate for a job with the NFL team, the—"

"Knights," I finish for her.

She nods then smiles. "My biological clock is ticking, and you might not hear yours, but you will one day soon." She shimmies her tights on. "Promise me something?"

Completely relieved, I nod. "Sure, Mal."

"Find a woman you see as more than a sexual equal and allow her to love you."

I chuckle. "Not happening anytime soon."

"Make sure she can also be your best friend and then marry her."

"Again, not happening anytime soon."

She slides her heels on, and I can't help but laugh at the fact that she went from evening attire to my jersey, with the same tights and heels, and she still looks put together.

Maybe too put together.

She points to my jersey that she's wearing. "I'm keeping this to add to my collection."

"A player can't hate a player." I wink as I walk over and kiss her cheek.

I toy with the idea of inviting her back if she's still around for the next event, but then I think again. She ended it and pulled the Band-Aid off quickly, too. Although that's not how these things normally work for me, I'm good with it. In fact, I'm elated that it's not messy.

"So, this might be the last time we will be …" Mallory struggles to find the word for what we have going, but in truth, there is really no term for it. We were just Mallory and Pope, hooking up.

"Yeah." I nod as she grabs her bag from the floor where she tossed it earlier. "I wish you the best Upstate."

"Oh, sweetheart, you don't have to," Mallory drawls as

she sashays toward the bedroom door, her hips swaying in that inviting way. "I *am* the best out there."

As I watch Mallory walk out the door, I decide to follow her down the hall. I stop at the landing, grab the railing, and watch her as she walks down the stairs.

"Thanks for tonight," she calls up. "I'm gonna miss that big dick of yours."

There is no respectful way to reply to that, so I go with, "Give them hell."

She blows me a kiss, opens the door, and walks out, closing it behind her.

WITH MALLORY'S UNSOLICITED ADVICE— SPECIFICALLY the *make sure she can also be your best friend and then marry her* part—now living rent-free in my head, I'm lying in bed, logged in to my original Instagram account, the account I had when Mom transferred my dad's phone number to a used phone she'd bought me.

I followed the wrong people, wanting to be liked and accepted like all kids do when trying to fit in. It didn't take long before I was getting DMs, trash-talking my shitty clothes and shoes, our home, and then my mom being a waitress. It was a hit to my already-bruised confidence, but then I got pissed.

After my father's death, we moved to Walton when our time expired to live on base. Mom had chose Walton because my dad's sister, Amy, lived about an hour away, and together, they found probably the only house in Texas that Mom could buy with the life insurance money she'd received.

I unfollowed everyone, yet the DMs didn't stop until I was pulled up to varsity in eighth grade. When I hit a growth spurt in tenth grade and broke every high school baseball record in our entire county, they all stopped.

There's a huge part of me that takes satisfaction in the fact that I have close to five thousand followers on that account. I only follow five people. Three of those people were friends before puberty hit and before my name was on the front page of all the local and regional papers. The fourth is our team captain and our coach's son, who graduated a year before me and pitches for the Sox, Leland Locke, and the fifth is Coach.

I only posted pictures of the scoreboard after every game. Pictures that my best friend had taken.

Whitley Mae Belington—or as she insisted on being called, Whit—was the only girl in my tight-knit group of friends, and she hasn't updated her IG in years, but her old posts are up — her softball team pictures and a few of her and her cousins.

Last time I saw her —or any of them for that matter—was at my mother's funeral. I don't remember much from that week, but thinking back, I do remember how different she looked—stunning. Just as beautiful as the women I've been with over the past few years. You wouldn't have known it when we were younger, since Whit covered it all up under baggy clothes. Except that last night, the night before graduation, which I missed because I had to leave for training camp with the Triple-A team, the Syracuse Mets, in Upstate New York.

There was a bonfire to celebrate graduation and the fact that both the baseball and softball teams took state championships at our friend Danny's hunting cabin. I remember how her brown eyes sparkled under the evening sky. She pulled off the baseball cap and let all those jet-black curls spill over her shoulders, hanging down to her waist. She was wearing cutoff denim shorts, which I'd never seen her wear before. I later found out she'd borrowed them from one of her cousins. She and the girls were dancing to whatever was playing on Danny's speaker system—country, of course—and she was swaying to the rhythm of the music. Not gonna lie, it was shocking to see her that way.

I'm pretty sure my jaw was dusting dirt when our eyes met, and when she laughed, I couldn't help but do the same. She was laughing so hard that her shoulders rocked her long waves all around her—*so much fucking hair*. And those freckles, bridged on her nose and sprinkled on her cheeks, were getting more pronounced, as they did when the summer sun was out. Whit hated them. My thought was always that they were a part of her.

She never tried to be beautiful. Hell, she did her best to hide her beauty. In fact, she was picked on, and just a week before that night, she was told she'd be holding her V-card forever by Sadie, a girl who liked me. Whit made me promise not to touch her, and I assured Whit that her nasty ass wasn't my type. I also remember telling her to hold tight to her innocence, because whoever got to love her was going to be the luckiest prick on the planet.

It was at Danny's party that she told me she wanted it to be me.

When I told her no fucking way, her smile fell. She was the one who had picked up my smile and turned it right-side up so many times, and the fact that I'd done that to her, well, it damn near broke me.

SHE WAS WEARING *those cutoff shorts, a baggy tee, the freckles, and all that fucking hair was down. She stomped her foot and crossed her arms. "So, I'm gonna go to college a virgin because you can't do*

with me what you've done with countless others?" I started to object, but she held up her hand, stopping me. "I'd never let you go out of here like that."

"We're best friends, Whit."

"And that's why—" She stopped and shook her head. "Never mind. I'll just ask—"

"I don't want to hear what undeserving piece of shit you're going to ask to bust your cherry—"

"And I'll never tell," she huffed and began to walk away.

Instinct kicked in, and I grabbed her hand to stop her. She turned and looked up at me, soft eyes full of anger when they caught mine. They changed right in front of me as she quirked her brow in challenge.

"Say please."

Her face screwed up. "What?"

"Say please."

"Fine, please."

"Let's go then."

In the back of my old truck, on a dirt road far enough away from everyone but close enough to see the fire and still hear the music, we awkwardly undressed ourselves.

When I leaned in to kiss her, she pulled back. "Just the sex part."

To say that night is etched in my memory because it was awesome would be a lie. It was quite the opposite.

She gave me the condom she'd brought, making it obvious that this had been planned, but she was pissed when I tried to joke about it. It was a wonder I even stayed hard with how she lay there, stiff as a board.

"You need to relax, or it's going to hurt."

"Pope, just do it already."

"Say ple—"

"Seriously?"

I nodded once.

"Please."

THINGS CHANGED AFTER THAT. We texted once a week for the first couple of months, then just once a month, and then birthdays. Then, Mom got sick. Whit was in nursing school. She noticed Mom had a cough that lingered. Whit was the one who insisted she go to the doctor. The diagnosis? Stage four lung cancer. She never smoked—ever.

I flew home anytime I had more than a day off. When I wasn't there, Whit, Danny, and my aunt stepped up in a big way. The day I got the call that the treatments were no longer working and that hospice was being called in, I left the team to be with her.

That was when I realized Whit and Danny were together.

The Mets took me back, but I played two more years in the minors, and I had just finished my first season with them. I haven't been home since Mom passed, and that was three years ago.

WHEN I WAKE up in the morning, I'm in a foul mood. I blame Mallory and Turner for sending me on that trip down memory lane, but the truth is that I've been putting off things I need to face.

It's the offseason. I have no real plans until the exhibition game in Vegas. There are no more excuses for not going back to Walton to take care of what I left behind.

Taking First

BEHIND THE WHEEL of the rented SUV, I see the sign—*"Welcome to Walton."* I spent from my seventh-grade year until I graduated high school making Walton the only community I lived in for longer than four years since I was born.

Less than a mile down the road, I pass by the First Methodist Church of Walton, a place we spent every Sunday after moving here. The place where I met Whit, who lived with her grandparents. Last I heard, her grandfather is still the pastor, and her grandmother, Mildred, still plays the piano every Sunday and leads the choir that Mom sang in. This should feel like home, yet it doesn't.

Just past the church, I flip on my blinker, pull into the cemetery, and follow the road that leads to the farthest row back, where Mom was laid to rest under the biggest tree on the property, with Dad's ashes inside her casket, just how she wanted it.

I sit in the vehicle for a long while, looking at the flowers in the pots on either side of the headstone. White lilies—Mom's favorites. I feel bad that I wasn't the one to put them there.

Deciding enough is enough, I open the door and step out onto the dirt, pulling my sunglasses down as I walk over to the large headstone with both my parents' names on it. Squatting down, I slide my hand over the smooth marble, etched with their names—*Gregory and Bianca Paul, Beloved parents.*

"Hey, Mom. Hey, Dad. Sorry I haven't been around. Life's been busy. I'm stopping by to tell y'all I finished my first season with the Mets. That wouldn't have happened without either of you. I know you would have been there if you could have. Swear to God, I looked for y'all." I fight back the emotions building up inside. "I miss and love you more than I could ever imagine. Thank you for being my parents. I hope I'm making you proud."

Not knowing what shape the house is in, I make the decision to check into the hotel just outside of town. When the front desk clerk's face catches fire, I know that it's just a matter of time before all of Walton knows I'm back.

I shower, grab the three promised jerseys—one to Ollie, one to Nancy, and the other to Coach Locke—and head back into town.

Pushing open the wooden door of Ollie's, it's like nothing has changed. The jingle of a bell hanging above the entrance still announces your arrival, but at this time of night, it's muffled by the laughter, clinking of glasses, and the Oilers game on the big screen. The chatter of locals fills the air as groups of familiar faces are illuminated by the warm overhead lights. Four kids, probably not old enough to drink, are engaged in a friendly game of pool. In one corner, the old-fashioned dartboard beckons with its well-worn darts and faded markings —Ollie never did put in the machines that require payment to play. Wooden stools line the aged mahogany bar, and behind it is Ollie, who has looked fifty years old since I was a teenager, no doubt talking sports as he uses his white apron to diligently polish glasses. The shelves behind him proudly display an array of liquor bottles, some dusty from lack of use while others gleam from recent popularity. The vintage jukebox in the corner is completely dark, because Ollie always unplugs it when there's a big game on.

My eyes stall on the couple who are sitting so close that she might as well be on his lap. A wave slowly flows through me that is always a prelude to a numbing feeling— a protective instinct I no longer have to call upon because it just happens. Novocain for the soul, anxiety relief when needed. His hand is on her cheek, pushing black curls away from her face and …

What the fuck?

Before I have time to think, I make my way through the bar to that corner and am barely able to stop myself from grabbing Danny's collar and dragging him off his stool.

"Hey, man, got a minute?"

He looks over his shoulder at me, his smile drops, and he sighs out, "*Fuuck.*"

Anger begins to boil inside of me, but that calm wave is still there, too—thank God. "Let's you and I go have a chat."

I head out the back, and he follows.

Once the back door is closed behind us, I ask, "You know what you have coming, yeah?"

"Look, things didn't—"

I jab him quick in the mouth.

"The fuck, Pope!"

Before I can reply, the door flies open, and the brunette walks out and looks at him. "Oh my God, you're bleeding!"

He spits on the ground and wipes his split lower lip.

I push a finger into his chest. "Whit deserves better than this, and you know it."

She throws her hands up. "Are you kidding me?"

I grab the door handle and pull it open. "Handle your shit. I'll be at the bar."

2

Saturday

Walton is a small community, and almost everyone knows everybody's business. It's not always as wonderful as the movies make it out to be. There's no doubt in my mind that Chloe is hating it right now.

"Over to you, Whit." Ruth, the head nurse, looks at me, and without using one single word, gives me an itemized list before patting my shoulder as she walks out the exam room door.

I'm the preacher's granddaughter, and my colleagues seem to believe I can perform miracles, which is what it often takes to get a victim of abuse to press charges, especially when it's against the man she still allows herself to believe loves her.

"How do you feel, Chloe?"

She wraps her arm around her frame and tries to blink a tear away. "I don't know how it got this far or what I did to—"

Instead of reminding her that she came in here in almost the same condition just four months ago, I proceed with the caution she desperately needs and deserves. "Did you ask him to hit you? To blacken your eye, bloody your nose, leave bruises around your neck, sprain your wrist?"

Her eyes dart around as she answers, "Dinner wasn't made. The house was a mess. Sometimes, I'm lazy, and he works hard."

"Chloe," I say softly, "there isn't one excuse you could possibly make for him that would make what he did to you okay."

"My friends, they told me to stay away from him. I didn't listen to them."

I watch her try to hold her emotions in.

"I'm so sorry this happened to you." I reach across the table, carefully observing her eyes as I gently take her hand. She doesn't flinch, so I squeeze it comfortingly. "You need to file an order of protection this time. That way, he will go to jail if he shows up anywhere you decide to go, including work. The officers can get your belongings from his place and—"

"Yes," Chloe states, and it shocks me. Then she looks up at me with a fierceness in her features that wasn't there the last time she sat in our exam room. "He needs to pay for this. I'm not going to let him do this to me, or any other girl, ever again."

"He does. I'm proud of you for being so brave. Let me go make that call and get you a drink. Dr. Pepper?"

Chin held high, she nods.

"I'll be right back."

As soon as the door closes behind me, I take off down the hall to grab my cell phone from the nurses' station. I immediately dial the police department, wanting to make sure that Chloe doesn't have enough time to change her mind.

"This is Whitley Belington. Could you send Officer York to Walton Med Center? We have a victim of domestic violence here who is ready to give a statement, and please tell her to hurry."

After depositing my phone back in my bag, I move to grab Chloe a drink.

"It's a busy day," Laurie, my work bestie/mom, states as I walk into the lounge, heading to the fridge.

"Full moon?" I ask, knowing Laurie fully believes in that theory.

"That's in five days." She sighs. "Chloe pressing charges this time?"

I hold up the can of coke that I grabbed for her. "She is."

"Doing the Lord's work, Whit," she calls after me as I make my way out of the staff lounge.

I head to the computer to find a way to either get Chloe into the women's shelter that I volunteer at in Hawkins, the next town over, or keep her here for the night to give Walton PD enough time to serve his ass.

I shoot off even more emails to shelters in the surrounding area, needing to ensure a spot for her, when I hear Laurie say from behind me, "York's here."

That was fast, I think as I stand. "I'll take her in."

"Thanks, Whit," she says, sitting down and diving into the pile of paperwork on the desk.

Making eye contact with the officer, I nod toward room seventeen. "Thanks for getting here so quickly."

"He needs to learn a lesson. Marks is at the station, waiting for me to give him the call. He'll head right over and arrest Spud's ass."

"I hope Marks's in a piss-poor mood."

York smirks. "Oh, he is."

When we walk in, Chloe is fully dressed.

Shit, I think as I hand her the Dr. Pepper and act like I don't know exactly where this is heading. "Officer York is here to take your statement."

She shakes her head. "I fell."

I feel anger well up inside of me as I see fear in her eyes then spot her cell on the exam table.

"He called you, didn't he?" I ask the question I already know the damn answer to.

"I called him for a ride," she lies as she turns around and walks over to grab her purse.

"Chloe, we can—" I stop when York elbows me and shakes her head.

"Sorry to waste your time." Chloe attempts to walk past me, but I block her.

York grabs my elbow and pulls me out of the way.

As soon as the door closes behind Chloe, I glare at York. "What the eff?"

She rolls her eyes as she taps on her phone then puts it on speaker. "Marks, it's York."

"And here I thought it was Scarlet Davies, confirming our date tonight."

She rolls her eyes. "Charges weren't pressed, but Spud is heading to Walton Med to pick her up. I'm gonna guess he won't pass a breathalyzer."

"Evil genius," I whisper, and she winks at me.

"And I'm gonna guess he has a taillight out." Marks chuckles. "Good work, York."

She ends the call and looks at me. "You secure a safe place for her to stay. I'll take her to get her clothes after Marks cuffs that piece of shit and tosses his ass in the drunk tank."

"I've got a call in at Hawkins. What time is your shift over?" I ask her.

"Eleven. You?"

"Same. Buy you a drink?" I ask.

She nods. "See you in two hours."

I'D LOVE to say the night got better, but …

Walking into Ollie's half an hour late, I spot York and head toward her. Then I stop dead in my tracks when I see her toss her head back in … laughter? York doesn't laugh. Heck, she almost never smiles, hasn't since I can remember.

Shocked, I glance at Charlie, who silently chuckles as he sets a beer on the bar in front of the empty seat next to hers.

Sidling up next to her, I see that she's laughing at Danny, which makes sense—he's a funny guy.

When she reaches across the bar to grab a napkin to literally wipe tears from under her eye, she notices me. "Well, look who we have here, the homewrecker herself."

"Excuse me?" I ask, totally confused.

"Not so much a homewrecker as she is a cockblocker." Danny leans forward, and I see his busted lip.

"Who'd you run your mouth to now?" I ask.

He throws his thumb over his shoulder. "No one. Just this guy teaching me a lesson."

And then a guy on the other side of them, with a full head of messy, thick, dark brown hair, rises from the barstool like a phoenix from the flames. "Hey, Whit."

I try my best not to fully take in John Paul, which is really, *really* difficult since he and I …

We'll just leave it there.

"Pope."

He saunters toward me with a different kind of confidence than I've ever seen in him, wraps his arms around me, and pulls me in for a hug.

And I can't help but laugh.

He looks down at me. "What?"

I step away and look him up and down. "You walk different now."

"I do not," he scoffs, dark blue eyes narrowing slightly.

York points her beer toward him. "Totally do."

Unable to hold back, I look at York. "Oh dang, my mistake. We've seen this before, haven't we?"

She nods to play along, but it's clear she's not following since she was a few grades ahead of us and graduated by then.

I tap my lip in thought as I reflect on John Paul winning prom king and how much he hated it. Regardless of the truth, we relentlessly picked on him about how his walk told a different story. "Oh yeah, that was a major league *promenade*."

Danny busts up laughing, and John Paul rolls his eyes.

I poke him in the chest. "Why does Danny have a busted lip?"

He looks past me and at Danny then back down at me. "You doing good, Whit?"

"I'm good," I assure him and add, "Maybe not major league good, but good just the same."

His lips twitch. He knows I'm dogging on him.

"Charlie, four shots of tequila," Danny says.

After doing the shot, I lean in and glance over at Danny. "Spill it."

"Let's just say we were greeted differently by our buddy, Major League."

Gasping, I glance back at John Paul, who's sitting next to me now, and ask, "You hit him?"

His lips purse together, and the muscles in his jaw flex. He doesn't say a word.

But Danny does. "I was talking to Molly Horner—"

York cuts him off with a gagging noise. "*Ew*, nobody *just* talks to Molly Horner."

She's not wrong.

Danny ignores her and looks at me. "Pope didn't know you and I called things off, and he thought I was stepping out on you."

"Wait—what?" I ask, confused.

Danny narrows his eyes in warning and continues, "I was just about to tell Pope about you and Kal when York walked in."

"What about me?" comes from behind us, and we all turn around to see Kal walking toward us.

The fact that Kal's awake and out here, in town after ten o'clock at night, is shocking. The fact that it's not our night to hang out, even more so.

I turn and smile, "Hey, it's a bit late for you, isn't it?"

He grips my hips and pulls me toward him. "It's never too late to see my girl." Then my fiancé lays a kiss on me … in public.

POPE

3

Saturday to Sunday

"You staying at a hotel instead of with one of us pisses me off almost as much as a fat lip," Danny quips.

I already explained to them that it was for one night, just until I see what needs to be done at Mom's house, and then I'd be staying there.

Marks chuckles as he looks at us in the rearview. "Pisses me off that I didn't get to see him give you a fat lip."

"Gonna piss me off if a picture of me in the back of a patrol car shows up on the internet because you couldn't walk three blocks from the station and drive my rental." I grip the cage between the front and back seat that separates us from Marks and give it a good shake.

"I can see it now, all over the socials—*Superstar MLB Playboy Arrested in His Hometown.*" Danny chuckles. "You'll be pulling in more ass than you were before. Chicks love a bad boy."

"That's horseshit," Marks huffs. "Just as many, if not

more, females wanna get down with a good man. Crazy is overrated."

"Marks, it's not about being a good guy; it's about the cuffs. You get off on crazy just as much as the rest of us," Danny jokes, and that pisses me off.

"That why you broke things off with Whit?" I ask, trying to bite back my annoyance that he fucked up a good thing, and now she's with a piece of shit like Kal Seward.

"You got it all wrong, man. She ditched him for Seward," Marks says as he takes a left.

"How the hell did you let that happen?" I snarl at Danny.

"Didn't we do this earlier?" Danny throws back at me.

I lean back in the seat, trying to control the anger that's been boiling inside me since that asshole laid his lips on Whit. "You went chasing after the girl, so, no, not really."

"Warning you both: if one drop of blood gets on my interior, I'm pinning the next Walton crime on whoever's DNA it matches."

"No one's throwing a punch," Danny tells him then looks at me. "We're square, right?"

I lift a chin, not fully committing, because although I'm not gonna hit him, I'm not sure how square we actually are.

"Kal Seward? How did you guys allow Whit to end up with his ring on her finger?"

Marks hits the turn signal, pulls into the hotel parking lot, and throws it in park in front of the hotel entrance. Then he turns in his seat and looks at me. "You needed to do your thing, Pope, and we understand. We all gave you the space to do that. You did a season in the majors, and we all hung back, cheering you on. You come back here and start dissing our life choices? Nah, man." He opens the door and climbs out.

I glance at Danny, who holds out a fist that I simply look at.

"Bump it."

I do so begrudgingly.

"I'll pick your ass up at seven so you can grab your rental and do whatever you need to do. I get out of work at four. We'll meet up then."

"Yeah, man, yeah."

Marks opens the door for me, and I slide out.

After shutting it behind me, I give as close to an apology as I can muster today. "Not trying to start shit."

"Understood," he says, rounding the front of the patrol car. "You'll get it tomorrow when you inevitably run into Whit and give her shit about that ring." He opens his door and taps the roof of the car. "Go easy on her. She's a single mom and doing the best she can."

I'm not sure what the hell is happening right now, but I'm pretty damn positive I'm on another fucking planet or in an alternate universe because I didn't drink enough to have imagined that Marks just said Whit is a mother.

By the time I wrap my head around the fact that I wasn't hearing things, Marks is rolling out of the parking lot.

I grab my phone from my jacket pocket to give him a call so I can get fucking answers, only to see the damn thing is dead. As I make my way inside, I also realize I don't have the key card for my hotel room. It's in the rental that Marks was supposed to drive me back here in.

I do not want to deal with this shit right now, I think as I pull my phone out of my pocket and see it's dead. I hold it up and show him. "Not possible right now."

Clearly annoyed about this, which, yeah, pisses me off because it's literally why he's here, he grabs another key and codes the card.

Why some people feel the need to give a lesson to everyone around is something I'll never understand. I don't walk into a ballpark and start doling them out unless asked. What happened to, *here you go, have a nice night* ... even though I won't.

Holding the little white envelope out, he arches a brow. "You'll return this and the other, and get the app, right?"

"The amount of these that get misplaced and go unreturned are horrible for the environment."

I'd like to explain to him how the actual phones we're all glued to are probably more harmful to the environment than a key card, but he'd argue that fact. Instead, I pull it out of the sleeve and set it on the counter. "I won't need this, and yeah, I'll do my best."

INSIDE MY ROOM, I realize I don't have a fucking charger because it's in the rental. Frustrated beyond belief, I'm ready to pack my bag and walk back to New York. But I can't because I came to face what I've been putting off. Add the fact that I just found out Whit's a single mom, and that ... that fucks with me on several different levels.

If it's Danny's kid, why'd Marks say she's a single mom and doing the best she can? Why isn't he being a man and stepping up? I know Danny, and a handful of years doesn't change a person that much. To my bones, I know Whit's not Danny's. I also know she's not living with that shitbag who locked up her finger because he asked her to stay with him tonight, which burned deep—really fucking deep.

So who's the asshole who made her a single mother?

Whit went to a local college to get her associate's degree in nursing instead of going with the plan she had in place before I left. That plan? She was going to Arizona

State to play women's softball and work on her degree to become a psychiatrist. The answer to my question—who the father of Whit's kid is—shouldn't be hard to find out. We live in Walton, where everyone knows everyone. She never left. He's gotta be from here.

I go over Marks's words in my head. "We all gave you the space to do that." On top of that, he said, "You come back here and start dissing our life choices?" And his "Nah, man," the answer.

My first thought is how took care of Mom because she insisted I follow *our dream*—Dad's, hers, and mine. Whit, Danny, Marks, Coach, and Leland Locke, they all but forced me to get back in the game.

So, all that and the fact that there was never one word about a kid leads me to believe they're hiding something from me, and I hate that I think I know why.

I SLEPT for shit and wake just as agitated as I was when I last closed my eyes. Instead of lying there, I hit the hotel gym at six and overhear someone mentioning they offer transportation service. I set that up, then call Danny from the lobby, letting him know my phone is dead, that I have a ride and we'll catch up later. Then, I shower and get ready to get some answers, and I know exactly where I need to start.

I time it right by walking into the First Methodist Church of Walton as the opening hymn begins.

"Praise God, from whom all blessings flow; Praise Him, all creatures here below; Praise Him above, ye heav'nly host; Praise Father, Son, and Holy Ghost."

Danny, Whit, Marks, and I were here every Sunday. We'd have to be half dead to get out of attending church.

We came up with ways to entertain ourselves, though. During hymns, we used to watch the Mitchell sisters in their weekly duel, to see who can sing the loudest. Today, it's Hilda.

Even with Whit being five-foot-seven, there's no way to spot her in the front row from here, and clearly, I can't see the child, either. For as long as I've lived in Walton, the second row has belonged to the McKinney family, who sit behind Whit and are all as tall as I am.

When I've settled on waiting it out, pressing down a strong desire to see her, my focus goes in a direction I wish it didn't.

Mom's service was here, and that day, the church was so full of flowers, all different varieties. I remember the mingled scents being so overwhelming that I swore they were stuck in my throat and, at times, choking me.

I was in the front row that day, with Whit on one side, and Danny and Marks on the other. Whit sat closer to me that day than she ever sat before, and she held my hand. At the peak of that feeling—the tightening of my throat and wanting to vomit—she somehow sensed it and gave it a squeeze.

"They're together again, Pope."

And they were. Mom had asked that Dad's urn be placed by her side in the same casket she picked out herself.

"They're with your great-granddad, talking about how much you take after him."

My great-grandfather on Mom's side made it to the minors but was then drafted. Because of that, he never got his shot at the majors. From what I heard, he'd have made it, too.

People say things to comfort you in times of loss, and

you grab hold of them, knowing they're mostly bullshit. But what Whit said next, I knew it to be true.

"They're going to be sitting on the bleachers in heaven and wishing on every fly ball that you make it to the majors."

When I'm at bat, I think of that. Every. Time.

Sitting here, I realize all the ways I got through that day, and it's not with the sorrow I expected; it's with remembrance.

I close my eyes and swear I can still hear Pastor B saying, "Our sister Bianca's heart no longer carries the worry of how she could leave behind the boy who meant the world to her. She knows her earthly family will always open their arms to John Paul. Sister Bianca is no longer in pain. Let us rejoice in her heavenly healing and reunion with her Lord and Savior. Can I get an amen?"

I didn't say *amen* that day with the rest of the congregation but find myself mouthing the word now. *Amen.*

"Before we sing our closing hymn, I need to acknowledge that one of our own is home this Sunday, and no matter how big of a success he's become, he and his ego still fit through the doors of this church. It's nice to see you, son."

Everyone turns, and I lift a hand and smile. "I'm happy to be here with you all."

"I'm sure John Paul has a few minutes for his church family after the service. Let us sing our closing hymn and end in prayer."

AS PASTOR B walks down the center aisle, all the kids follow behind him, as they always have.

Some things never change.

I try to pick out which one of the kids looks like Whit, one that I imagine has freckles bridged across their nose and curly black hair like hers. However, I don't get but a couple seconds to try because I'm immediately surrounded by people of the congregation, being herded into the fellowship hall through the side door.

First to approach are the older women, friends of Mom's. Next, the older men break down where I've messed up on the field and how to improve my game, and then the teenage boys. I try to stay engaged in all the conversations while still attempting to pick Whit's kid out of the crowd of a dozen or so of them surrounding Pastor B.

Getting antsy for answers, I promise the boys I'll stop by the school before returning to New York then head in the direction of the kitchen, knowing that's where Pastor B takes the kids and gives them snacks. On my way, I look around and notice Whit's nowhere to be found, either.

I step in and lean against the doorjamb, watching them all gathered around the massive stainless steel center island.

When he spots me, he laughs. "No matter the age, they always come for the snacks after the service."

Mrs. B walks past him and pats his belly. "And that's gospel."

Then she comes over and hugs me. "Good to have you home, Jonathon. You'd better hurry if you're going to get any snickerdoodles. These little disciples will gobble them up."

"They your favorite, too?" the tallest of the boys asks.

I walk over and grab one. "Always have been."

"Mrs. B makes them every week," another kid states.

"He knows that. He's been coming here since he was just a boy." Pastor B walks over and gives me a hug.

"Pastor B," someone calls from outside the door.

"Still on the clock." He nods toward the door. "We'll catch up."

I nod then take a bite of the cookie. "Delicious, as always."

"You'd better take more now while you can. Once the cookie monster gets in here, they'll all be gone." The tallest of the girls laughs.

"Is that so?" I smile.

"She can put them away like nobody else," the girl in the pink dress says.

"It's overindulgent," one of the boys, who looks awfully familiar, huffs.

"You happen to be related to Coach Locke?" I ask, grabbing two more snickerdoodles off the plate.

He nods. "He's my Popa B."

"Yeah? Who are your parents?"

"Lana's my mom, and my dad's Peter. They're not famous though, so you might not know them. But my uncle is Leland, and he plays pro baseball."

All the kids start hurrying out the door, probably to play games or something, but the Locke kid stays.

I swallow my bite of cookie. "I used to play ball with your uncle."

Then the sweetest little voice I've ever heard comes from behind me. "Hey, mister, you play baseball?"

I turn as a tiny little thing walks toward the stainless-steel island, wearing a ball cap, blue dress, and a scuffed-up tiny pair of white Chuck Taylors. Her eyes are a light brown with specks of gold, and her sweet little face is peppered with freckles.

It takes a few beats for me to respond, but when I do, she's at the cookie platter, grabbing a handful of snickerdoodles.

"I, um, I—"

"You can't take them all," the Locke kid snips at her.

She huffs. "Mommy made me wait so you'd all getta chance to grab some first. Not my fault if you didn't getta 'nuff, and don't go cryin' about it to nobody, neither."

She then looks back at me. "So, do you?"

I watch her throw a whole cookie in her mouth and can't help but chuckle as I nod. "I do."

"Are you my dad?"

Holy shit.

"You gotta stop asking people that," the Locke kid whisper-hisses. "You got God the Father, Nora. You don't need no dad."

Mouth full of cookie she narrows her eyes at him, "My mom told me my daddy plays baseball." She swallows and looks at me. "Well, mister, are you?"

There's no way the first thing I say to this little girl, who could possibly be my daughter, is going to be a lie. "Well, I'm not s—"

"Nora," Whit talks over me as she hurries into the kitchen and beelines it for the little cutie. She immediately snatches her hat off her head. "You can wear this when you get home. Now, scoot your boot out there. They're playing trivia."

She looks between me and her mother, shoves another cookie in her mouth, and then heads out the door. The Locke kid is right behind her, leaving me and Whit alone.

"How old is she?" I ask as Whitley grabs two trays of finger sandwiches.

"Going on five," she answers, heading toward the exit like she's trying to outrun her past, which is precisely what she's doing.

I grab the other two trays. "I gotta ask you, Whitley. Is—"

"You don't have to do any such thing, Jonathon Paul," she cuts me off with a curled-lip response.

"Whit," I hiss, following her.

"This discussion is not happening here."

"The hell it's not," I whisper as I set the trays on the table beside hers.

She turns and glares at me. "Does that little girl look like she only took three minutes on a back road to create? Now, again, not here."

"Never been a man who stepped up to the plate for the first time and hit a grand slam, Whit. Sorry to dis—"

"Everything okay, honey?" Kal fucking Seward interrupts.

"Of course it is." She picks up a quarter square of a cucumber sandwich and hands it to him. "Age-old debate —square or triangle? Pope and I never could see eye to eye on that."

He leans in, and I know that asshole is gonna put his lips on her again, but she leans back.

"We're in the Lord's house, Mr. Seward, not the local bar."

"Or my place." He winks.

Fuck this.

I turn, hell-bent on leaving out the back door, when my eyes catch Nora's, she's looking right at me. The Locke kid elbows her, drawing her attention back to the game.

I look back at Whit, whose brow arches in warning.

I make my exit.

Outside I take in a huge breath then exhale, "Fuuu-uck," as I head over to the cemetery to beg Mom to give me answers.

4

Sunday Night

I knew there would come a day when I'd have to explain Nora to John Paul, and last night, seeing him at Ollie's, I knew it would be soon. But I didn't expect he'd show up at church this morning any more than I thought Nora would ask him if he was her daddy. Even more surprising was the way he reacted to her, and not just the questions he asked, but how he asked them. It was as if he wanted her to be his.

My stomach has been in knots all day because of that.

To make it worse, Kal broke his strict schedule and not only came to church, but also to the house afterward and ended up staying most of the day. Knowing how he is about said schedule, I questioned him. He told me he wanted to spend more time with Nora, to bond, so that when we get married, the transition from Popa B and Gram's house to his place won't be so difficult.

Kal left after dinner, right before Nora's bedtime

routine. Once she had her bath, I tucked her into bed and read her three books.

As I reach over to turn off her bedside lamp, she yawns then says, "I love you, Mommy."

"Love you most, little slugger."

WALKING across the back lot of the church, I see the back porch light on at Pope's place and a fire in the pit. John, Marks, and Danny built it our junior year for Bianca's birthday. She loved sitting out there, making s'mores, chatting about everything from baseball to her Saturday bowling league, or just simply looking at the heavens, even more so when she got sick.

The back door opens, and I hear Danny laugh as he and Pope walk out.

"Should have called me."

"I'm not incapable of turning on the power. I just needed to know where the main power switch was located." He looks from him to the fire and spots me.

"Hey, guys."

"What's up, Whit?" Danny gives me that whole cat-that-ate-the-canary smile of his.

"Saw the fire and thought I'd come check it out."

"Well, I'd love to stay, but that school bell rings awfully early in the morning, and the old man gets pissed when I hit snooze," Danny jokes then turns and lifts an arm in a wave. "Night, folks."

"Night, Danny," I say.

"Thanks, D," Pope says. He walks over and sits in one of the chairs by the fire, opens the cooler next to him, and asks, "Beer or coke?"

"Got Dr. Pepper in there?" I ask as I walk over and sit in the chair closest to his.

"Happen to have one or two." He reaches in, grabs one, pops the tab, and hands it to me.

After he grabs a Dr. Pepper for himself, we sit in silence, watching the flames dance for a little while as I wait for him to speak.

When he doesn't, I look over and find that he's staring at me. "I know you have questions, and I want to give you answers to them."

He turns his ball cap so the brim is no longer covering his face, leans forward, sets his drink on the ground, and rests his elbows on his knees. "I've been back less than two days. On the surface, it seems like nothing's changed, but I gotta tell you, I feel like I've entered The Twilight Zone, Whit."

"I'm sorry, but—"

"How the hell did you end up with Kal fucking Seward's ring on your finger?"

"I needed some legal advice, and he just passed the bar and joined his father's law firm in Denton. We hit it off in a way that made sense."

"Legal advice on a little girl?" he more accuses than asks.

I nod. "Yeah."

"You remember me telling you about the asshole who shoved me in a locker my first day of middle school at Walton, yeah?"

"I do."

"You remember me telling you his name?"

I shake my head. I'm pretty sure he never did because that's something I'd remember. I remember everyone who was ever mean to him. "That was a long time ago."

"It was the man who put his ring on the finger of the

very first friend I made here—you." He scrubs a hand over his face.

"I honestly don't remember that, but he was a kid. People change."

"I was in seventh grade, and he was in eleventh. That's not just a bully move; that's a punk-ass bitch move, Whit."

"He's a good man, John Paul. He wouldn't do something like that now."

"Don't get it twisted. He stopped being a bully to me because, when he was a senior, he sat on the bench while my eighth-grade ass was on the field."

"So what? You want me to give him back the ring and call off the engagement because he was an asshole when we were in seventh grade?"

He huffs, "Maybe I do."

I roll my eyes. "Not your call."

He scowls and leans back in his seat, saying nothing, but his jaw is tense, those muscles popping, and I know he's angry.

"She's not yours."

His head whips around, and he looks at me. "She's five, Whit. You asked me to *rid you* of your virginity before you left for college. You stayed here instead of going. So, I know you weren't with anyone there. She told me her daddy played baseball, asked me if I was—"

"She's Nelly's."

He cocks his head to the side, like he doesn't know who Nelly is and then he has the audacity to ask, "One of your cousins from—"

"One? Pfft."

"You have dozens of cousins and—"

"The one you stuck your dick in right before you stuck it in me."

His head snaps back like I slapped him, and honestly, I

have done just that in my head at least a dozen times since Nelly told me that she and Pope had sex.

"Oh, come on, Whit. You know—"

"You could have told me that you had sex with my cousin, and I would never have *burdened you* with—"

"Let's call her up and straighten this out right now." He pulls his phone from his pocket and tries to hand it to me.

"Can't do that. She died in a car accident two years ago. She had a will, and in it, she named me as the person she wanted to raise Nora."

All the anger leaves his face. "My condolences, truly."

"After she had Nora, we mended what was broken in our relationship. It's not like you and I were a thing, but she knew my plan was always to make you ... *you know* ... before college. The fact that you and she had sex felt like a betrayal."

"Her telling you that about me should have held you back from standing on the edge of assumption, but you just fell into the lie like there was no guardrail." He pokes himself in the chest. "You should have asked me."

"We stopped talking and even messaging, and—"

"Yeah, and now I'm thinking I know why. Whit, that's not on me; that's on you."

"*That's on me?* You were busy; I was busy. That's life."

He stands up, shoves his hands in his pockets, and looks up at the sky.

"Your name was on Nora's birth certificate."

He jerks his head toward me. "Excuse me?"

"I was advised if I wanted to adopt her officially, I'd have to get a lawyer."

"You thought I had a kid for five years and didn't think to tell me?"

Taking First

I shake my head, pull my feet up onto the edge of the seat, and hug my knees.

"Don't do that shit, Whit."

"Do what?"

He points at me. "Curl into yourself and hide when we have things to discuss, and one of those things is going to be the fact that Kal Seward isn't going to raise a kid who has my name." He pokes himself in the chest again. "Mine, not his."

I pop up from my chair and stand toe-to-toe with him. "So, you *did* sleep with Nelly."

He holds up a finger. "One, I told you I never fucked your cousin." Then a second finger. "Two, do I think Nora's mine?" His head bounces up and down like a bobblehead. "Just as much as she is yours."

I throw my hands in the air. "What the hell does that mean?"

"Means Nelly gave you custody, and my name's on her birth certificate, so Nora's just as much mine as she is yours."

"But she's not yours because I—" I snap my mouth shut when I notice his face has gone hard and his eyes are filled with anger.

Teeth clenched, he seethes, "Because I didn't fuck Nelly."

I step back, cross my arms over my chest, and look away. "I don't believe you."

"Whit, clearly, you didn't catch the ball I tossed you earlier, but the minute you want me to prove it, all you have to do is ask nicely."

"What the hell are you talking about?"

He shakes his head as he turns and walks away.

"Where the hell are you going?"

He stops at the side of the back porch then turns and

walks toward me, holds up a hose, and sprays it on the fire, extinguishing it.

After he returns the hose, he says a sharp, "Good night, Whitley," and heads up the stairs of the back porch.

Heck no, I think as I march up behind him, stomping my feet the whole way. He knows damn well I'm following him, but he's completely ignoring me. I keep following him, too, as he walks around, shutting off lights, circling around, locking the back door, and walking to the front.

Standing in front of the open door, he waves his hand for me to go. "I said, good night, Whitley."

Anger boils inside me, and I snap, "When did you start lying to me, Pope, huh?"

In a flash, he steps to me, so close, too close. My steps retreat, and my back's against the wall. His hands slam against the worn wood, one on each side of my head. His nose, centimeters from mine, *almost touching*. His hot breath hits my face, and the smell? Intoxicating whiskey.

"I never fucked your cousin, Whitley Mae Belington." He inhales deeply, and I swallow down the saliva suddenly flooding my mouth. "I told you in God's house, of all places, that no man steps up to the plate for the first time and hits a grand slam. You need me to spell that out for you?"

"I … I think I, uh …" I'm stammering like an idiot because he's Pope, but he's Major League Pope, and he has me in some sort of tizzy.

"My first time up to bat was that night you stomped your damn foot and demanded it. I popped your cherry, Whit, and you busted my *guy-men*. I was never with Nelly in any way. I never let her give me a hand job, blow job, ride my finger, sit on my fa—"

"That's enough." I shove him as anger surges through me.

He doesn't budge. What he does is lean in closer—*real close*. His lips brush against my ear, and he whispers, "Your little dig about me lasting three minutes should have been your first clue as to how inexperienced I was. Now? Now, I could make your thighs shake, your toes curl. Hell, Whit, I could make you temporarily forget your name." A low growl escapes as he pushes off the wall and steps back, fists balling, jaw popping. Sapphire-blue eyes rake over my body as he leans against the opposite wall, checking out my boobs.

I cross my arms over my chest, attempting to hide the fact that my nipples are so hard they'd be able to cut glass. I lose the fight in stopping myself from glancing down at his pants to see if he's affected the same. He is.

Dammit, dammit, dammit.

That's when I notice his keys are hanging out of his jacket pocket, and I realize he's planning to drive. My eyes meet his again, and his nostrils flare.

He swallows hard, and his Adam's apple bobs. Voice thick, deep, *so sexy*, he says, "You let him kiss you at the bar. Gonna guess you and Danny did some of that, too. I was your best friend, Whit, the one you chose to be your first, and you denied me that first kiss, too."

I clear my throat as I push off the wall and square my shoulders. I completely avoid the Danny bit and glare at him. "Kal's my fiancé."

"That's fine. He can be that. What he can't be is Nora's dad when my name is on her birth certificate."

"You son of a—"

"Gonna stop you right there. You're in my mother's home. I don't want that regret to be added to the list of all your others." Again, he waves his hand toward the open door. "One last time, good night, Whitley."

"You, you … asshole!"

He bites back a smile, knowing darn well I don't curse unless highly provoked—and I am that.

"I think the walk home will do you good. Calm you down a bit so that you can get some sleep tonight."

"I highly doubt that, but it'll keep me out of jail."

Passing him, I look up then look him over, as he did to me, but only because a girl needs to do what a girl needs to do to prove she's just as strong as a man.

I'M MORE than halfway back to the house when I hear him slam the door to his rental. I clutch the keys that I snagged from his pocket without him noticing. I might be pissed off at him, but I certainly don't want him to get behind the wheel and drive.

I glance over my shoulder and see him speed-walking toward me. My heart racing, I pick up the pace.

When I hit the back porch steps, my heart in my chest, I take the stairs two at a time. I quickly open the door and walk in the darkened kitchen. I lock up behind me and lean against it in attempt to catch my breath.

"Everything okay over at John Paul's place?" Popa B's voice comes from the hall as he flips on the light.

"Popa B, turn off the light," I demand in a hushed plea.

"Why's that?" he asks as he walks to the sink, opens the cupboard, and pulls out a glass.

"Because—"

Tap, tap, tap.

Popa B looks at me, and I hold my finger to my lips, telling him, "*Shh.*"

"Whitley Mae Belington, I know you're in there. I'd be

much obliged if you opened the door and gave me my keys."

"You took the man's keys?" Popa B asks crossly.

Gram walks in, chuckling. "It's like the two of you are twelve years old again. Now, move aside and let that young man in."

"I'm not giving him his keys. He's been drinking."

"Planned on waiting a full hour more before heading out. But it's forty degrees outside. I'd really appreciate my keys, so I don't catch a cold." Clearly, he heard me.

Gram hip-checks me and opens the door. "You come on in, John Paul. You're always welcome."

He steps inside and smiles at Gram as she gives him a hug. "So good to have you home, son."

"Would you like a drink? Whitley and Nora made it fresh this afternoon when Whitley's friend, Kal, stopped over." Popa B pours him a glass of lemonade without him answering.

"Have a seat, John Paul." Gram insists, then looks at me. "You, too, Whitley Mae."

My blood is boiling at the fact that he still has me all tied up in knots. No, scratch that. *Knots* is too soft of a word to describe how tied up John Paul has had me since I kind of lost my mind, knowing I was losing him to the game that had brought us close from the day I met him. Gram sets the glass of lemonade in front of me, and I wrap my hand around it, welcoming the cold.

"Thank you, Gram."

"Much appreciation, Mrs. B." John Paul gives her that sugary-sweet smile he used to always give, the one that has been missing since he found out about Bianca's illness. It's back and, dear Lord, it's changed.

It's *major league.*

He takes a sip then clears his throat. "Whit's lemonade has always been the best."

"Sure is," Gram agrees.

"Now, what's this about your keys?" Popa B asks.

John Paul slowly turns his head so his eyes are trained on me.

I narrow my eyes. "No one should be drinking and driving."

"Wasn't going to drive until the"—he holds up three fingers, three thick and meaty fingers, fingers that he didn't let Nelly ride—"three drinks were out of my system. Was just gonna sit in the SUV to keep warm."

"Your house's not warm?" Popa B asks him.

"Not yet. Should be by tomorrow. I was gonna head back to the hotel and book the room for another night."

"Nonsense. You'll stay here," Gram insists.

Great, just great.

POPE

5

Monday

I fell asleep with my mind playing ping-pong. One side of the table was a version of myself, wondering what the hell was wrong with me, and the other side was a smug-ass version of me, telling me it's about damn time. I wake hearing the sweetest little voice.

"Why's he smiling like that?"

Whit huff, "Because he's insa—"

"Whitley Mae," Mrs. B cuts her off, "hush your lips."

She smiles at me. "The pastor and I have to head to the big house and spread some gospel. These two both tend to lollygag. See to it they get out the door on time."

I curl up to a seated position. "Mrs. B. Good morning, little lady." I scrub my hands over my hair, knowing it's sticking up all over, as it does when I need a cut. "I'll make sure they're on time."

Nora grins. "Did you get in trouble for that?"

I look around. "I'm guessing no since I have no idea what you're talking about."

"Writing on your arms? I got in trouble for writing on my hand, and it was only a little." She holds her thumb and forefinger less than an inch apart then stretches her arms far apart. "You wrote a bunch."

Whitley halts her steps to the kitchen and turns to look at me.

"I didn't write on my arm. It's called a tattoo."

"Which means he paid someone else to write on his skin." Whit sets a hand on her hip. "Now, why would you do that?"

Nora grabs my hand and attempts to pull me up, and I assist. "Can I pay them to write on my skin?"

"No," Whit says at the same time I say, "Not until you're a legal adult."

Confused, Nora looks between us.

"I'd make sure to listen to your mom, Nora." I stand. "Especially in the morning. If I remember correctly, she's never been a fan of this time of day."

"Things change." Whit glares at me, but the pink in her cheeks nudges a place inside of me that pushes hope out of the dark it's been hiding in.

"They do." I give Nora's hand a squeeze. "I need to fold up this blanket. You think you could help me out?"

She grins and does a little bounce. "Yepper."

"Nora, it's sweet to wanna help, but we need to make breakfast and get you fed, or you'll be late for school."

"Would like some breakfast myself." I give Whit a smile. "Haven't made it to Nan's. She still making those waffles and—"

Nora jumps up and down. "I wanna go, too."

"What do you say, Whit? Could I take you and Nora to breakfast this morning?"

"Yes, yes, yes!" Nora takes off running up the stairs. "I'll brush my teeth and get my bookbag and everything all by myself, like a big girl."

"Wait, Nora. We need to—"

"School still starts at eight thirty?" I ask Whit as I finish folding the blanket.

She crosses her arms and taps her foot against the hardwood floor.

"It's seven. Plenty of time to get there, eat, and get Nora to school on time."

"I'm not sure what game you're playing, but—"

"It's the offseason, Whit," I note, walking past her. "I'm not playing a game. Let me get my keys. I'll grab the vehicle, swing around, and pick you ladies up."

Stepping into the kitchen, I see them hanging on the hook next to hers. Both sets have the key chain Mom gave to Whit, Danny, Marks and I instead of a card for graduation. Mom wasn't a big fan of greeting cards, so she always did something else. Sometimes, it was a trinket, like the key chain, or a handwritten note. She thought cards were impersonal for monumental occasions. She preferred to use her own words, not someone else's. She also thought it was a waste of money. She'd write notes and put them in an envelope, often with a picture inside from a moment that she felt was something to remember.

I grab the keys as I slide my feet into my sneakers and head out.

Whit might not have given birth to Nora, but she looks just like her. Of all the things stuck in my head right now, all the shit I need to unpack, the fact that Whit's a mom and I didn't know fucks with me hard.

Focused on three things—pissing, brushing my teeth, and changing—I enter the house, which I really haven't gotten a chance to take in. Last night, when I decided it was time to face it, the sun had set before I arrived, and it was already dark. Then I was unable to find the breaker that I've flipped dozens of times to allow myself to take it all in.

I PULL into the driveway of the parsonage and hop out as they walk down the front porch stairs.

"You need a special seat, little lady?" I ask, opening the rear passenger door.

"Mommy calls me little slugger, and you can, too. She says I'll need one until I can drive." She rolls her light-brown eyes with little gold flecks in them.

"Gotta make sure you're safe."

Her jaw drops, and she gasps, "That's what Mommy says."

"All right"—Whit hip-checks me to make room for the pink booster seat—"we need to get a move on, or we'll be late."

I step to the front and open her door. "You think Mom needs a special seat?"

Nora laughs. "No, she's super tall."

"All right then, let's get at it."

Once Whit's buckled in, I look in the rearview and see Nora smiling at me. "You ready for waffles, little slugger?"

She gives me two thumbs-up and a huge smile. "Ready!"

Pulling out, I ask. "You ever have Miss Nancy's waffles?"

She shakes her head, little ponytail puffs moving side to side. "Nope."

I look at Whit and give her a you-haven't-taken-Nora-to-Nancy's look because, yeah, that's shocking.

"Nora's not a morning person," Whit explains.

"My bed is just so comfy, and all my stuffies want me to stay with them."

"Stuffies?" I ask.

"My friends."

"Stuffed animals," Whit whispers.

"Can't your stuffies keep each other company while you're at school?" I ask.

"They'll miss me."

"What about your school friends? Don't they miss you?"

"School's for learning. Right, Mommy?" she asks Whit.

Whit gives me a look of warning and answers, "It sure is." Whit then turns in her seat and smiles at Nora. "I'd much rather stay home with you and your stuffies, but we girls have jobs to do, and school's your job, right?"

"Yep, it's my job." Nora grins back and then looks at me. "You got a job, right?"

"Sure do."

"You play baseball *and* have a job?" she asks.

"Baseball *is* my job," I explain. "But before that, I went to school at the Walton Middle and High School with your mom."

"That's the big school right next to my school right?"

"Sure is," I answer.

"Were you friends?" she asks.

"Best friends," I answer.

Her little lips frown.

Feeling like I just stole one of her stuffies, I add, "We didn't become best friends until after we learned to read, write, and do lots of math."

She nods. "'Cause school's for learning."

"Once you learn to read and write, the whole world opens up, and everything changes."

"Like, what kinds of things?"

"The most important kinds of things," I answer as I hit the turn signal to park near Nan's place.

"What's the most important kinds of things?" she asks.

"Things like"—I kill the engine and turn in my seat—"what waffle toppings do you like the most? Are you a blueberry, strawberry, or banana girl?"

She grins as I hop out. I round the front of the SUV, intent on opening the door for both of them, but Whit beats me to it and has a smug smirk on her face. She's always been competitive, but never with me.

I turn to head for the door, wanting to make damn sure I get there to hold it open for them, but Nora grabs my hand. When I glance back, she's holding Whit's, too.

I glance at Whit and notice she's looking at the same damn thing. There isn't a doubt in my mind that she and Kal don't walk down Main Street while holding Nora's hand like this, and both Whit and Nora deserve better. They deserve more than that fuck is possible of giving.

"You wanna swing?"

She looks up at me, squinting. "At the playground before school?"

"Right here and right now." I look at Whit. "You got her?"

"She's got me forever. Right, Mommy?" Nora twitters.

"You betcha." Whit smiles then counts, "One… two … three!" Whit and I lift her up together, and as soon as Nora's little Chucks leave the ground, she lets out a belly laugh that should be scooped up and sold as happiness in a bottle. Her laughter draws the attention of everyone on the street.

When her feet touch the ground, she giggles. "Do it again!"

So, we do, all the way to Nan's place.

Taking First

WE ATE WAFFLES. Banana and whipped cream were her favorite toppings, especially when I drizzled some chocolate sauce on them. When we dropped her off at school, she asked if we could swing her all the way in, so we did. When she asked if I could pick her up, Whit interrupted by telling her that Popa B was picking her up, like he does every Monday.

I told her I'd see her around and gave her a hug.

As soon as I start the vehicle and pull out of Walton Elementary, all the warm and fuzzies turn to ice.

"Stop trying to date Nora."

"Excuse me?" I ask, confused because the past hour or so has been amazing.

Whit shoves her phone into her pocket. "I should have put my foot down before, but this needs to stop. She's going to get attached to you, and then you'll be gone."

"I'm not going anywhere, Whit. I'm—"

"I'm marrying Kal! Nora needs to bond with him, not you." She cuts me off.

"Let me ask you something, Whit. How long have you been engaged?"

"What does it matter?" she snaps.

"I've met Nora twice, and I already feel a bond growing. If he hasn't bonded with her—"

"I never said they haven't! I just don't want you coming in here with your big money and being a local hero and making her think you're someone who's going to be around."

"First of all, your soon-to-be ex-fiancé is the one who's always used his family money to make people think he's important. Local hero?" I huff. "Please, I'm no hero. And, Whit, I'll be around for—"

"That's a lie. When you left here, you were gone, Pope. Freaking gone. Your mom said you asked her to move with you, and she was planning to once you made it to the majors."

I scrub a hand over my face because all that's the truth. "Of course I wanted to make her life better, give her everything I could, have her closer."

"I know you did—she's your mom—but that doesn't change the fact that you left us. You left me, Danny, and Marks. We were your best friends, and you just left us. Nora isn't—"

I whip the vehicle over to the side of the road and slam it into park.

"Oh my gosh! What the heck are you doing?"

I turn and take her face in my hands. "You left me first! You, Danny, and Marks!"

She freezes.

I release her immediately and try to calm the hell down before continuing, "You all changed the plans we made before I left. When I came home that first break in season, none of you had time for me. You all had excuses and—"

"We had to work!" she yells at me.

"Then"—I throw my hands up—"I came home, and you were all picking up my slack and treating me like I was the one fucking dying. I mean, Jesus, Whit, you couldn't even tell me you were with Danny. Who'd you tell when you broke up, huh? Who? Because that used to be my role in your life. I was the guy you told when something was wrong, and I was the guy who made it better." When she doesn't say anything, I shake my head. "You're the one who wanted me to help you get rid of your—"

"How could I talk to you when I thought you'd gotten Nelly pregnant?" She pokes herself in the chest. "My cousin! And, yeah, I know that I had no reason to be upset with you—hell, you fooled around with several girls. None of us were anything special." She crosses her arms and slumps back. "And Danny and I were never together."

While I'm stumbling over the realization I punched Danny in the face—and wanna do it again because he never corrected my assumption—I trip on the fact that she thought I fucked Nelly and apparently several others. But the most important thing to address right now is the damn truth.

"You were always special, Whit."

Her phone chimes, and she shoves her hand in her pocket to pull it out.

Do I look? Yeah, I look. Kal's name is on the screen.

Fucking Kal.

Whit thumbs through messages, taps something out, and then shoves her cell back in her pocket. "I have things to do. Take me to my vehicle."

"Say *please*."

She scowls at me.

"I'm serious. Say *please*."

Arms crossed, staring out the passenger window, she huffs, "Please."

Not one more word is said until I pull in behind her little SUV because both of us are pissed.

She throws off her seat belt and all but dives out before slamming the door behind her. And I throw the vehicle in reverse and smash the gas, whipping around in the driveway, and peeling out.

When I left Walton, I felt like I knew what direction my life was going. Sex with Whit might have been underwhelming to her—and I would sound like a bitch if I ever admitted this to anyone—but it was all I thought about, even when our conversations started dipping off. Texts became shorter, less frequent. Then, I came home, and everything was different —everything.

Now I know why, but I also know more, and I'm pissed that she's acting like I did something wrong because I didn't do a damn thing but not be here.

Guilt is a feeling I know well. Not being here to take care of Mom every day crushed me, but everyone insisted I stay the course, so that's what I did. I stayed the course, and I made sure the bills were paid. I lived in shitholes. Hell, I never even bought a beater to drive, not that I needed one, until all remaining medical bills were paid off, which wasn't until I made the majors.

Whit thinking I'm going to hurt Nora, it stings me really fucking bad. I've always been no further than a phone call from Whit. I'm still the same damn guy I was. She changed that, not me.

But fuck her and fuck walking away with my dick tucked between my legs ever again.

She's not Kal Seward's. She's mine.

She and Nora both are.

IN NO HURRY THIS TIME, I allow myself to take my time as I walk around the house and look over Mom's flowers. She loved being outside, loved her flowerbeds, took great pride in them. Their vibrant colors are a stark contrast against the rustic ranch house that we painted the summer before my junior year, and it already needs it again. That's not all that needs work. The front porch looks like it is going to fall apart, the back porch needs to be stained again, and the small one-car garage, currently housing my old black Bronco, looks like it's leaning toward the house even more than before. I gotta get that thing out of there.

I open my Notes app and tap out a list of everything that needs to be done before I put the house on the market. The thought of selling no longer feels like I'm looking at the last page of a book I've been forcing myself to finish; it's more like reading one I don't want to end.

Mom's flowers were always beautiful. Clusters of cheerful sunflowers stand tall, their golden heads reaching toward the heavens, hoping for her to whisper to them, as she always did. Their bold blooms radiate happiness and a promise of brighter days ahead. Among the sunflowers are patches of orange marigolds. Their fiery hues always evoke memories of Mom, of a sunset on the horizon. Intermingled with the sunflowers and marigolds are cascades of bluebonnets—the state flower of Texas. Their sweet fragrance fills the air. I've always loved their scent, as they remind me of home, Mom and, yes, of Whit.

Heading back around front, I walk up the stairs, and the familiar creak echoes through the quiet Texas morning. Standing in front of the door, I add *keypad lock* to the list of things I want done. That way, I can give the code to a realtor *if* I decide to sell.

I open the door, step into the kitchen, and stand there. I can almost hear Mom singing softly, as she always did when she was baking. As I think back, it blows my mind that five, sometimes six days a week, she'd work from five in the morning until one in the afternoon, waiting tables, and she always came home and made an after-school snack for me and my friends then dinner every night, except for our once-a-month movie night when we ordered pizza and wings.

But she's no longer here.

Each step feels heavier than the last as I force myself to take in every bit of the place, silently begging for the walls to tell me what to do with this place.

The living room is small, but it was big enough for Mom, me, Whit, Danny, and Marks to hang out comfortably. With all the pictures and knickknacks boxed up, it feels no bigger, just empty.

As I move through the house, running my fingers over the familiar surfaces, I can't help but feel a pang of guilt for staying away for so long. Guilt for abandoning this place that was once a sanctuary, guilt for not facing my grief head-on before. If I had, then maybe I wouldn't have alienated my friends, and Whit wouldn't be in a position where marrying Kal fucking Seward seems like a good idea.

Amid the guilt, there is also gratitude. Gratitude for a community and my friends who took care of Mom and stood by me in her final days. Those who tended to this place with love and care in my absence. Gratitude for the memories that still linger in every corner, reminding me that Mom will never truly be gone when parts of her are still living. Me, the flowers, the huge Easter lily someone sent her after Dad's funeral—all very much still alive.

For the next several hours, I make even more notes, and then I send the list to Danny.

ME:

Schedule me in.

DANNY:

Done.

WHIT

6

Monday

I unlock the back door leading to the offices at the women's shelter and walk in, before locking it behind me and heading to the volunteer office.

When I walk through the open door, York is pulling her hair up into a ponytail. "You're early."

"Nora had more incentive to get out the door today." I set my brown leather bag onto the desk then drop my ass in the worn desk chair.

"Did you let her take two stuffies to school instead of one?" York asks, sitting across from me at the other desk in the tiny office.

I roll my eyes.

"Of course you didn't, hard-ass."

"Nan's place for waffles," I say as I flip on the computer.

"Wait—what? You diverted from the almighty schedule?" she asks, knowing how hard it was to get Nora on any sort of schedule when I first got temporary custody.

I lean back and pull my feet up, placing them on the edge of the seat. "I made the mistake of walking over to Pope's after Kal left last night and—"

She holds up a hand. "Pause. Kal was at your house?"

I nod.

"What was the occasion?"

"We're just months from our wedding. He wants to spend more time with Nora so they can get to know one another better before we move into his place."

She makes the same face she always makes when I mention moving out of Walton. "So, in other words, he knows Pope's in town, and he feels threatened."

I huff, "He knows there's nothing between Pope and me. He—"

"Bet? Pope punched Danny because he thinks he hurt you. There's something there, Whit, and it's not one-sided. You've been in love with that boy—"

"Loved him like family. Never in love," I correct.

"So, you're saying your *brother* popped your cherry?"

I launch a pen at her, and she catches it.

"Don't you have somewhere to be? Like the courthouse to get that order of protection and get it served?" I ask, knowing she pulled an overnight because Spud made bail and Chloe is here until we can get her into temporary housing and back into the workforce.

She stands, eyeing me suspiciously, and then a shit-ass grin spreads across her face. "You took Nora to Nan's this morning?"

"Yeah. So?"

"Don't answer a question with a question."

"Then don't ask leading questions, Officer York. Get to the point."

"Fine. Did Pope happen to be with you?"

I sigh and nod. "Yeah."

She plops back down in her seat. "Spill it, all of it."

So, I do, every detail and every filthy word.

TWO HOURS AFTER YORK LEAVES, I have all the meds sorted for the week and have talked to Chloe about finishing her degree in early childhood education. She's eighteen credits shy of getting her Bachelor's, and then she could get a job teaching. When she left the office, her eyes were brighter because hope had found its way back inside them.

Typically, on the one day I volunteer, after the meds are done, I go home and putter around until it is time to pick up Nora, but knowing Pope is close by and not wanting another argument—*not yet*—I turn on the sports network, grab a pen and pad, and make a list of things I need at the store.

When I hear the announcer say *Pope*, I look up at the small screen and smile, at the replay of his last game, chuckling as I watch him do the same little dance he always does when he's up to bat.

"What's so funny?"

I look over my shoulder to find Kal leaning against the doorframe, then glance up at the clock. "How long have you been standing there?" I turn in my seat as he saunters in, rolling his key to the shelter on one finger.

Kal is an attractive man, and he knows that. He is so conscious of his looks that, sometimes, I feel like I should be grateful he even looked twice at a girl like me who lives in leggings or scrubs. That out of all the women in Walton who light up when they see him walk into a room, it was me who he asked to be his wife. Although Kal has never said such a thing, he often makes remarks that he didn't even notice me in school, and had I not walked into his office, needing help, he would have missed out.

"Long enough to know your obsession with baseball hasn't gone away." He rests against the desk and unbuttons his suit coat before crossing his arms.

"I'm not obsessed with baseball. Softball, yes, but—"

"I'd love for you to start golfing. That way, we could see each other more often. You could join me and my clients on your days off."

"I don't have many of those, but sure." I smile even though his obvious irritation isn't putting me in the mood to want to take up golf and hang out with him.

"If the center needs extra funding so that you can spend more time with me, the firm will be glad to increase its donation."

"I enjoy helping out here."

He taps the end of my nose. "The future Mrs. Kalvin Seward needs to remember she's soon to be in a different tax bracket. Baseball"—he holds his hand about knee high—"is a different class than golf." He raises his hand to eye level.

"Baseball is America's favorite pastime," I retort a little bit forcefully.

He winks. "Only because very few have the privilege that would afford them to know a better game, like golf."

"You and I both played ball in high school," I remind him.

Kal laughs again as he rises from the desk. "I think I need to feed my future wife. You seem a little hangry."

I simply look at him.

He takes my hand and kisses it. "You're upset. I'm sorry. I don't think baseball is a lame sport. Are we good now?"

I nod, and he pulls me up into a hug.

"Let's go grab lunch at Ollie's."

I settle in his arms, breathing in the masculine scent of his aftershave. Although it is warm and familiar, it still doesn't do anything to take away how much of a jerk he just was.

Against my hair, he whispers, "I can't wait for the day I no longer have to share you with anyone else."

Wednesday

WAKING from the depths of a peaceful slumber, I'm not serenaded with the notes from Tracy Chapman's "Fast Car," but rather chaos outside my window. My serene morning is now shattered by the relentless sound of pounding hammers, the whirring of power tools, and the splitting of wood.

I must be having a nightmare, I think as I lie here, tangled in my sheets, feeling a mix of annoyance and resignation, knowing the few peaceful minutes I normally get have been taken from me.

With a sigh, I resign myself to the reality of the situation and slowly untangle myself, knowing I can't linger any longer. It's time to face the day, construction symphony and all.

Rubbing the sleep from my eyes, I roll over and grab my phone to see the time. "What the heck?"

I overslept. It's seven in the morning. I need to get Nora up, fed, and to school and myself to work.

Springing out of bed, I throw on my robe, hurry into the hall, and turn left toward Nora's room. And that's when foot hits something furry, a loud squeak startles me, my legs fly out from under me, and my butt hits the hardwood floor.

"Mother-father," I groan.

"You found Squeakers!" Nora squeals from downstairs.

"She found something." Gram chuckles. "You okay up there, Whitley Mae?"

Lying there, I see Nora's little pom-poms through the banister rails as she climbs the stairs.

I hold a thumb up. "I'm good."

"Morning, Mommy. Gram said we should let you sleep in." She holds her hand out like she's going to hoist me up and I take it and curling up to a painful seated position. "You got another long day, sleepyhead." She uses her hand to muss up my hair. "Pitter-patter, let's get at'er."

"Who are you, and what have you done with my little morning monster?"

"Popa B and my new friend, John Paul, are teaching me how to hit better."

Apparently, I should have been more specific about what I meant when I told him—no, insisted—that he stop trying to date my daughter.

"But John Paul, him told me the biggest secret." She leans in and whispers, "To be a great baseball playa is to get up early every morning, except Saturday." She shrugs. "He told me him and you hit the ball in the same yard 'cause you were best friends."

"You and I do that, Nora."

"But you have to work lots."

I'm so pissed at him right now. I told him to let her be, but I hold it back and take her hands. "You know John Paul isn't here for a long time. He is just here for a little bit to visit. Then, he'll be gone for a very, long time again. The last time he was home was three years ago, Nora. In three years, you'll be in second grade. You might even be big enough that you don't need your booster seat anymore."

She smiles. "But he'll be back, and I'll see him again. He's my friend."

I do not have time for this right now, I think as I try to figure out how to redirect this conversation and get us out the door without her being upset.

"Did you pick out which stuffie is going to school with you today?"

"Squeakers." She bends down and picks up the darn thing I busted my butt on and smiles.

That smile tells me I either did a great job of redirecting or she didn't hear what I said.

AT THE STOP SIGN, I immediately see where the annoying freaking noise came from that woke me up. I mean, yes, I needed to wake up, but still, freaking annoying. Also annoying is that I have to turn and drive past his house to get Nora to school.

Nora squeals, "Roll down my window, Mommy. I wanna wave to my friend."

"It's cold out," I tell her. "Wave with your window closed."

"No, he can't see me. He has to see me!"

Not wanting a breakdown right before school, especially when we're running late, I cave like a three-foot-tall tower of blocks when Nora decides to be a wrecking ball … but only halfway down.

Waving her little heart out, she screeches, "He doesn't see me, Mommy, he doesn't see me!"

"Looks like he's working on his house."

"'Cause he's gonna be in Walton lots, right?" she asks, still waving.

"Little slugger, I'm not sure."

"Popa B said he's our neighbor."

Great, just great.

"John Paul has a job and house in New York, too, so he won't be here lots."

She finally stops waving, and crosses her little arms over her chest, and legit quirks a brow at me. "He will sometimes, Mommy. He's our best friend."

"When he's in Walton, you and Popa B can see him. But remember, we both have jobs, and we have Kal, too."

She doesn't say a word.

DROP-OFF WENT WELL, considering how the morning had started, but as soon as I walk through the automatic doors at the med center, I realize that was the calm before the storm.

"Two ambulances on the way in," Laurie calls to me as I pass by the front of the desk and circle around to get behind it. "We need to move a couple of patients out of the rooms and relocate them."

I drop my bag under the desk and slide the hair tie off my wrist, pulling my hair up into a messy bun. "Which rooms?"

"Twelve's been treated for strep, and seven is a baby with asthma, but someone is supposed to be coming to take him to the pediatric wing. We've been waiting fifteen minutes."

"Oxygen tent?" I ask as I head toward seven.

"Yeah."

"Buzz them and let them know I'm bringing the baby myself."

She winks at me. "Such a mama."

My absolute favorite thing to be, I think.

"Whit," Laurie calls my attention back to her, and I look over my shoulder but continue walking. "Full moon tonight."

"Perfect." I force a big, fat fake smile.

I WORK FOUR TENS SO, typically, I'm home by seven thirty for Nora's eight o'clock bedtime. She's used to Gram and Popa B reading to her and tucking her in on my once-a-month, twelve-hour shifts on Fridays and Saturdays, but this is a switch she's not prepared for.

My ten-hour shift is turning into twelve, five of which I spent helping in pediatrics, as they were even more understaffed than we were in emergency. While I was rocking five-month-old Peter so his mother could go home to grab an overnight bag and pick her husband up from work, I called home on FaceTime. When she saw the little one asleep in my arms, she was just fine with me staying. Nora loves babies just as much as she does her schedule.

"I want you to have a baby for us, Mommy," she yawned out.

Kal and I haven't discussed kids, other than him mentioning he's not good with babies and is glad Nora is older. At that time, it didn't bother me. In fact, all I've prayed for since Bianca Paul passed away is to give Nora the best life I can and be able to take care of Popa B and Gram when they get older.

Whenever I talk about saving for retirement, they say they have "no use for money," so every cent they've ever made has gone into helping others, their whole lives lived in service of God's people. One day, they won't be living in the parsonage; a new pastor will be. Raising Nora and making sure she feels the love all kids should feel and taking care of my grandparents are a given. They raised me. Heck, I begged them to let me stay with them for the summer when I was five years old because my mom was incapable of being a mom.

My mother, Amy, is and always will be all about herself. My dad, Dion, still works all the time to give her everything she wants, and she wants a lot. When I lived there, he gave her flowers every week, bought her gifts, took her on weekends away—I'm sure *he still does*—not that she probably remembers half of them. She's either drunk or popping a pill. He was devastated when I didn't want to come home. Mom? Not so much.

Life was confusing, to say the least, with Amy as my mother, so I became good at reading people and situations and, oh yeah, I also became good at eavesdropping.

I remember Dad came and picked me up for a long weekend. He and I went to a batting cage, and then we picked up Mom to go get ice cream with us. That night, I was upstairs, sitting in the hallway, and heard her tell him that my inability to make friends was because I was different and that I'd have a better chance at happiness in Walton. I also remember overhearing Popa B and Dad exchanging words about the situation. Dad told him that he took his vows seriously. He said in sickness and in health was part of those sacred vows, and he thought my mother was ill in a way you couldn't see— *mentally*.

My grandparents took care of me, loved me like she couldn't, and I'll take care of them forever.

Holding baby Peter the first half of my shift makes me want more. Maybe not give birth to a child, but I really want to adopt and give love to kids like me, like Nora, who couldn't get it from the people who brought them into the world.

I lived with hurt in my heart for years because I hated my mother for not loving me until Nora came into my life. After Nora, I felt sorry for her.

Walking out the door after work, I dig in my bag that's full of things, like hand sanitizer, wet wipes, barrettes, ChapStick, tissues, scrunchies, a couple of emergency Beanie Boos. I pull my keys out, hit unlock twice for good measure, and then I dive back in to grab my phone.

Crossing the parking lot to my car, I'm kind of shocked at the number of missed calls and messages there are from Kal.

KAL:
Good afternoon.

KAL:
Again, good afternoon.

KAL:
I'm beginning to think you're avoiding me.

Really? I think.

KAL:
Jesus Christ, Whitley. That hick's been in town for less than a week, and already, he's causing a division!

I cringe at the use of JC. For me, it's more offensive than the use of *see you next Tuesday*. But calling John Paul a hick? I can't help but laugh at how absurd that is.

Pope's an athlete through and through, and he hasn't changed much. In high school, his hair was always super short on the sides and back and not much longer up top and his face was always clean-shaven. Now, he has a trim five-o'clock shadow, and his hair is still short on the sides and back but longer on the top.

Bianca always tried to get him to leave it longer, but he always convinced her to cut it for him. She would have loved how he has it now. That thick, dark, almost-out-of-control mess of waves is truly gorgeous.

And he was also so clean; he'd leave in the middle of a conversation, making me promise to stay right there, while he showered if he hadn't yet after school or during the summers when he worked construction for Danny's father's company. He always wore a crisp white tee and ball shorts, track pants, or jeans, except on Sundays, when he wore dress pants and a button-down. His sneakers were always clean, too, like oddly so. In one of our many conversations, Bianca told me her trick to keep them clean—peroxide and baking soda. I've used the tip ever since, especially with Nora, my little puddle jumper.

I glance down and read the next message.

KAL:
> Can't answer your goddamn messages or phone?!

"WHITLEY!" Kal yells my name, and I turn to watch as he storms toward me. I didn't even notice his car parked in the lot. "You can't answer your phone? Tell me you're stuck here?"

I put on a smile even though I'm far from happy. "It was a busy night. Really busy. Exhausting, as a matter of fact."

"No time to check your phone?"

"The only time I take it out of my bag is during breaks. I spent my break helping in ped." That's not one hundred percent true, but on days like today, I don't even bother putting my phone in my scrubs pocket.

"What if it was an emergency? What if …?" He pauses, and I wait for what comes next, hoping it's something redeeming, like *what if something happened to Nora?* "What if I needed you?"

It doesn't happen.

"Then you'd call here and have me paged, just like my family would."

When he steps toward me, I smell alcohol, and it makes me uncomfortable. "Where's your phone?"

"Somewhere in my bag. Why?"

He shakes his head. "I want to delete the message I sent. I was deeply concerned, and it doesn't represent me in a way I want to be represented."

Represent?

"It's fine. I won't read it."

He steps closer, wetting his lips and forcing a smile that I assume he thinks is sultry. It's not.

He narrows his eyes when I lean back then grips the roof of my SUV, caging me in. "You gonna give your fiancé a kiss?"

I kiss him quickly on the cheek. "I really need to get home." When I turn, he presses against me, wraps an arm around my waist, and pulls me into him.

"Come home with me tonight."

"You know I can't."

With a hand on the base of my throat, lips against my skin, his voice shakes as he asks, "This about John fucking Pau—"

I pull his hand away from my neck and turn. "This is about me having a ten-hour shift turn to twelve, and you coming here and accusing me of—" I stop when he steps back with my bag in his hand. "What are you doing?"

He begins rummaging through it, sputtering, "Deleting my texts. I wasn't bullshitting you, *Whitley*."

The way he says my name is with disdain—nothing I have heard before from him.

"Give me my bag." I reach for the strap and pull it. Kal pulls harder. "Let go of my freaking bag!"

"Jesus Christ." He grabs my hand and squeezes, causing my nails to sink into my palm. "Let go of the fucking bag!"

"Everything okay, Whit?" comes a female voice.

Laurie.

"All good, thanks." Embarrassed, I let go, causing him to jerk it, and then the contents dump all over the parking lot.

I quickly bend down to gather my belongings and reach for my phone at the same time that he steps on the screen, catching the tip of my ring and forefinger.

I jerk my hand back.

"What the hell, Whitley? Christ, why'd you do that?" he accuses—yes, accuses, as if it were my fault that he stepped on my fingers at the same time he was stomping on my phone to shatter it in order to hide text messages, most of which I already read and didn't want to admit to because I was too tired and sick to my stomach to deal with this ... this ... mess I've gotten myself in to.

Did it hurt? Yes. Does it still? Yes. But more than the physical pain is that it makes me angry. The kind of angry that burns your throat and the back of your eyes.

Laurie squats down and helps me pick up my belongings. "You okay?"

"I will be," I seethe, fighting back emotion.

"Oh shit, honey, your phone." Kal bends down to

snatch it up. "I'll get this fixed and have it back to you tomorrow."

I don't even look at him or reply. I dust off the Beanie Boos and toss them into my car, saving them from more abuse, as he says five words that make my hand start to shake.

"You should be more careful."

"Seward, let's roll, man. The wife's gonna be pissed if I'm late again," someone calls as lights flash a few cars away.

"You okay, honey?" Kal asks, lifting my chin with the hand that's not holding my phone hostage.

Through my teeth, I answer, "I'm fine."

He stands. "I'll stop by tomorrow and drop off your phone."

Standing, I hold out my hand. "I have insurance on the phone. I'll take care of it."

"I'm the one who stepped on it when your bag fell. I'll take care of you."

"Let's go, man!" whoever it is that brought him here yells.

"You have a driver?" Laurie asks, face pinched as she stands with my bag.

"Election year. My father wouldn't be happy if I got pulled over for driving after having a couple of drinks at the club." He leans in to kiss the side of my head, and my body stiffens. "Get home safe, *honey*. I'll see you tomorrow."

If Laurie wasn't standing here, I'd demand my phone and replace his empty hand with the ring that he gave me two months ago after a full year of promising me the only thing that would change when we were married was we'd spend every night together and not just once or twice a month when York took Nora.

I watch as his friend drives his Porsche out of the parking lot, wishing I could Carrie Underwood the damn thing.

"Whitley," Laurie's says, reminding me that she's still here. "You okay?"

I try like hell to pull up a smile, but I can't. I just freaking can't. "I need a shower and my bed."

She grabs my hand and gives it a gentle squeeze, and I wince. "Did you hurt your hand?"

I shake my head. "I'm good. Get home before Lex sends out WPD to find you."

"Sweetheart, for twenty-five years, that man has fallen asleep in his recliner after the evening news ends. I'm here right now."

"I'm good, I promise." I give her a quick hug. "See you tomorrow."

The convenience of working so close to home and Nora's school is wonderful, but right now, not so much. I want to either break something or cry. I can't do either because I don't have time to get my shit together before walking into the house, and I don't want Popa B or Gram to see puffy eyes and worry that something is wrong.

What a mess I've made. What a freaking mess.

POPE

7

Wednesday

Monday, after Whit handed me my ass and I sent Danny the text, I went and did some shopping for food and hygiene products then grabbed takeout before Nan's closed. I came home showered, then sat in the middle of the living room floor, looking through a box full of pictures and notes from Mom to me, and me to Mom. There was a notebook that I flipped through. Inside was the drawing of the back porch we'd saved for and eventually built. I grabbed a pencil and started doing some drawings of my own. Then I took some pictures and sent them to Danny with a text.

ME:

> This good, or do we need to have plans drawn up?

The next morning, on his way to his current job site, Danny drops off a storage trailer so that I can temporarily keep the items that are worth keeping and the few things that I can never see myself letting go of, like Dad's and Mom's ball gloves. They'll be stored in a dry, safe place until the garage is finished.

I need to keep busy because I'm feeling like shit now. Heavy shit, damn near crippling shit. For close to a decade and a half, I've kept my foot firmly planted on my feelings, holding them down. Until now. Suppressed memories are rising out from under the dust without warning each day. A volcano of emotions is slowly coming to a boil just beneath the surface that I can't seem to gain control of.

Tearing off the rotting roof and the battered boards to ready the garage for the addition is all that's keeping me from grabbing Whitley and demanding that we sort through the dirt and debris that was shoveled on our friendship—shit that was not within our control.

I'm exhausted. The sun is slowly making its descent in the west, but I would have kept pulling boards had I not heard a distinct sound. First, the crack of a wooden bat and then the deep laugh that could not be mistaken for anyone other than Pastor B.

I round the corner of the house and see him and Nora in the field, playing a little ball.

I hose myself off a bit, throw on the tee that I hung over the back porch banister, and walk across the lawn.

Nora drops the ball and runs to me. "Wanna play?"

"I'd love to," I admit.

And that's what we do —we play. And we play some more. Before they head back, I get a hug from her instead of a high— five.

After ball, I shower when I get back to the house. I am about ready to get at the garage boards again to stop myself from heading to the med center and faking a heart attack or some shit when Danny and Marks pull in, shining the headlights on the garage, no doubt checking on my progress. Then, they pull around back, which I can't complain about since the side yard is already gonna be rutted up from the storage trailer and the trucks delivering supplies.

The engine is killed, and two doors shut. I hear them commenting on my progress as they walk around and make their way to the front porch.

"Beer?" Marks asks, carrying a cooler in one hand.

"Wouldn't mind one."

He hands me a can of Crawford Bock.

"You go all the way to Houston to get this?"

"Always gonna hold up hope that you'll be back in Texas." Marks pops his tab. "Don't get to the stadium much anymore, so I'm bringing the stadium to us."

"Cheers to that." Danny holds out his bottle of water, and we all tap our drinks, then take a swig.

"You sure you need a crew here?" Marks asks.

"Looks like you got this under control." Danny chuckles.

"He needs an electrician." Marks nods to the front porch light.

"Lights work, but they draw the bugs," I explain.

Marks chuckles. "Not a lot of bugs flying around here in February."

"Right?" I scrub my hand over my hair. "Seems like spring here."

"Speaking of spring, when do you head to Florida for training?"

"Seventeenth of next month is day one. Preseason games start a week later." I take a long pull off my beer and clear my throat. "Wondering if you'd all like to come to Vegas and watch me play next week. There're two exhibition games, Thursday and Friday. It's closer than New York and—"

"The answer is fuck yes." Danny laughs. "We're going to Vegas, baby!"

"I'll make it work on my end. Wouldn't want you to have to deal with this guy alone," Marks adds.

I turn and look at Danny. "Not easy for a man who's seldom wrong to say he's sorry, but I hear I owe you an apology."

He lets out an amused laugh. "Still a self-righteous motherfucker."

I lift a shoulder and take another drink.

"What wrong are you admitting to?"

"Shouldn't have punched you. Should have asked you if you and Whit had a thing going instead of stewing about it."

He doesn't say anything, probably more afraid of Whit's left hook than my jab.

"She told me."

"Oh, yeah?" Marks asks. "She tell you anything else?"

"Couple of things."

"Like?" Danny asks.

"Cut the shit. I know Nelly lied and told her that—"

"It's about fucking time." Danny exhales like he's been holding his breath for years. Gonna guess he has been, in a way. Then, he starts talking, and hell yes, I let him.

"Fucked up she lied to Whit about one of her best friends. It's messed up she didn't ask you directly, but I understand not wanting to put more on your plate at the time. I told her there was no way you dipped it in Nelly." He holds up his hand defensively. "I didn't tell her why I knew that for certain. Didn't expose your secret."

"Not nailing every female offering it up in Walton wasn't a secret. You two might be okay with playing pass the ass, but I'm not."

"That was only in high school," Marks defends.

"And it was only because the ladies of Walton deserved a good time, and it just so happened that Marks and I could provide them with that."

"Such Southern gentlemen." I chuckle.

"Public service was always my calling," Marks jokes.

"Never did tell us who flipped your skirt first. Was it groupies in the minors, or did you keep polishing your cherry until you found someone *special*?"

"Quit busting his ass. Not a damn thing wrong with only fucking tens." Marks crushes his can and grabs us both another.

"I'm not asking for a roster, just your first. Spill it," Danny insists.

"All you're getting from me is I didn't leave here a boy." I pop the tab on my can and take a drink.

"We promised we'd all tell each other when we busted a nut inside an actual chick and not a hand or mouth or our own fist. So—"

"Danny," Marks cuts him off, "you should've been born blond."

"My hair's brown," he says, and I can't help but laugh. "What, man? A promise is a promise."

"Clearly not," Marks mumbles. Clearly, he's figured it out.

I say not a word, not one.

"Hold the fuck on," Danny says, apparently having a light-bulb moment. "Are you fucking kidding me right now?"

Marks snickers. "He's not saying a single word."

"You're the one who was all, *Whit is off-limits*."

Marks chuckles. "Guessing she still is."

At the same time, I say, "She still is."

Silence ensues until Danny has another epiphany.

"That's why Whit was so upset about Nelly, and you were so pissed, thinking I'd tapped that—"

"Never ever say *tapped that* in regard to Whitley Mae Belington *ever* again," I cut him off.

"If I were drinking instead of driving tonight, I'd have already hit you twice."

Lifting a shoulder, I admit, "I'd deserve both."

"You deserve more than that. You should have asked me, man." He pokes himself in the chest. "I'm the reason you stayed away for years."

"Step lightly, Danny," Marks says quietly, trying to defuse what he sees as a possible situation.

"I mean, Mama Pope, too, but—"

"Jesus, Danny, shut—"

"Nothing here felt like home anymore." I force myself to own up to my truth.

"And how's it feeling now?" Marks nods toward the church.

"Over there? Like winter in New York," I answer honestly.

"You gonna do something about that?" Marks asks.

"Made a promise to a little girl that I'd teach her how to play ball. Gonna make sure I'm around to do that as often as I can be."

"And what about her mom?"

My lips twitch up into a sneer. "There's no way in hell I'm letting her marry that piece of shit."

The next couple of hours are rather enlightening. I learn that Whitley broke some code or law by doing a DNA test with hair from my brush and some snippets of Nelly's. Whit was going to tell me about Nora, and then insist I tell my mom so that Mom wouldn't worry so much about me being without family. When she found out I was not her father, she made sure Mom knew that the four of us would always remain family.

Next, I find out that Whit apparently tried to remove my name— that Nelly had somehow fraudulently given the hospital an affidavit stating I was the father — from the birth certificate because she didn't want it to affect my life or Nora's down the road. And then I find out she went to Kal fucking Seward to start the adoption process.

"Now, all of a sudden, she's not so hell-bent on Nora's last name being the same as hers." Danny sighs.

"Why's that?"

"Because hers is going to change when she gets hitched to Kal."

"Again, she's not marrying that piece of shit—" I sneer. "Whit and Nora won't be dragged down by people who think they're better than everyone else when those people are far from it."

"Agreed. Now, what's the plan?" Danny asks.

"The more I know, the better I can come up with a solid one. So, I'll let you know when I hammer it out."

"Or you could *tap* it out," Danny suggests, trying to rile me up.

I don't bite. Not this time anyway.

"By hammer it out" —Marks nods toward the house I'm now balls deep into renovating—"this part of the plan?"

I nod and ask, "You think you can get your hands on a copy of the original birth certificate, the one with my name on it?"

"I can look into it."

We shoot the shit for a couple of hours, and we do so on the porch so I can see when Whit passes by. I know she works four ten-hour shifts, starting at eight thirty in the morning, but often gets stuck far past that. I'm guessing tonight is one of those nights.

When I see headlights coming down the road, I perk up, but when the vehicle slows to almost a stop and a window rolls down, I know it's not her. We all watch as something flies out the window, followed by a loud shattering of glass against my house —bottles— followed by several more.

"What the fuck was that?" Danny asks as I jump over the side of the porch while they peel out, laying rubber down the road.

As I run by the bucket of balls I've yet to put away from our little practice session tonight, I grab one and throw it as hard as I can.

"Jesus Christ, Pope," Marks spits right out after it smashes into the back window of the vehicle.

The streetlight above the car illuminates the shattered window. The driver hits the brakes and lights it up, showing the damage more clearly. Satisfaction takes over, and I smile at the fact that I hit dead center and the ball's stuck in the glass.

Of course I did.

And then reverse lights.

"Not a good night to leave my gun at home," Marks grumbles as I stand there, waiting for the punks to show their faces.

I hear Marks reading off the plate number and know he's called the station.

"Get here now. They're coming back." He then yells, "Get in the house and wait for York to get here. She's a minute out."

"You two head in. I'm not moving." And I don't.

I stand there as the passenger door flies open and see exactly who I hoped it would be—Kal fucking Seward.

Taking First

"You stupid son of a bitch! I'm gonna beat the redneck out of you!"

I raise my arms to the sides and stretch them out wide. "I'm right here. Take your best shot. I'll give you the first one free."

"The Seward family is going to make you pay for this," his buddy, the driver, yells as he takes in the back window of the car.

I don't even look in his direction. My eyes are locked on Kal as he storms toward me in Chinos and a Polo.

I stand there, arms still outstretched, with a smile on my face. Hell, I'm willing him to take the first jab so I can take care of the rest.

His knuckles crash into my lips, and the metallic taste of my own blood fills my mouth as he pops back then starts hopping around, fists raised.

This fool thinks he's Muhammad Ali.

I spit the blood out on the ground, and a low chuckle comes out before I taunt, "Let me know when you're ready to play ball, motherfucker. With a swing like that, your ass still deserves to be riding the bench, wishing you were me."

He swings again, and I lean back easily, dodging his fist.

"Strike one, *Sewie*."

8

Wednesday

Thankfully, the rain started after I filled up my gas tank, but it's coming down in buckets after I went inside to grab a cold can of soda—Dr. Pepper—and a "shareable" bag of peanut M&M's from the gas station. I have zero intention of sharing the M&M's with anyone, except my wounded ego and shattered pride. The can of soda, I'll wrap my throbbing fingers around.

Wipers set to *wow*, I pull out of the parking lot of the Gas 'N' Go and immediately tear open the bag with my teeth and begin the process of self-medicating. My hope is that the candy shoots me into a sugar high long enough to get me through a shower and drop my behind into contentment so that I don't mull over tonight's happening until the sun rises. I need to make time to schedule in a breakdown on Friday while Nora's at school. After today's shift, I don't have it in me to figure out what the heck I'm going to do next.

As I round the bend before the stop sign next to Pope's

corner lot, I swear I see flashing lights, but there's no way. I tell myself I must be seeing things. The closer I get, however, the more I realize I'm not seeing things. There are most definitely lights.

Before I can think, I'm jumping out of my vehicle and running toward a crowd —York and a group of guys. Pope, Marks, and Danny are unmistakable even though Pope is covered in mud. The other three men I can't make out ... until I can.

"What is going on?" I ask York, who is standing there, soaked.

"This asshole shattered the back window of the Porsche!" Kal sneers.

"There's more to the story than that," Marks spits back.

"And we'll sort it out." York looks at Pope. "Let's you and I take a walk."

Popa B walks over with his umbrella, puts an arm around my shoulders, and kisses my cheek. "Saw lights and thought I'd walk over and see what was going on."

"I do not want you around these people anymore. They're animals. No more, Whitley," Kal demands.

Shocked, I cannot even bring myself to respond to him. But when I do find my words, the first thing I say is, "I want my phone—now."

Teeth clenched, he replies, "I told you I'll be getting it fixed tomorrow and bring it to you at your work."

"What happened to your phone, Whitley?" Popa B asks.

"She dropped it," Kal answers. "The screen was damaged."

So were my fingers, I think as he wipes away more mud and flicks it onto the ground.

My eyes home in behind him, and I begin walking toward his car.

"What are you doing, Whitley?" he calls after me.

"Getting my phone," I state without pausing my strides.

"I told you—"

"And she told you. I advise you to let the lady get her belongings," Popa B cuts off his yell.

When I get to the car, I see who is driving, as Kal's friend Kris, steps in front of me. "You should think really hard about how you're going to proceed."

"*You* should move."

"He's a good friend to have. He'll give you a good life *if* you don't cross him."

I push past him and bend in to find my phone. I don't see it, but I do see white powder on the console and a tiny straw in the cupholder.

Cocaine.

The anger I feel at myself is changing to rage against him, Kal, and the situation. "Where is my phone?"

He doesn't answer.

Avoiding the drug residue but still digging around, I tell him, "You might want to point me in the right direction, or I can have York or her partner come over here and help me look. I'm not sure you want to be arrested for the coke and—"

"It'll be long gone before they get over here," he hisses. "Besides, there isn't enough for even a possession charge."

Under the driver's seat, I find a box of condoms, and I would assume several are missing. Latex. I'm allergic to Latex.

I move to look under the passenger seat and find my smashed phone shoved under it, but before leaving cokehead Kris, I want to make damn sure he understands something. "I'm not intimidated by you or Kal."

As I walk away, he says, "With what he has on you and your friends, I'd be real damn concerned."

I know I've never thrown any of them under the bus. Never told him they even knew. In fact, when Kal asked, I changed the subject to avoid the lie. Thinking of what I've trusted him with makes me sick to my stomach.

Could I lose custody of Nora for trying to hide a lie? I know the answer is yes, but there was no malicious intent. That's what Kal said. He actually praised me for trying to protect her. I should have seen right through him then, but I didn't want to. All I wanted was to give Nora a good life, a normal life and, yes, to protect Pope's reputation from my cousin's fabrication.

Walking back to Popa B, I see an ambulance pull up and wonder what the heck is going on.

"Why is there an ambulance?" I ask as I approach Danny.

"Kal wants his injuries documented."

"What?" I look from Danny to Kal.

"I want charges pressed against that—"

Before I have a chance to tell him what a complete and total piece of garbage I think he is, Marks forces a laugh. "Are you that clueless about reality, Seward? There was an off-duty police officer sitting on the porch when you and your boy pulled up and threw glass bottles at Pope's place. A police officer who watched you get out of your car and swing on Pope dozens of times, and he never once hit you."

"He shattered the rear window of a car that is worth more than his shack. He was begging for a fight. I was simply trying to find out who vandalized my property."

Voice shaking, I sneer, "You should leave."

He doesn't even look at me. He looks at Popa B. "As a man of God, would you remind Whitley what her role as a wife is?"

"She's not your wife," Popa B states.

"We're getting married in six months—you know this."

Not gonna happen, I think.

"I know what I've been told, but I don't recall ever being asked for her hand."

"*Excuse me?*" Kal laughs maliciously.

"Popa B"—I grab his hand— "it's all going to be okay, I promise."

"I know it will be, sweetheart." He points up. "Just have to have faith."

"Kal, the EMT will check you over now," York states, clearly annoyed she must provide him with any type of service.

As Kal walks away, Popa B closes his umbrella, as the rain has stopped. "I'll see you at home."

"I'll be there as soon as I can."

I stand here, looking around, wondering how bad went to worse. Like, truly, this can't be real.

York walks over, leaving her partner with Kal and the EMTs. "This asshole made me call out our volunteers to try to find a scratch when all Pope did was make him eat mud."

"He made him what?" I ask, trying not to laugh or maybe yell—heck, I don't know what to feel.

"Marks said Pope dodged all Kal's attempts to hit him after the first. Batted his fist out of the way when he came close, and then when the rain started to fall, it turned into a wrestling match, where John Paul restrained him, face-down in the mud, until I got here."

Taking First

I glance over and see Pope standing at the back of the cop car, arms crossed, looking murderously at Kal, who is sitting between the open doors at the back of Walton's volunteer ambulance's.

That's it, I think as I storm over toward him. "What the hell is wrong with you? You had volunteers called away from their families because you have the delusional idea you're going to get John Paul in some sort of trouble for something *you* started? Something you did? You, Kal, not him!"

"I picked a side. That was your side. You'd do well to remember whose side you're on."

I throw my hands in the air. "There isn't a mark on you! Leave him the heck alone, or you'll have charges of your own."

Eyes narrowed, teeth clenched, he sneers at me, "My friends were right; you lay with filth, and you'll start smelling like it."

I can't help but bark out an angry laugh. "I volunteer at a women's shelter that your family donates to. How well do you think the crap you pulled tonight—showing up at my work, demanding my phone, then smashing it, and—" I hold up my fingers so he can see they're swollen and red, but then the ring catches my eye. Pulling it off as if it were poison, I want to throw it at him. York must see that because she takes it from me and shoves it in his hand. "You can go to hell."

"What did he do to you, Whit?" Pope asks, grabbing me and turning me to face him. "You tell me right now. Did he hurt you?"

"Get them out of here," York says.

Suddenly, Danny and Marks are pulling Pope back as he lunges at Kal.

"Knock it off!" I yell at Pope. "Don't you let him win."

"Jesus, Whit," Danny grumbles, leaving Marks with Pope and, hoists me up.

"Gonna be a hell of a fight, getting custody of that kid, when you lose your job, your—"

"You motherfucker!" Pope roars.

"Goddammit, Pope," Marks grunts as he tries to rein in an angry John Paul.

Danny's still carrying me away as I try to get free when Kal remarks, "You're pissed, but you'll get over it and come crawling back."

And then, somehow, I end up in the back of the patrol car, locked freaking in. Within seconds, Pope is shoved in on the other side by Marks and Danny.

"Tell me what he did to you," Pope demands as they shut the door, locking us both in.

I shake my head, and he grabs my chin, turning it back to face him.

"Whit, tell me."

I force out, "I don't have a working phone. Text Marks and tell him there's white powder residue on his console, to make York document that. I … I … I can't lose Nora."

The dam nearly breaks, and he wraps an arm around me, pulling me into a hug, using his other hand to send the text. Then he wraps me in both arms.

"Everything's gonna be okay. I promise you, Whit. I'll make sure of it."

I want to believe him. I really do. John Paul always made things better. He could calm my nerves before a game and find me when I hid so well that even I didn't know where I was while playing manhunt. However, I'm not lost in the woods. I'm stuck right in the middle of a situational suckhole of my own creation.

"God, what have I done?" My voice is shaking. I

attempt to pull away to hide the fact that the dam is about to burst apart.

His big hand palms the side of my face, and he pulls my head against his chest. I can feel his heart pounding against my face.

"You've done nothing but try to make everything okay for everyone." Although quiet, his voice shakes in anger. "And you've made a mess, Whit, but I'm going to fix it—"

I shove his hand away and sit up, moving so my back is against the door, putting not nearly enough room between us. "I don't need your help!"

"Like hell you don't." He moves to the other side, running his hands over his scruff, up the sides of his head, and then gripping his hair. "Fucking Kal Seward, Whit?"

"Shut up. Just shut the ... hell up!"

And he does…for approximately ten seconds.

"No, fuck that. I'm not shutting up. You've been telling me what to do since we were kids. I'm not a damn kid anymore, Whit!"

I fold into a ball, angry at him, but more at myself, and tears of anger and frustration finally break through.

Pope bangs on the window, obviously trying to get away from me. "Marks, open the damn door!"

I glance up and see a tow truck, and then Kal throws his arms up, obviously pissed his vehicle is being towed.

Then I see a black SUV pull alongside the patrol car and stop. When the rear passenger window rolls down, I see Kevin Seward.

He looks from me to Pope and nods once before rolling up the window and pulling forward.

"He called his freaking father?"

"The man has pull," Pope states with zero emotion in his voice. He pulls his phone out of his pocket, starts tapping on the screen, then shoves it back into his pocket.

I swing my gaze back to the vehicle and see my ex climb in the back of the SUV, followed by his asshole friend. Then Kevin walks over and speaks with York before he returns to the SUV. York then begins taking pictures of the Porsche, and when she walks to the still-open passenger door, she takes more.

Pope glances at me as I try to wipe my tears on my soaked scrubs. Leaning forward, he reaches over his shoulder and pulls his windbreaker—or whatever the heck it's called now—over his head, along with a maroon, long-sleeved shirt. Walton's school color.

"Shirt's dry and mud-free. You should put it on—you're soaked."

"I'm fine." I sniff.

"You're shaking."

"I'm so pissed off I could scream!" I take the shirt he's handing me.

He leans forward and wipes the tears from under my eyes. "Right here is my kryptonite." He lifts his thumb as if he's looking at my tears and then makes an X across his chest—his bare chest.

I close my eyes in an attempt not to stare at Major League Pope's chest, abs, arms—those freaking arms—that ink that I want to hate.

"I'm not asking you this time; I'm telling you. I am going to make everything o—"

"It's not your pro—"

"Whitley, shut the hell up. This is what we do."

"No, we—"

"You took care of my dying mother, Whit. *My mother*." He points a finger at himself.

"I did that for her." I sniff as tears fall harder now. Then I carefully put his shirt over my head and manage to get my arms out of my scrub sleeves and pull it off without showing any skin. "I loved her."

"I know you did, and she loved you. But you also did it for me, and one day, you're going to admit to it." He leans back and links his fingers behind his head. "It will more than likely be after this bullshit is over with Kal."

"He's not going to let it go." I nervously fold my soaked shirt.

"He's not going to have a choice." He leans in closer to me. "And neither are you."

"And what makes you think I want to owe yet another egotistical male for helping out *little old me*?"

"Ego is something men like that create in their heads. I've worked for everything I have, and I'll never stop. You and I are the same; we have pride, and pride comes from the heart."

He reaches over and grabs my hand, giving it a squeeze, causing me to wince. He then moves his fingers around my wrist, stopping me from pulling it away.

"Let it go, Pope."

"He hurt your hand."

I glance out the window and see the SUV pulling away, following behind the tow truck. When I look back at him, he's leaning in with his phone light shining on my hand.

"The truth, Whit."

With Kal no longer in striking distance, I give him just that. "When I got to my vehicle after a twelve-hour shift, he was there. I hadn't answered my phone or texts, and he'd sent several. He regretted them. He asked for my phone to delete them, and it pissed me off."

"As it should." He nods his agreement.

"We played tug-of-war with my bag." I fight back more tears of frustration and anger, continuing, "It spilled. I bent down to grab my phone as he stomped on it to make sure I—"

"He stomped on your hand?" he asks, lip curling.

"He said it was an accident."

"What does my very smart and intuitive friend think?"

"You saw me give him back his ring." I start to pull my hand away, and he holds it up and rubs his lips back and forth over it. "What are you doing?"

"Holding on to the only thing stopping me from kicking out a patrol car window, hunting him down, and stomping on his face."

"Well, I can't hold your hand forever, Pope, so …" I leave it right there.

Unfinished.

His phone chimes, but he doesn't release my hand. In fact, he links our fingers and pulls his cell out of his pocket with his free hand and taps the screen.

Music comes through the speakers. "*There was something 'bout the way the blue lights were shinin', bringing out the freedom in your eyes. Too busy watching you going wild child to be worried about going to jail …*"

Face burning, I'm annoyed at whoever sent that, ready to kick out a window myself. Pope's laugh surprises me. I narrow my eyes at him, and he nods to the front. I lean over and look out the windshield, where Marks, Danny, and even York are singing along.

Pope pulls me into a surprising hug and kisses the top of my head. "Promise you, Whitley Mae Belington, it's all gonna work out."

York opens my door, and I pull away, slide out, and shut the door behind me.

Even over the music still playing from Danny's or Marks' phone, I hear him laugh. I've always loved John

Paul's laugh, and right now, I realize how much I've missed it.

Marks opens the door for Pope, and he gets out, still smiling.

"You sure don't look like a man worried about getting arrested." York shakes her head as we walk around the back of the car.

Looking at me, he shakes his head. "Not a lot I can do behind bars, is there?"

I look away.

York steps to him and hands him a card. "Senior asked me to give you this. Said that you should give him a call tomorrow so you can sort this out."

I watch his chiseled jaw tense, muscles popping.

"Thanks, York. Sorry about tonight."

"Gave Gavin here a chance to—"

"Huge fan." Gavin, her rookie, cuts her off.

Pope shakes his hand. "Nice to meet you. Sorry it had to be under these circumstances."

Danny snorts. "And what circumstance is that? Shirtless with nips poking out—"

"Danny, what the heck is wrong with you?" I ask.

"Sober, for one. Fucking cold, for another. And, yeah, a little intimidated by the fact that I'm not a dad, yet here I am, rocking a dad body, and Pope here's in better shape than he was in high school."

"I get paid to stay in shape," Pope deflects the ... odd compliment.

"Well, put a shirt on, man," Danny says.

"Anyone want a beer?" Pope asks. "Marks brought Crawford Bock, and we haven't even finished a six-pack. Be a shame if it went un-drank and got warm."

"I'm gonna head home. Popa B is probably worried."

"We'll follow you and make sure you get there without incident," York says.

"It's right around the corner," I huff.

Pope quietly says, "The other options are: you let me walk you home, or you could always stay here with me."

I glare at John Paul.

"Not even trying to be smooth," Danny states, clearly having heard him, as I'm sure they all did.

WHEN I WALK into the house, Popa B and Gram are sitting at the table, sipping hot lavender tea, and a third cup is waiting for me.

I hang my bag over the back of the chair and sit down as Gram asks, "Are you all right, Whitley?"

"I will be," I answer, picking up the cup and inhaling the calming scent and heat.

"I'm not one for violence," —Popa B starts what I know is going to be a sermon, but then his deep laugh fills the room— "but I've always enjoyed comedy. I couldn't help but stand in the shadows and watch John Paul give that Seward ample time to stop acting a fool "—he chuckles—"and then subduing him facedown in the mud when he just wouldn't comply."

I take a sip of tea then set the cup down.

Gram puts her hand over mine. "Popa B told me you called off the engagement."

I nod, confirming.

"I know that's gotta sting a bit, but I also know it's what's best for you and Nora."

"I sure hope so, Gram."

Fifteen minutes later, showered and lying in bed, I pull the long-sleeved tee up to my nose and inhale Pope's scent.

A scent I spent the month after he left for the minors trying to decipher and then imitate. The primary note was the scent of wood mixed with leather. That night we spent together in the back of his truck, I remember a light musk scent, as well. The notes are all the same, but bolder.

Just like him.

I want nothing more than to trust that everything will be okay—I truly do—but it's so hard when I can't even forgive myself for the choices I made yet.

That's not on Pope. That's on me.

POPE

9

Friday

Yesterday, I avoided all calls from Kevin Seward, Kal's father, and fought my instinct to go sit outside the med center in the shadows, to make sure Whit made it out and to her car without incident. Marks is on patrol tonight, just like he was last night, and promised he'd make up an excuse to be there when she got out.

Today, the crew showed up to wait for the concrete truck to arrive and pour the floor. Then they'll start in on the walls.

Me, I head out for a run. After running through the cemetery and saying my good morning to my parents, I head back out onto the road, and run harder.

Midway through, I get a text and hit my watch app.

I slow to a walk to read what *unknown* has to say.

UNKNOWN:

> I hoped that we would have a conversation, but it seems that isn't going to happen. I've contacted Officer York, and she's aware that my son will not be pressing charges if none are pressed against him. We'd like to put this behind us and move forward. I have always respected your mother and you as an athlete. I hope that you can give me the same. Regards, KS

Kevin Seward.

The respect for my mother that he's referring to came in the form of having breakfast at Nan's three mornings a week and leaving large tips. It spilled over to talking with her after and sometimes during ball games and him praising my game. I liked that praise, at first, especially when I saw how pissed off it made his son, who I didn't care for and clearly still don't. When he continued showing up at games after his son graduated, it became apparent that it had nothing to do with me; it was Mom. That suspicion was confirmed when he showed up at our home one night with flowers, and I heard my mother tell him that she had told him several times she wasn't interested in anything more than a friendship. He asked her how the team would manage without his donations and how she would manage without the tips he left.

Ever the respectful Southern woman, she responded, "I thank you for your generosity and concern, but I'll manage just fine. Now, you have a wonderful night, ya hear?" As she stepped into the house, I hid back around the corner and heard her whisper, "What an incredulous asshole." She then walked into the living room and saw me lurking.

Before she could say anything, I told her, "I don't think Dad would want you to be alone forever."

She smiled softly. "John Paul, I could never date a man

who wasn't even half the man your father was, and I've yet to meet one, not that I've been looking, but women know these things. That man? He's not even close to that, and even if he were, he's a married man, and I will never be somebody's mistress." And then she ended that with, "Bless his heart."

She was never wrong—ever.

I shoot him back a text.

ME:

> I'll be in touch on Monday after I've discussed this with Whitley. Tuesday if I decide to get my lawyers involved.

His reply is immediate.

UNKNOWN:

> I do not think that is necessary.

Blood boiling, I start to send a reply when I hear a horn blast behind me.

Pulling out an AirPod, I look back, and only then do I realize I'm no longer on the side of the road. I'm almost in the middle of the right lane. The person who blew the horn? Whitley, and she's wearing a seriously sexy messy bun and shades that are hiding her whole face.

"What are you doing?" she yells—yes, yells—at me.

"Yeah, what are you doing?" Nora's little voice asks, making me smile.

I step to the passenger side and open the door. "Looking for a ride."

"I gotta go to school. Gonna be late. Pitter-patter, Pope."

"Pitter what?" I ask, setting my ass in the seat without invitation.

"Pitter-patter, let's get at'er. Means we're runnin' late.

Buckle up, buttercup. We gots to go." She starts laughing, and Whit just shakes her head as she puts the vehicle in drive.

I turn and smile at the little slugger. "You're full of it this morning."

"Full of what?" she asks.

"Excitement for school and learning," Whit says. "Hold on to that while we swing back around and take Pope—"

"Can't be late. I'll ride along."

"Yay!" Nora claps.

"Yay," I say and clap, as well, gaining a side-eye from Whitley.

Still clapping, Nora asks, "Are we playing baseball again tonight? Mommy doesn't have to work, and she can play too."

"You ever been to a batting cage?" I ask, fully immersing myself in Nora's excitement, my proximity to Whit, and the plethora of opportunities I seem to be having this morning.

"No!" She grins as her eyes grow bigger. "Can they fly in there?"

I chuckle because she thinks I'm talking about the mammal. "Yeah, they sure can."

"I wanna go! Can we go, Mommy? Can we?"

"Can we, Mommy?" I ask.

"I need to look over my schedule and—"

"Love for you both to go, but if you can't make it, Whit, I think Nora and I could manage."

She flips on her blinker to pull into the school. "I will look at my schedule."

"What about my schedule?" Nora asks.

"I'll look over yours, too," Whitley says, putting the

vehicle in park, opening the door, and sliding out. "First, you have to—"

"Get to school and learn, learn, learn." She unbuckles her own belt, hops out of her seat, leans over the console, and grins. "You and Mommy are my best friends."

"You and your mommy are my best friends, too."

"So, we're all best friends."

"Yeah, we are."

When Whit comes out of the school, she's still rocking shades. When she gets in the vehicle, she says, "This isn't a good idea."

"Do me a favor?"

"What?" she says in a way that is so un-Whitley like as she shifts into gear.

"Take off the sunglasses so I can see your eyes."

"What?" Then she immediately asks, "Why?"

"Because."

"No." She pulls out of the parking lot.

"You're not gonna make this easy."

"*This*? What is this?" she says with anger in her voice now, but at least she sounds alive.

Us—me, you, and Nora, is what I want to say, but that's pushing it too far, too soon, and although time is of the essence, it's important to walk as easy as I can—well, until I have no other choice.

"I'm gonna be here as often as I can from now on. I was gone too damn long." I shake my head. "I've missed you, Whit. Missed home. As fucked up as last night was, it might have been the best night I've had since the night before I left. And Nora, she's amazing."

"She's gone through a lot. She had a very difficult time adjusting." I see tears fall down the side of her face. "I can't lose her; she can't lose me."

"I won't allow that to happen."

"What makes you think you can do a thing? This all happened when you came back. He changed when you came back."

That stings.

"I know it's not you. He's different—"

"He proposed to you after, what — a year of you two seeing each other once or twice a month? I mean, I get it. You're amazing, and hot, and—"

"Would you stop with all that? Pope, I need a friend, not—"

"Okay. That's what you'll get." *For now.*

"I mean it."

"Fine, so hear me out. Not trying to rub salt in a wound, Whit, but he hasn't changed one bit. He could only hide it for so long. I want you to press charges against him, put a fucking restraining order on him—"

"He knows what I did, John Paul. He knows—"

"Which makes him culpable. He's not going to risk his law degree, Whit. He's not."

She pulls up in front of my house, and I reach over and put it in park. Turning to face her, I take off her glasses, and she closes her eyes, but not before I see how red they are.

"I was told there was nothing filed."

She sniffs. "He has her birth certificate, the one I—"

"Whit—"

"He said he'd have her taken away. That he'd make sure she was in foster care and have this held up in court for years."

"He can't do that."

"Yes, he can, and he will. Then what? I'm supposed to lie in court?"

"No, he can't, not when my name is on her original

birth certificate. Ask me if I'd think twice about lying in court to keep you and Nora together."

"I know you; of course you wouldn't."

"I know you, and I'd never have thought you'd go to the extremes you have to protect my name, either, but you did, Whit, and so will I." I pull my phone out of my hoodie pocket. "And it's not going to get that far. His father's called several times, and today, he sent a message. Read it."

After she reads the message, she holds my phone to her chest and closes her eyes. When she opens them, her worry is back. "He's not gonna stop."

I grab her keys and get out. Then I walk around the vehicle, open her door, take her hand, and say, "Let's go."

"I have so much to do," she says but follows me.

Once inside my house, I turn and wrap her up. "Cry, Whit. Let it all out, and then we decide how you want me —or *us*—to respond to this text."

When she releases all that frustration and fear in the form of tears, it's heartbreaking. Her body begins shaking so badly. I lift her up so her feet are just off the floor and walk us to the couch, where I sit beside her as she curls into a ball.

"I'm not weak, or stupid, or—"

She stops when I pull her into another hug.

"You're perfect, Whit."

WHEN I FEEL someone poking me in the arm, my eyes flutter open, and I realize I dozed off after Whit cried herself to sleep with her head on my lap.

"Got a minute?" Marks nods to the other room.

Carefully, I slide out from under her, surprised she

doesn't wake, but also grateful for it. I'm guessing she hasn't slept since I've been home.

I follow him into the kitchen, where he pulls an envelope out of his inside pocket and hands it to me. "I might have lied and said I was you when I called and requested it. Had it sent to your PO Box."

I open the envelope and see Nora Mae Johnston, born March 22nd at 7:37 p.m. She weighed seven pounds, ten ounces, and she was eighteen and a half inches long. Her mother is listed as Nelly Anne Johnston, and her father, John Paul.

"Guessing she didn't know your middle name?"

"Apparently not," I say, staring at my name on Nora's birth certificate.

"Got something else."

"Yeah? What's that?" I ask, looking at her little feet prints.

"Whit's amazing—we all know that—but the fact that Kal is becoming unhinged, that couldn't be all about you."

"What are you implying?"

"Just wondering who Nora's biological father is, aren't you?"

"No." I run a hand through my hair. "Fuck, now I am."

"I'll look into it on the down-low."

"If there's any chance it's going to hurt Nora or Whit, I'm not sure you should."

"I know a guy," he states.

"Yeah, but do you trust him?"

"Of course."

OVER AN HOUR LATER, when Whit wakes up, she can't even look at me. She then insists she has to go grab groceries and get a new phone before she slices her fingers open on the shattered glass of her current one. I grab Mom's cell out of the kitchen drawer.

"When I upgraded my phone, I upgraded Mom's, too. Use it for a while. Keep it if you want. Regardless, I think you should consider changing your number so he stops harassing you."

I pull it out of the box, power it up, tell her the code, and hand it to her.

Shaking her head, she asks, "Why'd you keep it?"

After placing it in her hand, I lean back against the counter and cross my arms. "When Mom gave me my first phone, it came with Dad's number; she didn't want someone else to have it. I think she took comfort in being able to call and text his digits. Guess I just adopted that attachment from her."

"She loved him so much," Whit says, looking down at the phone.

"Wanna see something cool?" I ask, opening the drawer and pulling out the large manila envelope.

"Socorro, Texas?"

"Yeah."

She sets the phone on the counter and pulls Nora's birth certificate out of the envelope. And just like she did with my phone after reading the message from Kal's father, she holds it to her chest and closes her eyes.

"You saying a prayer or allowing yourself to remember where hope lives?"

Her eyes open. "What?"

"When you do that—hold something tight against you like that—you're holding hope. Don't you dare let go of it."

"Tell me you won't take her from me."

I hold out my pinkie. "I promise."

She hooks hers around mine, never breaking eye contact.

I pull her closer and wrap my arm around her. "Stop looking at me like I'd ever do anything that would hurt you. I'm still me, Whit, and you're still you. We just have a few years on us."

She allows me to hold her a bit longer before she steps back and picks up Mom's phone. "I'll use this, but only because if I mail mine in for repair, I'll save the headache of them trying to sell me on a plan at the store. When it comes back, you get Mama Pope's back."

That's a start, I think. But instead of saying that, I just nod.

Then she looks at me, and I see a hint of a smile.

"What's making you want to smile?"

"You've changed."

Glad you noticed.

"How so?"

"You would have never delayed taking a shower immediately after returning from a run. You used to leave in the middle of a conversation and make me wait when you were sweaty."

"Wasn't about the sweat, Whit. It was about control."

Her eyes narrow. "That's so messed up. Rude, actually. What the heck?"

"Not about controlling you."

"You know my headspace is a little bit messy. Could you be a little less cryptic?"

"After a game, a workout, busting my ass for Danny's old man, my testosterone level was pretty damn high. Then, there you were."

She still looks confused.

"I needed to take care of myself."

"Oh my God, shut up."
I wink. "Say *please*."

AFTER A SHOWER, I go to pick her up at her place. She's still getting ready herself, so I sit and drink some sweet tea with Pastor B and Mrs. B while waiting. Nothing much has changed at all with them. Monday through Thursday, they visit jails and rehab centers to spread the Word. Sundays, they spend all day at First Methodist, and on Fridays and Saturdays, they prepare for the week ahead.

I let Pastor and Mrs. B know that I invited Whit and Nora to go to the batting cages near Fort Worth and that Whit is still working that out. I also invite them, but they decline.

WHIT

10

Friday

Elbow on the console, one hand on the wheel, hat on backward, he checks on Nora at least once a minute. Nora who passed out after spending two full hours at the batting cages, and then going to dinner at a barbecue place we'd gone to dozens of times with Bianca after she had taken us to the same place. Then, we hit the ice cream stand that all four of us always got huge sundaes. I can't believe Nora ate as much as she did.

"Mom ever meet Nora?" he asks.

"A few times. She was at the baby shower the ladies of the church hosted for Nelly. Then, after she gave birth, Nelly spent the first few months here. She then moved away, got her own place, and then she ..." Whit shrugs instead of saying *she died*. "I have a picture of Bianca holding Nora."

"Yeah?"

"I took more but gave them to Nelly. They might be in

one of the boxes with her belongings in storage that I plan to one day let Nora sort through."

"Nora ever talk about Nelly?"

"She knows Nelly was her mom first, and then she had to go to heaven and wanted me to be her mom."

There's so much more that I could tell him, all the incredibly sad things, the things that make me angry, and the miracle that Nora is. I know he adores her, and she talks nonstop about him. No need to muck up the beauty of that. Not yet anyway.

"You have fun tonight?"

"Yeah, it's been a while."

"You've still got it, Whit. I can't believe you didn't get to play in college."

I glance back at Nora. "She's better than softball."

"I get that."

I'm not sure he does, but he needs to. "I love her more than I have ever loved anyone or anything in my entire life."

His lips turn up. "Always knew you'd be an amazing mom."

"Oh, please." I huff.

"How many more do you want?" he asks.

I quickly answer, "I'm good at one."

"That's not fair."

"It's totally fair. I'll be able to give her so many opportunities and—"

"Siblings?"

"Never part of the plan."

"Totally understand that when you were making plans with—"

"Do not ruin tonight with his name."

"Wasn't planning on it. I was just going to say the wrong person."

Taking First

This is not the first time since he's been home that I've had butterflies fluttering around in my tummy—*or further south*—but just like the other times, I picture myself capturing them with a net and tossing them right out of there. I do not have the luxury of being smitten with Pope, *not again*.

"I just know I wish my parents had had more. They were happy with one." He smiles. "Mom loved you like a daughter, and Marks and Danny like sons. You took care of her when I—"

"If the roles were reversed, you'd have done the same for us."

"I love this game, but my dream was a ten-year career in baseball, and then I always planned to come back here and ask the girl to marry me. Have at least two before we were thirty, beg her for a couple of more before thirty-five."

"Come back here and ask the *girl,"* is what I heard, but I'm sure he said *a* girl.

"Your type doesn't seem to be the kind who'd want to live in Walton, let alone birth four children."

"Gotta ask," he says with his major league smirk. "What exactly do you think my type is?"

"Blondes with C cups that probably aren't real. Ones who have never missed a spa appointment, who wear designer clothes and actually choose to wear shoes that look more like torture devices. Women who would never eat a doughnut hole, let alone two whole doughnuts—and most of the time want to grab a third and devour it because it's so much easier than making a salad when they've been on their feet for twelve hours."

"Is that right?" He chuckles again.

"I've seen the women you date."

"You've seen the women I take to functions that require a date."

"Oh yeah? They leave right after?"

"Sometimes, but I can promise they never stayed the night or expected anything more than a good time."

"So, hookers."

"Jesus, Whit, is that what you think of me?" he asks as if he's offended.

"It's an assumption. Prove me wrong." What the heck is wrong with me? Why can't I just shut up already?

"Three is my number. All of them after Mom passed. None of them were interested in dating or a relationship. All wanted the same thing I did—to get off."

"Gross."

"The last woman was the one I spent the most time with—"

I cover my ears. "I do not want to know these things."

Grinning, he grabs my hand and holds it against the leather console. "After attending a charity event where a ton of little ones were running around, she told me it was obvious I adored kids. I was worried—nah, *worried* doesn't quite describe what I was feeling." He widens his eyes. "I was freaking out that she had gotten the rules twisted."

"Rules?"

"No overnights, no attachments."

"That's horrible."

"Don't judge. All of them were as career-focused as me."

I can't help but laugh out a big fat lie. "I'm not judging."

"She told me that I was a settling-down type and that I should find a woman who would be my best friend and marry her." He glances over at me. "How do you feel about that?"

Don't feel, don't think, don't, don't, don't.

"I think your best friend—Nora—is too young to get married."

He pulls my hand up and kisses the back of it while silently laughing. "I've missed you, Whit. Missed us, this, so damn much."

"I missed you, too, but we're older now, and a lot has happened. I'm not the same person I used to be, and—"

He cuts me off with a laugh. "I can see you've changed. You're all grown up. You're Major League Whitley. You're a MIL—"

I cover his mouth. "Don't you dare."

THE REST of the ride home was quiet. Quiet in the way that allowed the voices in my head to scream lies about how *your dreams were always the same as his* and how *things could work out*. I just hope those screams were unheard by Pope because the rational and logical part of me knows that it would never work.

I'm not the naïve little girl who thought, one day, that boy would love me and he'd love me forever. He's a major league baseball player. He has women around him who follow "rules" that the boy he once was would have never dreamed of setting.

John Paul carried Nora inside, up the stairs, grabbed her pajamas as I changed her out of her sweatshirt and little jeans, and tucked her in with me.

Outside in the hall, with the door closed behind us, he whispers, "You think you could sneak out and come hang by the firepit? I'll burn you some marshmallows."

"I need to get some sleep. But thank you for tonight."

He licks his lips, wetting them as he looks me over.

"Understood." He nods toward the stairs and winks. "I could really use a shower, anyway."

I pretend I don't understand what he's alluding to, but I'm not sure he buys it because the temperature in the house rises ten degrees due to the heat that's being thrown from my face.

He walks down the stairs, chuckling, and I stand at the top, listening to him talk to Popa B and Gram for long enough that I'm sure I'll fall asleep.

Sleep doesn't come easy, especially after I receive a text.

JOHN GREGORY PAUL:

> Goodnight. Sleep well, Whitley. X, JP

I hold the phone to my chest and realize that Pope must have had everything transferred from the old phone to the one he upgraded when he decided to keep her number, because I can't imagine he'd have put his full name in the contacts.

Something I've had to work on all my life is not letting the way I perceive others' feelings about me mold me into who I am. This has caused me to become acutely self-aware. I know that I have a deep need to understand things, including different people's perspectives, and often spend way too much time contemplating why they feel or act the way they do.

The day Bianca Paul told me that she felt sorry for my mother because she was missing out on the greatest gift a mother was given—the ability to watch me grow into an amazing and beautiful woman—was the day I adopted that same belief. That was also the day I got my period and felt like I couldn't talk to Gram about it and the day Bianca took me into the city to have me fitted for my first bra, which, looking back, I know was way overdue.

This need to understand people sometimes causes me to have a tendency to dig deeper into things that might not be my business at all. And sometimes, like right now, I can't rest until I find the answers. Right now, I have an overwhelming desire to know just what's on this phone.

I tap in the code he gave me—1259—and make sure to avoid the messages app because I don't want him to know I read his good night message, but I do hit the photos app.

My eyes immediately fill with tears when I see photos of Pope and Bianca. The way he looked at her with such love and grief in those last few days is beautiful in the saddest way.

I keep scrolling and see pictures of them at a few games she was able to attend before she got sick, and the pride in her eyes is exactly like it always was when she looked or even spoke of him. The most captivating thing about them was he looked at her in that same way. He was so proud of his mother and who she was. He loved her in a way you just don't see many people loving a parent.

I scroll through and keep looking at the beauty that was Pope and his mother's relationship, the same one I hope to build with Nora. I find pictures of Bianca at my college graduation, and the pride in her eyes for me is nearly the same. The high school graduation party in the empty lot beside their home, under a giant tent, two weeks before he left, one she and Pope had demanded would be both mine and his even though I didn't really want one. The close-ups of him and me and ones of him looking at me when I was talking with Gram or one of the church ladies—and those, they are plentiful. And so are the ones of me watching him, one in which my lower lip is caught between my teeth. How embarrassing is it that she not only saw but captured that moment? Super, super embarrassing, so much so that I scroll back and increase the size of the ones where he's looking at me to see if I can catch something as telling, but all I see is how proud he seemed of me. Then I see the one of us wearing our ball uniforms, and the number on both of our jerseys— 22.

"Gotta be fate Whitley Mae Belington," he had said, and even though I'd let myself soar on that cloud way to many times, on cloud 22, I never thought he really meant it the way I took it.

I WAKE in the same position I fell asleep, with the cord attached to the phone lying on my chest. The phone that is vibrating.

I pick it up and see a text.

JOHN GREGORY PAUL:

> Good morning, Whit. Mark, Danny, and I are headed to the lake. Pastor B and Mrs. B are planning to make the trip. You and Nora up for some fishing?

"Mommy"—Nora, who has become a morning person in a week's time, slides across the hardwood floor and into my room—"Popa B said he and Gram are going fishing. Can we go? Huh? Can we?" She dives on the bed and wallops me in the nose with her stuffie as she goes in for a hug.

"Isn't it too cold for fishing?" I ask, pulling her in tight as my eyes water from the impact.

"Popa B said it's too cold for swimming, but he didn't say nothin' about fishing." Her little mouth opens in an O before she asks, "How can the fish swim if it's too cold?"

From my open doorway, Popa B chuckles. "Certain ones swim year-round."

She moves off of me, grinning. "Which ones?"

"If I remember correctly, at Danny's family's lake, there are lots of speckled trout, and spotted ones, too."

She jumps up and down. "Are they pretty?"

Popa B gives me a look, which I read as, *You wanna handle this one?*

"It's not about how they look, little slugger; it's about how they taste."

Her nose scrunches up.

"We eat fish almost every Friday." Popa B laughs. "These days, we usually catch them at the store."

WHEN YORK SHOWS up at the house at eight thirty in the morning, it suddenly hits me that we planned to take Nora out for a girls' date because she didn't want her to think Pope was cooler or more fun than us, and I agreed.

"You forgot," she says, walking in.

"It was set as a reminder on my phone," I admit.

"Your phone that you mailed in to get fixed."

"Exactly."

"Morning, Miss Gwen." Nora, who is the only one I ever hear calling York by her first name, beams as she walks into the kitchen. "Mommy let me eat cereal in the living room in front of the TV, like she did, when she was little like me."

"That's so cool." York squats down at eye level, and I take the empty bowl with a built-in straw from Nora—it's the only real way to get her to drink milk in the morning. "You know what else your mommy thinks you're grown up enough to do?"

"Go fishing?" Nora jumps up and down. "Can we, Mommy? Can we?"

York grabs her hands and looks at her nails. "We're doing something way cooler than fishing. We're going to have a girls' day at the spa and get our nails and toes painted."

Nora's little face scrunches up. "Then, can we go fishing at Uncle Danny's lake?"

"I mean, maybe, but do you really want to get fish yuck on your pretty nails?"

Undeterred, Nora states, "Yeah."

"Guts and scales and—"

"What's guts and scales?" she asks York.

"The parts you don't eat."

"All right," I cut off the conversation before York doesn't simply change her mind, but scars her for life. "Go brush your teeth and put on some clothes. We don't want to be late for our appointment at the spa."

Nora's off in a flash.

"Appointment?" York laughs at me.

"You called the nail place, which sits between the liquor store and a tattoo shop in a strip mall, a spa," I defend.

"They're amazing, and they only charge twenty bucks for a pedicure."

"I'm not complaining."

WE HAVE fun at the burger joint where, when you step in, you feel like you've walked back in time. Even the waitstaff plays the part. The music is a bit too loud but works in the '60s atmosphere.

Heading to York's car when she receives a message. After reading it, she hands me her phone.

Taking First

CHLOE SHAW:

> Sorry to bother you, but Spud has found out my new number and said if I don't call him, he's going to come here and make me talk to him. He says he has this address.

"Call her." I hand York the phone. "Tell her we're picking her up."

"Who, Mommy?" Nora asks.

"Miss Chloe. She used to play softball with me."

"Does she like to go fishing?" she asks.

I look at York, who shrugs.

"I bet she would love that."

"Awesomesauce!" She jumps up and down. "She can sit next to me. Is she short? Does she need a booster? She needs to be safe, right, Mommy?"

She sure does.

AS I EXPECTED, Nora talks Chloe's ear off the entire forty minutes to the lake, but Chloe seems to enjoy it, encourages it even.

Nora has a way about her that makes you forget all the bad things that could be lurking in the dark corners and instead reminds you of all the awesome surrounding you. I suppose all kids have that effect if allowed. I certainly didn't get to feel safe enough to do that with my mother, but Popa B and Gram made up for it in spades.

I swear it all changed when I became a preteen. The first time I asked what a period was at the dinner table, Popa B nearly choked to death—and not in a figurative sense. Gram wasn't much better. She told me a lady of her age wouldn't be of much help in that department and suggested I ask the school nurse. It was the right call, but it was also the weekend. Thank God for Bianca Paul.

When we pull down the dirt road, it's close to two in the afternoon, and Nora is all but bouncing out of her seat.

York smiles. "Unbuckle and stick your head out the window. Feel that—"

"What?" I gasp, but it's too late. It's also the moment I find out Nora can unbuckle herself, and I don't like it at all. "You're a cop."

"We're on a private road to a private home," she scoffs.

I reach back as Nora leans out the window and see that Chloe has moved and is holding her around the waist.

"We're here!" Nora calls out.

"And just who are you announcing our arrival to? The trees?" Chloe laughs.

"Trees and fishes, we have arrived!" Nora yells, and then she continues, "Let's get this party started!"

All of us are still laughing when we pull up to a stop beside Popa B and Gran's car.

Pope walks around the corner, smiling. "No need to get you a bell, little slugger."

He pulls her out through the window as she asks, "What's a bell for?"

"So we hear you when you're coming," he explains and gives me a wink as he walks away with her on his hip.

"Please tell me I'm not the only one whose ovaries just exploded," Chloe whispers.

"Gonna check for wet spots as soon as Whit—"

I smack York in the arm. "Don't be nasty."

"Are you two finally official? Please tell me yes because so many of us wanted to kick you square in the ass just to watch you fall into that boy's open arms back in school."

"What are you even talking about?" Okay, so I'm playing dumb. I do kind of know what she's talking about since going through Bianca's private photos, but there is no chance I'm admitting to that.

"The only male who's ever looked at me like John Paul has always looked at you is a dog I had growing up."

"Golden retriever?" York asks.

"Yep, old Max." Chloe leans forward. "Rumor has it, you dumped Stewie, so what's the holdup?"

"She's an idiot," York states in that tell-it-like-it-is way of hers.

"How do you really feel?" I ask dryly.

Chloe turns to her and accuses. "So are you."

York's head whips around. "Excuse me?"

"Leland Locke? You two were as in love as they come, and then it all just fell apart."

"Are you gonna be okay?" York deadpans.

"Not for nothing, but some of us have to live vicariously through the Whitleys and the Gwens of the world. We didn't all come out of the womb looking like you two. The rest of us have to get up two hours early to primp in order to look halfway decent."

That just pisses me off. "You're insane, Chloe Shaw. You're a freaking bombshell. I have no idea why you ever allowed the likes of Spud White within arm's reach of you."

"Well, what do we have here?" I turn and see Danny standing there, looking at Chloe. He stretches out his arms. "Welcome to the lake, Miss Shaw." Then he reaches over and opens the door. "Can I get you a drink?"

Sliding out, she huffs, "Pick your jaw up out of the dirt, Danny Aiken. You didn't look at me twice in school. You don't get to now that I've lost weight and bought tits."

"I'll look at you three, four, five—hell, I'll look at you a million times to make up for my youthful blunder."

"Well, shit." York laughs as she gets out.

"Don't think you're off the hook, Miss Thing."

"What are you talking about?" she asks.

"Leland Locke. How did I not know anything about that?"

"Wasn't a secret. You just never pulled your head out of *cloud twenty-two* long enough to notice anything else going on in Walton." She nods to Danny and Chloe. "We should probably let Chloe know Pastor B is here so she can retract the claws, or she might never walk into the church again."

I link my arm through hers. "But her claws sure do look good out, don't they?"

She wags her brows. "Maybe Danny can help Chloe get her groove back."

POPE

11

Saturday

"You sure they're sober enough to deal with an issue if it arises?" Whit asks as we pull onto the main road.

"Chloe turned off her phone, even though there's little chance that he has her location. She has two cops who are, without question, smarter while drunk than old Spud is on any given day. They'll be fine."

"I hate him for hurting her, and maybe even more because not one single part of him didn't know he was a monster and that she deserved better."

"Danny sure seems to want to see her happy." I chuckle in an attempt to lighten the mood.

"I'd chop off his balls if he touched her before she was ready to move on."

"Mom used to say, you never meet the right person at the wrong time. She believed that we *never* meet the wrong person at all. Each person serves a purpose, they're either a blessing or a lesson. Either way, they are the right person at that time." I shake my head and continue, "Maybe they are the right person to hurt us so we raise our standards, learn what our boundaries or non negotiables are. Maybe they are the right person to leave us so we will realize we can stand on our own two feet. Maybe they are the right person to break us so we can build ourselves up on our own. Maybe they are the right person, but for a different reason than we expected."

"I miss my talks with her," she whispers.

"Right now, she'd assure you that life doesn't give you the people that you want; it gives you the people that you need. So, maybe Danny is exactly what Chloe needs."

"I'd love a sweet tea and biscuits chat right now. She'd help me figure out why on earth Kal was part of my life. I find it hard to believe he should have been part of it."

Fucker, I think, and right then, something inside my gut turns. "He have access to the women's shelter?"

She huffs, "His family donates a ton of money; of course he does."

"Are there security cameras there?" I ask.

"Why? What does this have to do with—" She stops as realization hits. "Chloe's name and new phone number are in the system. I think I'm gonna get sick."

"Any reason we can't get Nora tucked in and go check it out?" I ask.

Hands to her belly, she shakes her head.

This motherfucker, I think as my grip on the steering wheel tightens.

"Let York know your suspicions," I tell her.

"Don't credit me for something I didn't think of."

Taking First

"BASEBALL OR FISHES?" Nora yawns as I carry her up the stairs.

"Both," I whisper.

"Me, too," she says, leaning her head against my chest. "Mommy, do I gotta take a bath?"

"You can wait until tomorrow morning before church."

"You're the best."

"No, you're the best." Whit peppers kisses on her cheek as I sit down on her bed and situate Nora, who's pretty much boneless at this point, on my lap.

"I think you're both the best."

"That's 'cause you're the best, too." Nora lifts her arms as Whit pulls her shirt off. "Mommy, I'm so cold."

"Footies tonight?" Whit asks, moving to her dresser.

"Uh-huh." Nora slides off my lap and shimmies out of her little jeans while Whit grabs fuzzy pink pajamas then a white tee, which she tosses to me.

"Arms up."

She yawns, putting them in the air, and I slide the T-shirt over her head.

"Feet in," Whit says, and within seconds, she's all zipped up.

I stand and pull back her comforter then grab her up and set her in the middle. "You do prayers?"

She yawns again as she nods, and then Whit yawns and, yep, they're contagious 'cause I'm doing it now, too.

I pop a kiss on the top of Nora's head. "I'll leave you ladies to it. See you at church in the morning."

"Kiss Mommy's head too."

"Nora, it's—" Whit stops mid-sentence when I do just that, and Nora starts giggling.

Downstairs, Pastor B and Mrs. B are sitting at the table.

"We had a great day today. Thank you for inviting us." He smiles.

I shove my hands in my pockets, and I have no idea why, but I'm feeling anxious as hell right now. "Thank you both for coming."

"She's got you twisted up, doesn't she?" Pastor B chuckles.

Being as honest as I can, I ask, "Which one?"

"Son, Whit's had you twisted up since you walked into our church the very first time." He smiles. "And now, Nora, has you by the heartstrings, too."

"Won't deny either one of those things."

"What are you going to do about it?" he asks, eyes locked with mine.

"Arthur Belington," Mrs. B tsks. "You need to stop meddling."

"Will I have your blessing when I figure out how to untangle it all?"

Mrs. B giggles. "Well, now."

"Will you wait until she's ready?" Pastor B asks, eyes narrowed a bit, lips in a straight line.

"I'll try my best."

His face breaks into a smile. "You have our blessing."

"You sure do," Mrs. B says.

"You two mind if Whit and I head over to the women's shelter to look into something?"

"Got anything to do with Chloe Shaw?" Pastor B asks.

"It does."

I hear Whit coming down the stairs, and Pastor B says, "Heard talk about a couple of games in Vegas next week."

"Love to have all four of you there. You could fly in with—"

"Our weekends are the Lord's, but I'm bettin' Whit, Gwen, and Chloe would love to see you play."

"Popa B," Whit gasps, shaking her head.

"Don't shake your head at me, young lady. You haven't been away from Walton since you became a mom. Gram and I are gonna take a few of the kids to that new water park near Fort Worth. She won't miss you one bit."

"Work," Whit says.

"You work one weekend a month. You have next weekend off. Use a personal day for Thursday."

"Well, I don't know if York and—"

"Whit, come on. You'll have fun. So will Nora." She narrows her eyes at me, and I hold my hands up. "It'll be a girls' trip."

WALKING OUT OF THE HOUSE, I can't help but laugh. "How's the air up there?"

"What?" she snips.

"You've done that since I've known you. You get pissed, and you stick your nose up in the air. Not gonna lie, I worry that if you do when it rains, you might drown, Whit."

"You're not funny." She starts toward her vehicle, and I move around her, scoop her up, and throw her over my shoulder.

"You big jerk, put me down before I kick you in the junk," she growls.

"No way we're driving separately."

Her fingers knot in the back of my hair. "No kidding, but the residents know my car, and it won't freak them out if they happen to see it."

"My bad." I make a U-turn and head toward her vehicle.

"Last warning, in three… two—"

"Fine," I concede as I put her on her feet. "You changed your clothes."

"I smelled like camp."

"You smell like bluebonnets right before they fully blossom—always have."

She turns back and scowls. "Can we focus on the task at hand?"

"Sure can, Whit." I open the passenger door and wave my hand in front of me. "But only if you let me drive."

It's silent as I drive until Whit finally breaks it. "Did you know Leland Locke and York had a thing?"

"When?"

"In school."

"No, I must have missed that."

"You worshipped him." She sits back. "How did you not know this?"

"Don't get it twisted. I didn't worship him; I admired his talent. Learned what I could from him. I didn't tell you because I truly didn't know."

"Danny and Marks never mentioned it?"

"Not to me."

Silence again. This time, it's me who breaks it. "Fish or baseball?"

She smiles. "She just couldn't pick."

"Says it was her first time getting her nails done."

She nods. "Yeah."

"You never did that girlie stuff before. Just that once for prom."

"Sure didn't, but York insists we treat ourselves once in a while."

"She and you got close," I state.

"Yeah, she's a good friend." She leans forward as we turn down the road toward the women's center. "Pull into the back. I'll go in the front and let you in the back door."

"You hiding me, Whit?" I joke.

"No need to get them nervous or riled up."

"You saying I still got it?"

Sliding out of the car, she replies, "Pfft, I never said you had it to begin with."

As Whit heads in, I look around and see way too many issues that need to be addressed, like the fact that the lighting back here sucks. I don't like the idea of Whit walking out here and some angry ex going after her.

Leaning forward, I also notice there's no light on the camera above the door. Does the damn thing even work?

It feels like forever before the back door opens and Whit waves me in.

Inside, she leads me through a small corridor and points toward an office. "That's where I do meds once a week. Make sure everyone has everything they need and put each person's in their weekly pill organizers. We tell them it's to make it easier for them, but it's also a safety measure. People can be at their lowest of lows when they're going through such a difficult time. The computers are in here." She flips on a light to a small room with a couple of desks and computers. "I looked at the physical logbook when I came in, and no unusual people have signed in, so grab a chair and get comfy."

I pull over a wheeled chair that looks extremely uncomfortable, and lo and behold, it is. "What's it take to fund this place?"

"More than the state is willing to cough up," she says as she taps away at the keyboard. "The building was donated by the town. Back in the '50s, it was a school. It would have caved in eventually. Aiken Construction donated the materials and labor to fix the roof. We got a few grants to cover windows and entries, and security cameras were covered, too. The furniture and clothes for those who come in with nothing are all donated. Hygiene products and food can typically be bought with fundraiser money. We do four fundraisers a year. Bianca was on the board until she got sick."

"She never said anything."

"I'm not surprised. Are you?"

I can almost hear Mom saying, "Don't brag about the good deeds you do here on earth. Reap your rewards in heaven."

"Was she always religious?" Whit asks as the program opens up with four squares, showing the building's entries.

"We went to church every Sunday. All three of us when Dad wasn't deployed. But I wouldn't say she was religious. She just believed in the power of faith and doing good things. I think when Dad was killed in action, she leaned into it more." I nod to the screens. "Tell me more about this place. What else does it take to run it?"

"Not much more to tell. Donations help pay utilities and some of the staff. The Sewards have been generous. It was implied they'd be even more so once we were married." She all but cringes when she says that last bit. "York and I have discussed some ideas, like increasing the fundraising efforts and looking for more grants."

"Been thinking more and more about starting a charity in my parents' name. Mom and I talked about a charity to help families of soldiers killed in duty, and when Mom was sick, I realized if I didn't have you all, I—" I stop, not wanting to get too deep. "My point is, she was clearly also passionate about this place, and so are you. I want to help."

She pauses what she's doing and looks at me. "You're being serious?"

"With money, of course. And when my name gets out there some more, my old jerseys will be worth a hell of a lot more to a place like this than a storage box. What else am I gonna do with them?"

She smiles.

"In both the minors and majors we've done so many fundraisers. People pay thousands of dollars for a seat and a few hours with their favorite team. They also love knowing their money is going to do some good. It's also a tax write-off. Most would rather donate to a good cause than pay more taxes."

The way she's looking at me right now makes me feel so damn good that I can't even describe it, but I know that's how I want Whitley to look at me every time she glances in my direction.

She clears her throat while she stands, cheeks pinkening. "You want some coffee?"

"You asking me on a date?" I ask like I'm joking. *I'm not.*

"No, I'm asking if you want some coffee." She rolls her eyes as she makes her way to the coffeepot.

I cover my heart with my hand. "Ouch."

"Get over it."

"I'm still gonna let myself believe it's a date."

"I thought Major League Pope didn't go on dates," she says, making light of what she knows is going on.

"There's only ever been one person I'd make an exception—"

"How far has the footage gone back?"

I look at the time stamp. "Still rolling back through yesterday."

"I think we should go back a few days, don't you?"

I watch as she puts just a shot of vanilla creamer in her coffee. This is new. Whit used to only drink coffee if half of the cup was filled with milk. *Major League Whit takes it strong.*

"I'm good with going all the way back to when Chloe moved in here. See how long he's been—" I stop speaking when I see a Porsche roll up to the front entrance and hit pause. "Come here and tell me if you think this is your ex's vehicle."

She walks back over, two cups in her hands, and sets mine down. "Black, two sugars?"

"Thanks, Whit."

She sits beside me and hits a few keys, rewinding the frame until the vehicle is backed out of it, and then hits some more keys, making the frames move slowly. She again pauses then zooms in on the license plate and whispers, "Too blurry."

As the footage rolls slowly, we watch as someone walks out to the car, pulls something out of her pocket, bends over, and hands that something to the driver something.

"You know who that is?"

Swallowing hard, she nods. "Unfortunately, yes, I think so." She leans back from the screen as the car takes off, and the woman turns and walks back in. "That's Alice. She's one of the nine paid employees. She works nights."

"You okay?" I ask, knowing damn well she's not.

"She's working tonight." "I know exactly what I'd do. I'd question Alice immediately. Ask her why I'm looking at her handing something off to who I'm damn sure is Kal Seward the day before Spud obtained confidential information about a woman who should have felt safe here."

"That's exactly what I'd like to do." She looks back at the screen. "But I can't make that call on my own."

"Talk it out," I encourage.

"We never bring a woman to a shelter this close to her abuser. I just knew Chloe needed to get out of there. This was my push."

"I'm sure you did what was necessary."

"I thought so. I need to talk to York—tomorrow when she's sober, of course. Then we'll call an emergency board meeting. This has never happened. I can't leave here when I'm questioning if the women are safe. Overnights, there's one person on, and that one person knows they never leave the building unless there's an emergency and the police have been called."

"As of right now, you're a hundred percent sure that Alice broke at least one rule last night." I point to the monitor showing the evidence.

She nods.

"That's a safety and security issue. I'm guessing that alone calls for an emergency meeting."

"I can't leave them," she states, eyes glossing over.

"We're not done going through the videos, not even close. We're not going anywhere."

"I can't expect you to sit here in a mess of my own doing."

"You didn't create this issue. I'm not leaving, Whit." I hit the keys, rewinding the footage further. "We're figuring this out, but I gotta tell you, this date is going to be the last one your ex gets to be a part of."

POPE

12

Monday

"The board asked Whitley to step down?" Danny asks. I simply nod, not trusting myself to speak because nothing good will come out of my mouth if I do. "And York?"

Marks answers that one. "York's not being portrayed as a scorned ex, nor would they say that's the reason behind them asking Whit to step down. York will be leaving once she figures out why the hell Kal's been stopping by once a week since Alice was the last full-time hire, which didn't happen until after the Sewards started donating to the shelter."

"Glad shit flows downstream. We wouldn't want that local shit in Seward-ville to flow upstream and taint the waters of Walton," Danny grumbles and looks at me. "So, how's Whit?"

"Not good, I'm sure," I answer.

"How do you not know?" he all but accuses, which pisses me off and pleases me at the same time.

"Because she's working a ten-hour shift."

"And you're sure Chloe's staying with them?" Danny asks ... *again*.

"Yes," both Marks and I answer... *again*.

"She going to Vegas with the girls still?" he asks.

"York seems to think so," Marks answers. "You hear anything?"

I give him a thumbs-up, and he chuckles, knowing that's all I've been getting from Whit in reply to my good morning and good night messages. "Shit's not funny."

"It's Whit."

"Yeah, well, it didn't used to be." *Before Nelly told her little lie, one in which I can't hate her for, not at all.*

"You giving up already?" Marks ask

I just look at him.

"You get in touch with Kevin Seward?" Marks asks.

I shake my head as I look at the phone to check the time. It's nine. Whit should be driving by soon on her way home. "Hasn't been a good time to talk to Whit about what she wants me to do, and I'm not going to do a damn thing until I know it's in her best interest."

"You stopped at the school today?" Danny asks.

I nod. "Pastor B reminded me on Sunday that I promised some of the youth of the congregation. I tagged along when he picked up Nora today, and the three of us went over."

"Is Nora calling you Uncle yet, like she does with us?" Danny taunts.

"I know you think it's cute that we're on different levels with Nora, and you're not wrong." I hold a hand about chest high. "You're here." I lift it to my nose. "And I'm about here."

"Such bullshit," Danny groans.

"What's bullshit is just about everything that comes out

of your mouth, Danny Aiken." This comes from behind us, and we all swing around to see Chloe walking down the street.

Danny hops over the porch railing and damn near falls. "What the hell are you doing out at this time of night, all alone?"

"I'm not under house arrest, you damn fool. I'm a guest."

"And you have an ex who—"

"Is no doubt afraid of Pastor Belington? He's not coming around these parts."

"You, of all people, know what he's capable of. I'll not have you—"

"Damn right you'll *not have me*." Chloe cuts him off. "We established that Saturday night, or did you forget?"

Both Marks and I chuckle.

"You got a beer for your neighbor?"

"We're on the H2O for the week." Marks nods to the cooler. "A soda if you think you can handle the caffeine at this time of night."

She looks at Danny, and he holds his hands up. "Not sure we could handle two weekends in a row if we got into the sauce on a Monday night. We're lightweights."

The slight upward twist of her lips tells me that she likes that, and I can't blame her, knowing now that her ex got really heavy-handed when he drank—and he drank often.

"I think I can handle a Dr. Pepper, if you have one."

"Pope keeps that on hand."

"Smooth," Chloe scolds Danny as Marks pops the tab and hands her one.

"What?" he asks, clueless to the fact that she obviously caught on that I keep that brand in stock for Whit.

And now, I also have vanilla creamer.

"Smooth as a cat's tongue," Marks says dryly.

Chloe rolls her eyes at Danny and takes a sip, sliding her gaze to me. "Pastor B was saying there was record attendance at First Methodist yesterday." Then she looks at Danny and Marks. "He was very happy you two were there."

"Everyone needs a good dose of Jesus and Pastor B to get them on the straight and narrow," Danny states, like it's the gospel.

Marks and I exchange looks, both obviously aware that Danny is in hot pursuit of Chloe Shaw.

"Some more than others," she quips at him.

We all look left as headlights start coming down the street, and behind it is another set.

My heart stays stuck right in my damn throat as I wait to see if it's York. I grab a ball out of the bucket next to me.

"You damn fool." Chloe snatches it away. "Sometimes, a girl needs to feel like she's her own hero in order to heal."

I narrow my eyes. "Why the hell do you think I've been keeping a distance?"

"Watch the tone with the lady, Pope," Danny snaps.

Chloe rolls her eyes at him and looks back at me as she holds up one finger. "You've given her less than a day."

"I've given her much more than that." *So much wasted time.*

"Let her come to you." Chloe insists as Whit's car pulls to a stop in front of the house, and York pulls up behind. Chloe quirks a perfectly shaped brow. "Give her as much as she needs."

"I have a window of opportunity that's closing day by day."

She nudges me with her hip and whispers, "I always

thought the Pope and Whit I knew back in the day had a lifetime."

A smile tugs at my lips as Whit steps out of her vehicle, pulling a hoodie over her head. "I really hope you four fools stop sitting out in the cold like you're waiting for the annual parade."

"My bad," Chloe says, taking off down the stairs. She hooks her arm through Whit's and the other through York's. "I snuck out after reading approximately eight bedtime stories."

"Eight?" Whit gasps. "She's playing you."

She used the Mommy-has-to-work-late-again card with those big brown eyes and her pouty bottom lip. I caved like a sandcastle at high tide."

"You're going to be a teacher; you'd better learn how to recognize a master manipulator." York giggles.

"Maybe I should finish my hours and get my cosmetology license."

"What?" Whit laughs as I hand her an open Dr. Pepper then hand York one, too.

"Two-time loser here. Quit college then became a beauty school dropout."

Danny pipes in, "Don't talk shit about yourself. You had circumstances surrounding both situations."

"What do you know about my situation?" Chloe laughs.

He gives her a look like she knows the answer to that question. Then, highly un-Danny like, he avoids stepping further into shit and asks the right question. "Which job would make you happier?"

Whit and I look at each other and share a smile.

Wanting to keep her attention, I ask, "How was work?"

"Busy," she says before taking a drink of her Dr. Pepper. Then she asks, "How was your day?"

"Good." I nod to the garage. "Electric's updated. Plumbing's tomorrow, and then insulation and walls."

"I can't believe you're doing"—she shakes her head—"all of this."

"I can't believe I didn't start as soon as I got that signing bonus."

She looks down to hide a smile but then gives it to me. "She would be so proud of you."

"No doubt she is." I take the opportunity to push a bit, just a gentle nudge. "Wish she could be in Vegas this week."

As Whit does, she sees right through me. "I know another girl who wishes she could be there."

Smiling, I tell her, "That other girl can be there. And I really hope she shows."

Brow arched, she responds, "She's going to a waterpark with a few of her church friends."

I lean in and whisper, "Stop trying to date me through your daughter."

She shoves me gently and whispers, "You don't get to use my words against me."

"I'll use whatever I can to steer us back to good, Whit, all three of us."

Her brows turn in slightly.

"My hands are on the wheel, but it's your foot that's in control of the gas."

After that message has been delivered, I force myself to focus on something else.

Nodding toward Danny and Chloe, I chuckle. "And then there's these two."

Whit smiles as she shakes her head. "He'd better not hurt her."

"Pay closer attention, Whit. It should be his heart you're worried about."

Wednesday

"WHAT'S GONNA BE UP THERE?" Nora asks as we pass the garage, heading toward the house to use the bathroom so she and I can get washed up to go grab a snack in town, which was approved by Whit with a thumbs-up emoji.

"A couple bedrooms and bathrooms," I answer with a smile.

"And a high-up porch?"

"Yep." I smile.

"What about the other bedrooms inside?"

"The inside's gonna change, too. But I'll need a place to sleep while that's happening."

"'Cause you're gonna live in Walton, too?"

We have similar discussions daily. She needs reassurance that I'm not going anywhere, and I'll give her that as often as she needs.

"When I'm not working, I'm going to be here as much as I can be."

"You gotta work in Florida and then in New York?"

I open the back door and we walk into the kitchen. Then I pick her up and set her on the counter before turning on the faucet.

"Just like you've been practicing throwing, catching, and batting every day, I have to do that with my team, too."

"And you'll teach me all the things you learn when you come back and sleep in the upstairs of the garage?"

Squirting soap in her hands, I answer, "Baseball season ends before all the big holidays, except your birthday and your mom's. I'll be here even more then."

"And you'll see me or call me on my birthday?"

"You bet I will."

"And Mommy?"

"And Mommy," I concur.

"You gonna get a tree at Christmastime?" she asks, beaming.

"Might need someone to help me find one."

"I'm a good tree finder." She grins. "The best!"

"Perfect." We finish rinsing our hands. "Then you can teach me how to pick the perfect tree."

"You promise?"

I hold out my pinkie, and she looks from it to me curiously. *Seriously adorable.* "When your mommy and I were younger, when a promise was very, very important, we used to hook our pinkies and shake them, like this." I curve her little pinkie around mine and give them a shake. "That's an unbreakable promise." I lift her off the counter and set her on her feet. "Whenever I'm here, I promise that I'll ask you to go get the Christmas tree for this house."

She bounces up, arms in the air, which is Nora for *catch me*. Her little arms wrap around me. "I love you."

Ever had the air taken right out of your lungs, but instead of it hurting, it felt good? Me neither…until right now. It's been too damn long since anyone has said those words to me.

"Love you too, little slugger," I whisper against her hair.

She leans back, takes my face in her hands, and says, "I know."

"No doubt you do." I force a laugh, hoping to keep the emotions her words have brought on at bay.

IT'S midnight when I walk into the five-star hotel and resort in Vegas to check in and make sure everything is set for the others when they get here tomorrow.

York assured me that Whit will be with them. She also promised if Whit backs out for any reason, they won't leave her back home, not alone, not when I feel there's still a threat. And I'll be feeling that until Whit and I have a chance to talk about what she wants so she doesn't feel like I'm stepping on her toes. That's unlikely to happen this weekend, but ready or not, it has to happen before I head to Florida for training camp and then the regular season begins.

"You made it, man." Turner clasps my shoulder. "Most of us have been here three days, soaking up the free rooms and all the city has to offer."

I look around. "No kids this trip?"

He shakes his head and looks down. "Twenty-seven years old, a three-time divorce—"

"Thought you and Claudia were working through things?"

"Thought so, too. Went back to the LA house, and the locks were changed. Called her, all, *what the hell?* She fed my divorce papers through the mail slot and then a positive pregnancy test." He holds up six fingers. "Six kids. Three exes with fat pads, alimony, and child support. I have a two-bedroom apartment in New York the size of their closets."

"Kids are a blessing. Those women—"

"All gold diggers," Frankie, who plays centerfield, says as he takes my other side.

"My first wife, Kathleen, wasn't," Turner admits.

"Forget about them. Let's go hit the tables and then the strip clubs. At least professional women take the money up front. Am I right?" Tony, who plays shortstop calls to the guys. "Let's make it rain for the honest ladies of Vegas."

"I'm whipped, man." Which is code for hell no. I have shit to do to prepare for tomorrow.

At the same time, Turner says, "I'm hungry."

Tony throws up his hands. "We're in Vegas."

"So is the rest of the team." Turner lifts his chin. "I'm sure they'd love to help you two *make it rain*."

"No doubt." He holds up his phone as he walks away. "You have my number when you change your minds."

Turner looks like hell, like he hasn't slept in days and like he shouldn't be left alone.

"Wouldn't mind eating before I get some shut-eye."

As I follow Turner toward one of the restaurants, I look at my phone to see if Whit has replied to my good night text. I mean, hell, I didn't even get a thumbs-up last I checked. But there's one there now, and that makes me giddy—*fucking giddy*.

After we each order a prime rib, I watch him, sitting across the table, as he looks down at his hand, twisting his ring around and around in circles. The fact that it's still on his finger is telling. He loved her, and probably still does. I know they split up mid-season, but she was at our last game.

"People warned me that she was playing the same game ex number two did. Guess I should have listened." He looks up at me. "Love's a bitch."

"You have five, going on six, kids. The kind of love they give isn't a bitch. It's the best."

"Until you're not around because you're out here playing ball in order to afford the lifestyle they've grown accustomed to."

"I'm not gonna pretend I know what that looks like."

"Sucks because they're involved in everything, so

there's never enough time, but you don't want them to not find their passion, you know?"

I lift my chin.

"My exes can't even get along so that the five I have now can be at a game once in a while together. My oldest is eight, the youngest three, and now a baby is coming." He leans back, scrubs both hands up and down his face, then leans forward. "At least when the others were babies, I was with their moms. I got those hours after I got home late from a game, and I'd just scoop them up and hold them on my chest as I watched highlights. Feed them when they woke up and let their mom sleep. Kathleen and Sharon, too. I won't have that this time."

"I'm sorry, man, truly."

He waves his hand in front of himself. "Not gonna bring you down. Talk to me. Tell me something good."

I shake my head, the corner of my lips twitching up before I can stop it.

He chuckles. "Spill it, man."

"It was finally nice to be home."

"Yeah?" He picks up his water and takes a drink.

"Started fixing up the house and plan to spend as much time as I can there."

"Got family there still?" he asks.

"Yeah, I do."

WHIT

13

Thursday

"Well, shit," Chloe says as we walk into our room at the Marriott in Vegas. "Aren't we all fancy now?"

Looking around the spacious hotel suite, I have to agree. The furnishings are all contemporary with sleek lines and rich fabrics.

"So, this is what being indulgent feels like," York says.

"It's like sophistication and indulgence made a baby, and that baby was a hotel room." Chloe continues walking around, and York and I exchange amused glances.

Chloe has admitted she doesn't drink, but she certainly did at the airport. She and I have never flown, but unlike me, who was excited, she was extremely nervous. Therefore, shots.

She opens the curtains, and we all stand at the wall of windows, taking in the panoramic view of the glittering city skyline, with its towering skyscrapers and neon-lit streets stretching out as far as the eye can see. It's breathtaking.

"Well, hello, Vegas. We're in you," she whispers her greeting to the city, which is kind of adorable.

To stop myself from looking at York, knowing we'd both start laughing, I turn and look around. In one corner, is a sleek workstation, equipped with all the amenities you need to stay connected during your stay—high-speed internet, a spacious desk, and a comfortable chair. I cross the living area to the bedroom. Two plush queen-size beds are covered with crisp linens and plump pillows.

Chloe rests her chin on my shoulder, yawns in my ear, and then sighs, "That looks so comfy."

And it does.

"There's no sleeping. Pope's game starts at seven, and the stadium is about twenty minutes away. It's five now," York says as she starts peeling off clothes, walking into the bathroom. "I call shower first. Chloe, you're next."

"Why am I last?" I ask.

"You're going to take the longest," she calls out to me.

"How do you figure?" I ask.

"You have two and a half days where you don't have to hurry."

Chloe dives headfirst onto the bed so she can *rest her eyes*, and that gives York and me a few minutes to chat while she showers—or more accurately, me to freak out because, again, I haven't had the time to do so.

"York," I begin.

She cuts me off immediately. "We're not doing this. You're sticking with the plan."

"It's not a plan. It's playing Russian roulette with three—"

"We've overtalked this, you've overthought this, and

there's no other option. Now, turn it off and get ready to have some fun."

DRESSED in jeans and my Walton Wolves long-sleeved tee tied at the side, I start to put on my ball cap.

"Do not mess with perfection." Chloe, who's currently suffering the beginning of a hangover, snatches it out of my hand.

"She's not wrong, Whit. You look like a freaking supermodel."

"I know I look good, but supermodel is overkill." I lean in close to the mirror. "And so was waxing my brows."

"But not your kitty?" York asks.

I lift a shoulder. "Although it hurt like a bitch, and I'll probably never do it again, there's something liberating about it."

"Damn right," Chloe says loudly—too loudly because she's now cradling her head.

"All right, let's message the boys to meet us down in the lobby and go find Chloe some pain relievers."

WALKING INTO LAS VEGAS BALLPARK, I'm immediately reminded of the games Bianca and Danny's parents took us to in Houston when we were in high school. I can picture the way Pope looked around, taking it all in and him allowing it to take him in. I remember telling him that he'd play there someday. Being a rookie, he didn't play when they were in Houston last season, but there's still no doubt he will one day.

Marks points to a screen and beams. "He's starting on first tonight."

"Let's grab some beers before we head to our seats." Danny nods toward the concession stands.

When he looks back and, without words, asks what I want, I shake my head. "I'm good."

"Like hell you are," York insists. "You need a drink or ten."

"They have wine slushies." Chloe smiles. "We should get wine slushies."

"Feeling better?" York jokes.

"I'm about to, and I'm buying." She sashays her behind up to the counter.

"Put the card away, Chloe Shaw. I've got this," Danny scolds her.

"I don't need your charity," she huffs.

"It's a damn wine slushy, not a house in the Hills." He boxes her out.

"We'll get the next round." York grabs her hand and pulls her back before she biffs him.

"He's infuriating." She glares at the back of his head.

Marks and Danny grab the first round and half a dozen hot dogs, which is good because Chloe hasn't eaten anything since she started drinking at the airport. Me? I ate my weight in peanut M&M's.

Walking down the stairs to our seats, my heart pounding, I see the players on the field, warming up. It's not Pope's team, New York; it's Oakland. But I'm still taking it all in.

The atmosphere is absolutely buzzing with anticipation. The stadium is alive with the sounds of enthusiastic chatter, the crack of the bat on the field, and the roar of the crowd above us, cheering on their favorite players, helping to get them hyped up for the game. From the sides of the field, the bright lights of the stadium illuminate the early evening sky, casting a warm glow over the diamond and adding to the sense of magic in the air. Every now and then, the Jumbotron lights up with advertisements and stats on some of the players, adding to the excitement of what's to come. I can't wait to see John Paul's name up there.

The scents surrounding me are all familiar and bring me back to the days when we all knew he'd be on a pro field, playing in the majors one day. It's the smell of popcorn, hot dogs, and roasted peanuts, mixed with the smell of dirt, and even though there's turf and not real grass, I swear I can still smell it.

As we take our seats, my eyes heat up, and I have to fight back tears as my face breaks out into a huge smile, making it even more difficult to keep the tears at bay.

From my vantage point, I have the perfect view of the players as they come out of the dugouts, and when I see blue and orange, my already-pounding heart beats faster.

Marks leans over. "You gonna make it?"

"It's different, knowing we're going to see him play live and in person, doing what we could have been doing all along. That's on me." The first tear falls. "God, I was so stupid to believe that he and Nel—"

"We're here now, Whit. That's all that matters."

"Ladies and gentlemen, welcome to Las Vegas Ballpark and tonight's first major league exhibition game of the season between New York and Oakland! As the players take the field and the anticipation reaches a fever pitch, get ready for a night of heart-pounding action and unforgettable moments. So, sit back, grab your peanuts and Cracker Jacks and let's play ball!"

The stadium erupts in applause, and all five of us rise

to our feet as the dugout empties. I immediately see Pope doing his major league jog to first. Facing away from the crowd, he bends and taps the base twice with his glove, holds it to his heart, and points it up to the sky.

"Same Pope." Danny grins.

It's basically true. He always did that in high school. Except now, he taps the base twice—once for his dad and once for his mom.

When he turns, he scuffs his feet on the dirt like a bull before charging, and I swear he's looking up at us. He holds up four fingers, and the three of us do it back, just like in high school.

Chloe grins. "Y'all are so damn cute."

"Yeah, we are." Danny winks at her, and we all laugh, except Chloe, of course.

The first batter up gets walked, which is total bull.

"At least two of those were strikes," Marks yells over the crowd.

He's not wrong.

The second batter hits a ground ball, and the shortstop totally overthrows first base when he should have gone for second to begin with, but Pope leaps in the air and catches the ball.

"You sure this is the majors?" Chloe asks. "What the hell was that?"

"A nervous rookie," Marks answers over the boos. "Kid just got pulled up after a year."

"Gonna get dropped if he keeps that shit up," Chloe huffs.

The next batter up hits it to left field, and it drops before the left fielder can get to it, but when he does, he guns it to third. The third baseman's foot hits the base, and then he hurls it to second for a double play.

Taking First

The next batter hits it to short, and this time, the rookie doesn't overthrow it by much, but Pope doesn't get it in time, which is not his fault. But then the player on first steps off the base, just for a split-second, and Pope somehow sees it and tags him out.

"Hell yes!" Danny jumps up, cheering, and the rest of us follow suit as New York jogs back in.

When John Paul gets close enough, he lifts his chin and smiles at us before ducking into the dugout.

The batting lineup flashes on the screen, and we see Pope is sixth. Everyone knows that spot isn't where they put the best hitters, and that can mess with a player's head. High school Pope was always up to bat in either second, third, or fourth position. When I could get the minor league games on the TV or when I was with Bianca and John Paul would FaceTime her and prop up his phone, hoping she could see, he was never toward the bottom, either.

I glance at Marks who reads me well.

He leans over and chuckles. "Chill, Whit. He's on a team with men just as good and some better than him. He's batting in the majors in sixth position. He made close to a million dollars last season. As soon as this season starts, he'll be making even more. He's not sweating it."

"That's insane," I say, wondering why I never even thought about how much money he was going to make. I only thought of how happy he'd be doing what he loves.

"Deserves it. The minors pay shit."

And yet, he made it work.

The first batter up strikes out. The second hits a single and, in my opinion, could have gotten to second had he put forth more effort. *Pope would have.* The third batter gets to first, advancing the last to second. The fourth batter pops out, and the fifth gets to first base. Now, the bases are loaded, and Pope is up.

As he walks to the plate, he looks over his bat, no doubt made of maple—it was always his preference. He runs his hand over it, gripping the end tight and sliding it down.

"Why does that look sexual?" York asks.

"What?" A laugh bubbles out of me. She begins to ask again, and I cut her off. "It doesn't. It's his thing."

"Yeah?" She snort-laughs. "What else is his thing?"

I don't play into her twisted little game, but I do share what I know. "He's going to tap his helmet with it, which reminds him to focus."

Less than half a second later, he does just that.

"He'll tap the plate before getting into his stance, which grounds him."

"Jesus." She shakes her head when he does it.

"And then he'll point the bat to the sky before kicking back some dirt and getting back into his stance."

Everything I told her happens moments after I said them.

"He's going to swing on the first pitch, and more than likely, it'll be"—I pause as he swings and misses—"a strike."

She looks at me, and I nod toward the game.

"He steps back and says a little prayer, then gets back in his stance."

"And what's going to happen next?" she asks.

As he swings, I smile. "Magic."

The crack of the bat echoes through the air, and he doesn't hesitate like the others did. He puts everything he has into making it to first, then second, and he wants to continue but is forced back to second.

We're all on our feet, cheering for him as he crouches down.

Taking First

"Two RBIs." Danny holds up a hand, and we all high-five each other, as if we'd gotten them ourselves.

The next batter hits a single, and Pope gets to third and a few steps to home when he has to go back.

The next hit, he makes it home, and the batter is out at second.

For the entire game, John Paul defies the stereotype that first base is the easiest base to play. He doesn't just stand there and wait for the ball to get thrown to him; he dives, leaps, and does his best the entire nine innings.

The game ends with New York winning by seven. Pope batted a thousand, had four RBIs, and rounded the bases three times. Anyone who can do basic math would come to the same conclusion we all do. He was the MVP of the game, and tomorrow, he'll be the same.

On our way to the waiting car, York whispers, "How hot are you for that boy right now?"

Slightly tipsy, I smile. "We're in the desert— everything's hot."

Halfway back to the hotel, I decide to send my first text to him.

ME:

> You played an amazing game. Your parents would be so proud.

HIS REPLY IS IMMEDIATE.

JOHN PAUL:

> And what about you?

ME:

I type and delete, then type and delete again because everything I want to say sounds sexual, and it's not like that, so I give him a thumbs-up.

When Marks chuckles, I glance over and see him shaking his head.

"What?"

He gives me a thumbs-up, and I give him an elbow to the side.

As soon as we get out of the car, Chloe looks up. "I wanna ride that Ferris wheel. Danny, do you wanna ride the Ferris wheel?"

"You want a ride? I'll give you a ride," he says.

She totally misses the sexual innuendo and grabs his hand, pulling him in the direction she thinks will take us to the giant wheel.

"We're not walking all over Vegas at ten thirty at night, Chloe. We'll take a car," York grumbles, trying to keep up with the two of them.

"Is Pope coming back here?" I ask Marks.

"After press, yeah."

"Don't you think we should wait for him?" I ask wanting nothing more than to do just that.

"Could be an hour, and I'm not thinking Chloe will last that long," he says, tapping out a text. "I sent him a message to let us know when he's ten minutes out and that Chloe Shaw wanted to ride the giant wheel —the High Roller— with Danny. Let's roll."

We end up walking the one-point-two miles and stopping at three different refreshment carts to get drinks and snacks.

"I can't believe they sell wine on the street here," Chloe says, sloshing the red liquid from the plastic cup onto the sidewalk.

"I can't believe you didn't want a frozen chocolate-covered banana," Danny says, taking a bite of the one he bought for her.

"You think I don't know that you want to watch me eat that banana to fuel some sexual fantasy you have about my mouth and phallic objects, Danny Aiken?"

He nearly chokes on the bite he took, and we all laugh.

"And why didn't we get a car? I have money, you know. I could have paid."

"I'm pretty sure you're the one who can't stand still long enough to hail a cab," York points out.

She raises her hands in the air. "It just feels so good to walk around and not worry about anything. I should move to Vegas. Go to school during the day and pole dance at night in one of the fancier clubs, where you're not expected to grind on some asshole's lap for a twenty."

"There's no chance in hell that's happening," Danny tells her.

"Why not? I'm a liberated woman, you know."

"That you are." I laugh as I link arms with her to stop her from passing by the reason we've walked a mile.

When I turn us and point, she looks at it in awe. "That's huge."

"Biggest Ferris wheel in the world." York holds up her phone and shows her what Google says about the *High Roller*.

"Long line. You sure you want to wait here?"

"You bet your bippy I do, Danny boy. I'm gonna ride that beast, just like I rode the plane."

"By just like, you mean, drunk?" I joke.

She grins. "Exactly."

We wait in line for what feels like forever, maybe because Chloe now has her head resting on my shoulder or maybe because I'm anxious to have the conversation I need to have with John Paul, whose heat factor just rose from Texas to Vegas hot. Major league hot.

What the hell is wrong with me?

I glance over at York. "Do you think we should head back, go to bed, and come back tomorrow?"

She smirks. "No way in hell."

I don't like that smirk, mainly because it makes me feel like she's in my head, doing her detective work without permission—*again*.

I narrow my eyes at her. "Don't you think it's rude that we're not going to be there when he gets back?"

"Oh my God, it's me. I'm the rude one." Chloe pouts, sounding like she might cry.

"I'm glad you all came here. I saw this last night from the hotel and thought it looked like a good time."

I turn my head and see Pope, all freshly showered and in jeans and a Henley.

He holds up his phone. "We've got a skip the line pass. Let's do this."

As he passes by me, he takes my hand, and we move swiftly through the line with all the other's who purchased tickets ahead of time.

When we get to the front, he holds me back as the others step into the large, round glass cabin, and the doors close.

He looks back. "Ours is next." *Ours.* "Getting you alone is not an easy task."

My mouth is suddenly dry, and I'm not sure I want to get in the damn thing, let alone tell him what I need to.

But he moves us in and to the center, and the doors close, leaving me no way to escape.

"You played like I always knew you would."

He sits down on the bench in the center. "Felt numb

most of last season. Tonight was different." He pats the bench. "Sit and relax."

"I'll sit, but I'm not promising I'm going to be able to relax."

He nods to the glass in front of us as the wheel begins to move a little bit faster, lifting us higher and higher above the streets of Las Vegas with its millions of twinkling lights illuminating the iconic landmarks that, until right now, I've only seen in movies.

"John Paul, I need to tell you something," I begin.

"Not yet," he says, linking his fingers with mine and pulling me up with him as he stands. "Let's get one full rotation under our belts first. Just take in all of this place."

So, that's what we do. We rise to five hundred fifty feet above ground, where time seems to stand still for a moment as we sit in a bubble made of glass, swaying ever so gently as we stand together and take in the panoramic view. The giant wheel continues a graceful descent, offering a new perspective on the spectacles below.

I glance over and see him looking at me.

"What do you think?"

"As kids, we were fearless, but when Nora came into my life, that changed. Outlets needed to be covered, cords hidden so she didn't see them as a toy. Her crib couldn't be near the blinds, or she might get the strings caught around her neck."

I can't help but fall a little bit more when I see the look on his face.

"That's terrifying."

I nod my agreement. "Once she was out of that and crawling, then walking, gates were needed so she couldn't get to the stairs, the kitchen, or the bathrooms. Her bed needed railings so she didn't fall out and hurt herself." I look out over the spectacular view before us. "Nora's hundreds of miles away and surrounded by water, and I'm not stressing. I made sure she learned to float and swim before she could even walk. I know she's happy because she's with people who love her like I do." I nod to the glass. "This? This should terrify me. The thought of some freak thing happening while I'm up here, causing me to be a little unable to be there when she no doubt needs stitches one day or just needs a hug because it's been a rough day at 'work' or when she falls for a clueless boy who breaks her heart and didn't even know she'd given it to him to begin with."

He frowns.

"But I'm not afraid we're going to fall out of the sky." I don't add that it's because he's here, but I think he knows that.

He runs his thumb the back of my hand as we're again stopped, suspended in the air, watching the twenty or thirty people from two cabins, pods, cars—whatever they're called—empty out onto the platform. I'm jealous of them in a way. Their feet are on the ground, and they're feeling relief while I'm standing here, feeling all the warm and fuzzies being overtaken by the anxiety that's lived inside me since Pope returned to Walton.

When the wheel begins to move again, we bypass the platform.

Fingers still entwined, he walks us back to the red cushioned bench and sits, clearly prepared for our chat. "Do you mind if I go first?"

"Yeah, sure, go ahead." I sit as I think, *Because I'm in no hurry to see you look at me differently than you have been for the past week.*

"I have a meeting with Kevin Seward scheduled for Tuesday morning. I can't put him off any longer." I nod, and he continues, "I want you to press charges. Kal physically injured you."

"I'm fine. It only hurt for—"

"And then they hurt you here"—he touches the side of my head—"and here"—he places his hand above my heart—"when they asked you to resign. They don't get to do that to you."

"I don't think it would be smart for me to go up against them."

"They have nothing on you. They've done all they can do. I don't give a shit if they take me to court for a busted window. I'll win."

Without warning, I feel wetness on my face, and he quickly swipes away the falling tears.

"I promise, I'll make sure you and Nora—who told me she loved me the other day, Whit, and you can get pissed, but I said it back because I do. I love her, will make sure he's safe, and she's—"

"She's his. She's Kal's," I cut him off, unable to let him continue.

He looks at me like I slapped him, and my heart starts to crumble as anger etches his face.

"So, we're going backward now, and I have to play the only card I have and remind you, that that's not what the birth certificate says?"

I take his face in my hands to stop him from turning away. "She's Kal's biological daughter."

He shakes his head, anger leaving and shock and sadness taking its place as it sinks in.

I force myself to continue. "When I got my phone back, dozens, maybe hundreds, of messages popped up with him threatening to sue for custody of 'that kid.' He stated he'd get the right judge and make sure I never saw her again. When I told York about it, she asked if I thought Nora was his." I sit back and wipe my tears away. "I thought she was crazy and told her so. She said she hoped she was wrong, but then told me she had some things of his from that night at your place and wanted to do a DNA test to prove her theory was wrong."

He sighs. "Jesus, Whit."

"So, I either play nice or I chance—"

"Or you fight. We fight." He cuts me off.

"Do you think that's smart?"

"If there's anything worth fighting for, it's your little girl. Yours, not his." He stands and starts to pace then turns and hits himself in the chest. "Fuck, Whit, she's mine too."

My bottom lip begins to quiver.

"We're going to fight for her. There is no way that bastard is getting a moment with her."

"I'm all about fighting for her, but if I lose—"

"That's not gonna happen."

"You can't be sure—"

"Like hell I can't. Kal is four years older than us. Nelly was your age, right?"

I nod.

"So, he fucked an eighteen-year-old girl and got her pregnant, wanting nothing to do with her. Even after he knew Nora was Nelly's, he said nothing? I don't believe for a second that either he or his father wants that to be public knowledge."

"I can't lose her," I repeat.

"Neither can I!" he roars, which startles me. He sits beside me and takes my hand. "Fuck, Whit, I'm sorry."

"Don't be. I was … I am just as angry, but now, I'm more afraid than—"

"I need to work out a plan."

"You need to focus on this weekend."

"Right now, I don't give a shit about this game," he seethes.

"I need you to be the stable one because they're already painting me to be a crazy ex." I inhale a deep breath. "And if they manage to do that and some of his threats, including the one to get her taken away from me, come true, your name is on her real birth certificate. The one I gave him that I'd removed your name from when I first went to get her name changed, it's been replaced."

"You went to him?" He growls.

I shake my head. "No, but a friend of mine might have figured out how to get into his office. I should have asked, but you got a copy of the original. I hope you're not upset people are going to think—"

He rolls his eyes. "Anyone I give a damn about knows who I am, so like I said, I don't give a shit. I love her."

"I'm already being seen as some scorned, crazy woman to the people I don't give a darn about, so I plan to tell anyone who asks that I didn't tell you and—"

"I'm not gonna let you do that."

"You don't get to make all the decisions, John Paul." I place my hand over my heart. "She's mine."

He nods then lifts a shoulder. A smile tugs at his lips for just a second. "Walking into church that very first time we attended, I was still angry that He took Dad, but when I saw you outside with a glove, throwing a ball up in the air and catching it over and over…" He holds his hand over his heart. "You've been mine since that day, and I've been yours."

I hold out my pinkie. "Best friends forever."

He links his with mine. "Best friends for always."

I inhale a deep breath. "I need to ask for a favor."

"Anything."

"If we're going the route of fighting together … York

thinks it might be a good idea"—I scrunch my eyes shut for the next part—"if you and I get married in case he does try to have her removed from my custody. You being named as her father and us being married would give us a better chance of—"

"Open your eyes, Whitley Mae."

I open them one at a time. "In name only. I'll sign a prenup. You being on the road, it won't be weird that Nora and I are living with Popa B and Gram."

Mischief plays in his blue eyes. "I have conditions."

I roll my eyes, knowing exactly what he wants from me. "Fine, I'll say it. *Please*."

"That's not it, but I like the way you're thinking."

"Okay, shush and tell me this condition."

"When we say I do, I get to kiss you."

My face starts to heat up. "Fine."

"You'll let me make decisions with you to keep you and our Nora safe."

"Okay."

"I won't be around a lot, but I want you and Nora to live in the house when it's finished, and I want your help in making plans for the rest of the expansion."

"Only if I can pay some of the bills."

"That's fine, but when I'm home, we have to act like we're a real couple. I want Nora to see us as her parents together. I know I can handle that. Can you?"

I nod. "And I have a condition. I mean, I'll have more, but one right now."

"It's only fair. Go ahead."

"We get married soon. Like, really soon. Like, before your meeting with Kevin. I want them to know we're not messing around."

"Like a-little-white-chapel-in-Vegas soon?" he asks, clearly amused.

"I mean, yeah."

"I'm game, Whit, but we do a little something at home, too, for Nora."

"Okay."

"You'll stay with me tonight."

"I'm not sleeping with you."

"Yes, you are, but we're not fucking unless we both decide that's what we want. And by not fucking, I mean anyone else, either."

Oh. My. God.

POPE

14

Friday

I hold Whit's hand as we step off the High Roller and walk down the ramp toward our friends. None of them seem at all shocked at the fact that our hands are linked up. It's kind of mind-blowing to me, and it serves as a warning. This might be a marriage of convenience in Whit's eyes, but to me, it's the beginning of forever. I will never again be so focused on the game that I lose sight of what's really important, and that's Whit, Nora, and my family in Walton.

I glance down at Whit walking beside me. Her face is tinged pink, and she's fighting a smile as she rolls her stunning gold-flecked brown eyes. "You have always been so damn good to look at."

She elbows me. "This arrangement doesn't have to be mucked up with bullcrap."

"You and I both know nothing about this is—"

"Well, it's about damn time." Chloe claps her hands and bounces on her heels.

I see York with her phone up, either taking a picture or a video, and, yes, I'm gonna need her to share that with me.

"It sure is," I agree.

Danny and Marks walk over and give us each a half hug because I'm not letting go of her hand to allow more. York and Chloe are next, both yawning as they step back. Then, as yawns do, they spread to Whit and me.

"Car will be here in two minutes to take us back to the hotel," Marks calls us to follow with a wave.

"EVERYONE TIRED?" Whit asks as we drive back to the hotel.

All of them answer *yes*. I simply nod because I should be fucking exhausted, but I'm not sure I'm going to be able to sleep.

At one point, Marks, Danny, and I tossed around reasons—aside from the fact that Whit is a smokeshow—that Kal was obviously obsessed with her. We knew he was hiding something. We easily dismissed the fact that he could still be trying to get back at me for taking his spot on the team all those years ago or because of his father praising me and not him. Danny was the one who mentioned the possibility that Kal knew I wasn't Nora's father and maybe he knew who was. The mess at the women's center happened, and Marks is convinced—as am I—that the Sewards are paying off the board or have something over them to have pulled that shit with Whit, who truly gives a shit about those women and volunteered her time because she gives a fuck.

I now know York is doing what she can to gather information, and Marks is also doing some digging. He thinks the Sewards are running some illegal shit through the shelter; he just doesn't know what. The fact that they're doing this for us blows me away, but I also want to be sure all of us are on the same page and that the endgame is to make sure Nora's with Whit and I, the people Nelly wanted to raise her if she couldn't.

Stepping out of the SUV, I still have her hand in mine, and she's yet to ask for it back.

Walking into the hotel, we run into Lou, Frankie, Turner, and a few other guys from the team, and they're not going to let me just skate by—the assholes.

"Guys, this is my, uh, Whitley and our friends Danny, Marks, York, and Chloe."

"Told you she was taken." Lou hits Frankie in the chest.

I glare at Frankie, and he holds his hands up. "How would we have known that one of the stunning women in the bleachers, wearing the high school swag, was yours, man?"

"It's okay. He didn't know he was mine until he came home, either," Whit says sweetly.

They all laugh.

"We knew. We totally knew the whole time." Chloe stops and holds her hand to her stomach. "I don't feel very good."

Danny swoops her up. "Let's get you upstairs." He lifts a chin to the guys. "Excellent game today."

"Pope played his ass off today. You all should try to do the same tomorrow," Chloe calls back.

"All right, Miss Shaw, that's enough." Danny laughs as he carries her away.

I chuckle. "She's had a lot to drink."

"She's not wrong. He killed it today." Turner winks at

me. "This beautiful woman must be your lucky charm. Hope you bring her to all the games."

"I'm sure she'll be at a few, but we have an almost five-year-old who has a bedtime and—"

"Wait, you have a kid?" Frankie asks.

"He—"

"Name's on her birth certificate and all," I cut Whit off.

Turner looks at Whit, who shakes her head. "It's complicated."

"Life is complicated. Love should be easy." Turner smiles at her then looks at me. "Come on, man. Show me some pictures."

"He—"

I pull my phone out, cutting her off. "Whit calls her little slugger, and she's got one hell of an arm on her." I scroll through the pictures, showing my teammates, and then I show them a couple of clips of her railing the ball and throwing, too.

Turner chuckles. "So, she's got your game and her mom's looks."

"Her mom has just as much game as I do. She had a scholarship to Arizona to play D1 ball, but went on to nursing school, and took care of my mom when she was still here."

"Women in professional sports don't get paid to play like you boys do," York says, bringing all their attention to her.

"York, right?" Frankie asks.

"Frankie Frangula, center field. RBI is 218, but could be better if your follow-through wasn't piss-poor."

He holds his hand to his chest, as if he's in physical pain. "Fuck, that hurt. Come on, little lady, give me some props."

"You have one hell of an arm."

"I have other skills I'd love to—"

"Respect, man," I cut him off.

York turns and looks at me. "You know I'm older than you, right?"

"Nah, he's right. My bad."

I look down at Whit, who's transfixed on my photos. I look at the screen and see she's looking at the ones I took of her alone and with her and Nora at the batting cage.

She looks up at me, as if seeking an explanation.

"No apologies."

She looks me over. "You hungry?"

"Starving," I admit.

She looks at the guys. "Nice meeting y'all. We'll be cheering you all on tomorrow."

×

THE FOUR OF us decide we need a place to talk privately and to check in with Danny and Chloe, who doesn't answer the phone when Whit calls to ask what they want to eat. We hit the buffet and load some takeout containers before heading up to the top floor.

The smell of vomit immediately assaults us when we walk into the room. As if that isn't bad enough, the sight of Danny pacing at the end of the bed in nothing but a hand towel covering his junk, is now and forever etched in our minds.

He won't leave Chloe, who apparently threw up on him and then was choking on her vomit when he returned from his and Marks' room where he changed.

York and Whit offered to take care of her, but he is wigged out and refuses to leave. We manage to get everything bagged up, and housekeeping brings up new linens and also takes Danny's clothes to be laundered.

Sitting around the table in my room, which is on the other side of Danny and Marks, just two doors down from the women, we discuss being on the same page. Then Whit and I listen to York and Marks snap at one another for not telling the other what they were doing.

By the time that is finished, the four of us eat some.

"It's one in the morning. You need to get some sleep."

As Marks stands, he tells York, "You can crash in Danny's bed."

"Sounds good." York grabs a fry and pops it in her mouth as she stands. "You two try to get some sleep."

"Wait—what?" Whit all but jumps out of the chair.

I catch the chair that's falling over and then Whit around the waist. "We've already slept together since I've been home."

Laughing, York and Marks make their exit.

"My intentions have always been PG with you until you changed that up." I walk around to stand in front of her. "After that, all I could think about was what I wanted to do to you."

She swallows hard, and I step back.

"You've got nothing to worry about, Whitley Mae Belington. We're going to sleep tonight, maybe cuddle a little. I'm going to get up early and head to the field, and you can sleep in."

I head to my bag where I pull out a T-shirt and bring it over to hand it to Whit. "Bathroom's right over there if you want to change."

She walks away, and once in the bathroom, I allow myself to feel how fucking good this is gonna be when we get through this, and yeah, the moments like this in-between.

I'm just finishing cleaning up the empty containers and setting them outside the door when she walks out in my tee.

"I used your toothbrush."

"Yeah? I'm going to use it now."

Walking to the bed, she looks over her shoulder, catching me checking her out. "Preference for a side?"

"Doesn't matter to me."

After taking a piss, washing my hands, and brushing my teeth, I head out and find Whit on the side closest to the door.

"What?" she asks.

"Nothing." I smile to assure her all is well.

She sits up. "Wrong. You just did the fake smile, the kind that doesn't show a dimple."

"The fact that you can decipher the meaning of my smiles is kind of cute."

"Nope, you're not turning this around on me. Why the face?"

I run a hand through my hair. "I didn't have a preference, but now, I do."

"I'm not going to sneak out, run back to Texas, and take Nora to Europe. I don't have that kind of money."

"That's oddly specific, Whit." I watch her ass as she moves to the side closest to the window as I continue, "That whole thing was clearly thought out."

"Again, what's the reason for the change?"

I pull my shirt over my head and toss it on the chair. "I like the idea that if someone walked in here, they'd have to get through me first. It might sound ridic—"

"I understand. My bedroom is smaller than Nora's because it's closer to the stairs. It's not ridiculous; it's being protective. But I can assure you that I've been protecting myself since I was Nora's age."

Shedding my jeans, I shake my head. "One day, maybe you'll trust me with that heart." I look up when she doesn't reply. "I'm not pushing."

"Why are you naked?" She pulls the comforter up to her chin.

"I have boxers on."

"Barely. They're like a second skin and tiny."

Smiling to myself, I lie back and link my fingers behind my neck. I smirk as I turn my head to the side and can't help but laugh at the fact that she's nibbling on her lower lip.

"Don't laugh at me. And cover up!"

"I respectfully did the laughing silently, and how the hell am I supposed to cover up when you have all the covers?"

Her brows furrow, but she doesn't look away or say a word, and then she states. "It's a wolf tattoo."

I glance down to where her eyes are fixated. "It is."

I roll to my side, facing her, holding my arm out. "The wolf is our mascot—home, us. The wings, obviously Mom. The colors—camo—for Dad."

"And this is Walton, too?" Her nail touches one of the *W*s.

I slide my hand over my now-hard nipple from just her nail touching my bare skin in bed. "Look close enough, and you'll see an *M* and a *B* in there, too." *Her initials.*

Her face flushes, and she sits up. "Why?"

"I'll explain it one day if you really need me to."

"So, this"—she motions up and down my body—"needs to change."

"I can promise you, that this isn't what I typically wear to bed."

"Good, because Nora doesn't need to ask why John Paul has a bat in his undies."

I don't even try to hold back my laugh this time.

She moves to lie back, grumbling, "That confidence you have seems to be quickly becoming cocky."

My chest heaves in another silent chuckle. "Whit, stop while you're ahead."

"How is it you think I'm gonna get behind?"

"Your previous comments included *my bat* and then the use of cocky. One might conclude that you're thinking a whole lot about my—"

"That's not what I was implying." She smacks me with one of the dozen decorative pillows. "I was talking about pajamas and your big fat ego."

"I don't have any pajamas. I sleep naked. I'll let you pick out appropriate ones."

"Fine," she huffs and throws part of the comforter over me.

"And I'll pick out yours."

She makes to swat at me, and I grab her hand, holding it against my chest.

She remains still, quiet. Looking right at me, she finally asks, "You sure about this?"

"You know I am." I lift her hand and brush my lips across her knuckles. "And, Whit?"

She cocks her head to the side in question.

"If shit starts going in the wrong direction, I have enough money to keep us in Europe. But instead, I think we should keep going east. Playing ball in Japan would be pretty amazing."

As tears fill her eyes, I pull her closer and wrap her up tightly.

"You and I have got this. Everything's going to be better than fine, Whit."

✕

Taking First

THE SOX HAVE BEEN UP by three since the top of the fifth inning, when they put Bares into pitch. At the bottom of the ninth with one out, Lou and Frankie are on second and third, and I'm up to bat. My aim is to hit a ground ball between first and second to right field with just enough gas behind it to make the centerfield man work to make a play and to get Frankie home. I'm hoping to get to first. Being that Turner's on deck, there's a chance he'll hit a home run, and we'll win this one, too.

The first pitch Bares throws, I'm gonna swing—I always do. When I feel the ball connect with the bat, I'm a bit surprised as I head to first. Luck is on our side because Betts stays deep and has to haul ass to get to the ball. He guns it to home, but Frankie scores a run, and I'm safe on first.

I've done real good, keeping my focus in the game, but when I see Whit jumping up and down, foam finger in the air, I can't help but think about her falling asleep in my arms. Can't help but smile because she stayed just like that all night and didn't wake up until I was coming out of the bathroom, wrapped in a towel to get dressed before meeting the team to catch the bus and head here.

When Turner steps up to bat, brows furrowed, I take a small lead in anticipation of him nailing it, but he swings and misses, so I tag back. The second pitch is another strike. He lets the third go by, and the fourth, he rails it, sending Louie and me home, tying the game.

Joel is up next and pops out.

I glance up at Whit and the rest of them, and all I can think about is that an extra inning would suck because, today, I'm going to kiss Whitley Mae Belington after she takes my last name.

When Scoot hits the ball, it doesn't get far, and

although there's no force and Turner doesn't have to run, that's exactly what he does.

WAITING for my mandatory press time, I see that Whit sent a text.

> WHIT:
> Another amazing game, but we didn't expect any different. Your parents would be so proud.

And another.

> WHIT:
> If you've changed your mind about this whole thing, I understand, and there will be no hard feelings. I'm probably overreacting.

That message was just five minutes ago, and I hit her back.

> Me:
> When you get back to the hotel, there's a dress waiting in our room. Marks knows where we're meeting, and he has strict instructions to handcuff you and drag you there if need be. Because today, I'm marrying my best friend, and I'll get to call her my wife.

What's her reply?
A thumbs-up.

15

Saturday

"Stop fussing with your hair." Chloe bats my hand away as I run my fingers through the waves, trying to loosen them up a bit. "It'll relax all on its own."

"The fact that you're even upright today blows my mind," York says, zipping me into the dress that Pope sent to his room.

The dress is honestly something that would catch my eye, and I might have picked it out for myself, if I ever had an occasion to wear a dress somewhere other than church. It has a halter-style top and sheer long sleeves with flouncy cuffs. It's more fitted than I'm used to, and it reveals some skin, as there's a slit on each side of the waist. The bodice top attaches to the skater-style skirt that hits just above the knees. The entire dress is covered in the same sheer material as the sleeves, which classes it up in a way.

"I expelled all of the poison I put in my system last

night, and I will not be doing that again for a very, very long time." Chloe, who is being a trooper today, smiles.

"You've got fifteen minutes in there," Marks calls to us from the living room area of the suite.

"I still wish one of them were with him."

Danny pokes his head in the room. "We both offered. He wanted us with you."

Bianca's phone, which I'm still using, makes a sound, alerting me of a call, and I know it's Nora.

"Okay, act normal and just, you know, be normal."

I accept the FaceTime request and smile when I see her sweet little face.

"Hi, Mommy." Before I have a chance to say hello, she leans in. "You look so pretty. Are you, Miss Gwen, and Miss Chloe goin' on a girls' day?"

"No, actually, I'm going on a date."

Her nose crinkles up. "Not with Mr. Seward, right? You said you weren't gonna marry him anymore."

"Nope, not with him."

She smiles. "Is it with our best friend, John Paul?"

"Would that be okay with you?"

"Is he gonna be your new boyfriend?"

"I think so. How do you feel about that?"

She laughs a deep, excited little laugh. "I would feel really good, 'specially if you married him instead of Mr. Seward. He's way more fun, and he loves me, Mommy."

"He told me he loves you, and I was like, 'of course you do. She's the most lovable little girl in the world.'"

"Yeah." She shrugs, trying not to show just how excited that makes her. "I am lovable."

"I miss you and can't wait to see you tomorrow."

"We're leaving the water slide place and going right to church. Will you be at church, Mommy?"

"I might not be, but I'll be there to tuck you in and read you books."

She frowns. "You gotta work?"

I hate lying to her, but I also don't want her to feel left out. When it comes to Pope, that girl wants to be right in the middle of it all. He makes her feel special, and I know how good that feels. And this is why I didn't tell her I'm not in Walton.

"Maybe."

"Okay, Mommy. I love you. Have fun with John Paul. Tell him I love him."

"I will, but you can tell him that tomorrow, too."

"Can we play baseball?"

"Maybe."

"Awesome. Bye, Mommy."

"Bye, Nora."

"You three ready?" Marks asks.

"York, you have the rings, right?" I ask.

"Of course I have the rings."

I let out a slow, deep breath, hand York my phone, and smooth my hand over my dress. "Let's do this."

GETTING out of the car in front of the marriage license bureau with the printed application already filled out and all the documentation needed in an envelope, I can't help but feel like I'm once again demanding something from John Paul that he's not ready for.

"You're not allowed to overthink this." Marks hooks his arm through mine from one side.

Danny takes the other. "He's waiting inside, Whit."

I glance over my shoulder at York, and she mouths, "*Smile.*"

I can't smile, not feeling this way. "We have time for a drink?"

"After you become Mrs. Pope," Marks says, opening the door.

I see John Paul immediately. He looks amazing in his black suit, holding white lilies, the stems wrapped in a thick white ribbon, as he walks toward me, looking me over.

Once he's at my side, Marks and Danny release me, and Pope hooks his arm through mine.

"You're stunning."

"You look pretty good yourself." He starts to say something, but I cut him off. "Pope, I'm not gonna stomp my foot and—"

"Whitley Mae." He smiles, and it's the kind that makes my knees wobble. "You're not making me do something I don't want to do today any more than you did back then. And we're not doing this back-and-forth thing anymore, either. We're two adults who know nearly everything about each other. We've been friends for decades, and we're going to get married. Married." He smiles. "We'll be the best parents any kid could ever want."

Unable to speak because I know I'll cry, I nod.

"I get to kiss those lips today, Whit." His tongue swipes across his own, wetting them. "And after I do that, after my lips and tongue enter the picture, the only thing you'll ever wonder is when it's gonna happen again."

I open my mouth to remind him that this marriage is for the purpose of our—my ... well, for Nora.

"Number twenty-two," comes over the speaker.

John Paul holds up a ticket, blue eyes so bright they're sparkling, "That's us."

Of course it is.

Taking First

WITH OUR LICENSE IN HAND, we walk outside, and he holds up the envelope and chuckles.

"Two weeks home, and I've already got you walking to the altar." He nods down the street. "Well, a gazebo. Based on that alone, it should only take a month or less to talk you into letting me plant baby number two inside your—"

I smack him with the flowers. "We're doing this for Nora."

His lips twitch up. "Of course we are, and we'll be doing each other so she can have the siblings we didn't."

"Um, not part of the deal."

"Fine, then I'll just speak for myself. I'll be doing you. You can just lie there."

When I go to whack him with the flowers again, he catches them and wraps his hand around mine gently.

"You know the significance in the flowers I chose?"

I didn't even think about it until right now, but I know. Of course I know. I nod.

"I'm guessing it was you who put those flowers at my parents' grave, for Mom."

"She'd have done it for me."

"You didn't just take care of her when she was sick. You continued taking care of her after she was gone. That means more to me than I can ever tell you."

"You don't need to tell me. I know."

He moves in front of me, walking backward, smiling as he holds one of my hands, watching me smell the flowers. The he stops in front of a gazebo that sits in a flower garden in the middle of the city in January —this is Vegas after all— and I watch as he unbuttons his suit coat and takes a knee.

"What are you doing?" I ask, looking around, shocked when I see our friends all standing behind us, all with their phones up, either shooting a video or taking pictures.

When I look back at John Paul, he's still on his knee, but this time, he's holding a ring box.

"Whitley Mae Belington"—he opens the box—"will you marry me?"

"I'm pretty sure that's why we're here instead of celebrating your wins, Major League."

He gives me a seriously sweet smile. "Whitley. Mae. Belington. Will—"

I cave to his charm, as well as the effort he's put in. "Johnathon Gregory Paul, yes."

As he puts the ring on my finger, I hear cheering and laughing, and then more cheering as York walks up and shows me the screen.

"Mommy, you said yes!"

"I did."

Nora's smile grows as big as her face.

She turns and looks behind her. "Can we go now? Can we?"

I see Gram dabbing a tissue under her eyes. "Yes, baby girl, we can go."

"Where are you going?" I ask.

"You're gonna get married at church tomorrow!" Nora shouts as she jumps up and down. "So, we gotta go home and get everything ready."

In the camera screen, I see Pope move behind me, and he leans in, resting his chin on my shoulder.

"Love you, Nora. See you tomorrow at church."

She claps her adorable little hands. "And then you'll be my daddy."

"Yes, little slugger, you'll be my little girl."

"Love you." I blow her a kiss, and she catches it.

"Love you, Mommy." She smacks her hand on her cheek, placing the kiss there that I threw her.

Once the screen is black, I turn my head and look at Pope, who hasn't moved. "You did that?"

"Damn right I did. She needs to see how a man should treat the woman he's going to call his wife."

"Thank you. Now, let's get this show on the road, shall we?"

He stands at his impressively full height, and I turn and look up at him.

"I'd really like to wait and have Pastor B marry us in the place we first met."

"That's adorable," Chloe says, drawing my attention to our group of friends.

I look back at Pope. "Yeah, I think we can do that."

He winks at me and takes my hand. "Let's go grab a meal and a bottle of champagne to celebrate me being the luckiest man on the planet."

Before my face can turn bright red, York shoves her phone in her bag and says, "Yeah, yeah, yeah. Let me see that ring."

With everything going on around me, I haven't even looked at the ring. Truth be told, I was too busy looking into John Paul's eyes and wanting to live in the moment. The moment where I'm not as terrified that, one day, he'll see whatever it is my mom said is in me that made her believe I just don't fit in with her lifestyle.

But now, I'm looking at it and ...

"Holy effing crap."

York snort-laughs. "You had to go bigger than Kal's, didn't you?"

"Damn right I did," Pope answers with a nod.

"I can't wear this."

"Whit, you're going to wear it."

"What if I lose it?" I ask, feeling myself start to panic.

"It's insured," he says, as if it's no big deal that I have a giant diamond on my finger, along with the platinum band that is also covered in diamonds.

"Cars and houses are insured, Pope. This is ... insane."

"But, Whit, look how pretty it looks on your finger," Chloe swoons.

I glance at Pope, and he winks—freaking winks.

WALKING INTO THE ROOM, I'm feeling the effects of the expensive champagne and the alertness of how close we've been all day. Pope's hand held mine most of the day, and as silly as I know it is, how easily he could break my heart, I've allowed myself to feel his touch so deep that it's probably going to leave another John Paul–size scar—a *major league* scar.

"I'm going to use the restroom," he says then finally lets go of my hand before he walks away.

"I'll be here," I say, looking down at the ring that no doubt cost more than the land I've been saving for two years to buy. The half-acre lot where the guys and I, and now Nora, Popa B, and Pope, have hit balls and played catch, where I plan to build a house for Nora and me, and Gram and Popa B. I never want them to have to live in some retirement home far away from the church community they love and who love them, and they will not.

I slide my kitten heels off and walk over to take in this city that is stunning, but not home. John Paul will live in these types of places for at least ten years if he sticks with his goal, which of course he will, because he's Pope.

In the window's reflection, I see the bathroom door open, and he walks out.

"Makes you miss home, yeah?" he asks, walking toward me.

He stops beside me, and I turn my head and look up at him.

"It's beautiful. I bet New York is, too."

"Not a bad view from my place across the bay in Jersey." He smiles when he sees the confusion. "Never been a big city boy." He chuckles. "Not that Weehawken is like Walton, but it's a twenty-five-minute drive, or forty-minute train ride in. The house is a two-family Colonial in Kings Bluff. It's an older home. Twelve-foot ceilings, marble floor, restored mahogany walls and staircase. I rent the other side to some CEO who lives in the city. He's never there, but his rent check is."

"I'm surprised you're not living it up in the city as a bachelor and—"

"Are you really, though, Whit?" he asks.

"I mean, yeah." I shrug.

"That was never the plan." He shakes his head. "Love the game, and it loves you back, right? Play until I can't, and then come back and ask the girl to marry me. Plan got a little twisted, but in the best possible way. And you know what I did today, Whit?" I force myself to swallow as he walks around behind me, rests his hands on my hips, and whispers in my ear, "Asked the girl to marry me."

Trying to keep this light, I joke, "She say yes?"

His chest vibrates against my back in a silent chuckle that acts as a match being tossed at a tinderbox that is my entire body.

"She did." His voice drops an octave, but it's just as smooth as ever. "I'm marrying *the only* girl I ever would, and there's a good chance I'm gonna make a fool of myself."

"How's that?" I ask, nipples straining against the bra under the dress he bought me.

"When I kiss her for the very first time, in front of

people we both love, I'm not sure what's gonna happen, but I'd like to know I'm not going to pass out, pop wood, or make a mess of my pants."

I bite my bottom lip to stop from laughing.

"Are you gonna laugh at me or let me kiss you so I know what to be prepared for?"

"I think a kiss would be accept—"

"Hands on the glass, Whitley Mae."

The fact that I don't hesitate to do what he told me to do at a breakneck speed should be embarrassing, but with his arm across my center, pulling me against him, I feel he's just as affected by this as I am. His large, strong, calloused hand is at the base of my neck, gently positioning me as his hot, wet lips touch my skin, stealing my breath as I'm pinned between the window and Pope's major league body. His mouth moves from my jaw down my neck, where he sucks and nips at my collarbone. My body takes over, and I arch into him, a wordless petition demanding more.

He turns me now so I am facing him, completely breathless, panting. My eyes devour his body as he reaches behind his neck and pulls his T-shirt over his head. My knees clench as I take in his chest, the mountains and valleys of muscle lining his abdomen, the ink running from his biceps to his wrist. He has and always will be a work of art.

In the blink of an eye, he grips the back of my head and pulls me into a hard, hot, and demanding kiss that causes me to whimper into his mouth and him into mine.

Both of us needing a breath, he pulls back, breaking our kiss. Then, resting his forehead against mine, he twists his lips in a sneer. "I knew—I fucking knew—that the taste of you would be my undoing. I'll never be able to get enough of you, Whitley Mae Belington. I'll feel starved, like I'm going to die, until our lips touch again. Your taste is my new obsession. I'm going to make damn sure you feel, the same about me."

I open my mouth to tell him that he's already done that when his lips crash into mine again. His hands are on my waist as he turns me back toward the window. Palms flat against the glass, I hold myself up as his teeth lightly graze the back of my neck. I feel the heat between my thighs intensify, and my nipples are so hard that they ache. I have never been so turned on in my entire life—*never*.

I feel the zipper on the back of the dress begin to descend, and my body tenses.

"I asked for a kiss. Now, I'm begging for you to let me continue worshipping your beautiful body with my mouth and my tongue. I promise, until you and I exchange vows, I will not be fucking you, no matter how much I know you want me or beg for my cock."

White satin pools at my feet, and my body is covered with goosebumps as his lips sear my neck, my shoulders, and my upper back. His thumbs hook into the band of my underwear, and he begins pushing them down.

"Can't get enough of you, Whit. Never gonna stop wanting to taste you," he murmurs, his lips pressed against my ear. His tongue skates down my spine as he pushes my panties lower and lower. His lips and tongue cross my body from hip to hip, right before his teeth nip one of my ass cheeks and then the next. He growls against my skin, "Fuck, you smell good. You want me to touch you, don't you?"

I don't know why I can't just say the word *yes*. Perhaps because my heart is stuck in my throat, but I do arch against his touch, against his mouth on my ass.

"Hell yes, you do, just as badly as I need to touch you." His finger traces my soaked seam as his hot tongue runs down the back of my thigh. "Step out of your panties, Whit."

"Say *please*," I manage, and his deep, dark rumble comes from behind.

"Please," he groans.

I step out of them, and my breathing becomes labored as his touch against my aching center becomes more intense. His lips move back up my body, kissing, nipping, and sucking over my ass, my hips, my spine, my shoulder, and now against the sensitive spot behind my ear.

Finger still stroking me, his own labored breath at the shell of my ear, his hardness against me, he whispers, "More."

Again, I arch against him, and this time, he nips my earlobe, eliciting a whimper from deep inside of me.

His finger sinks between my folds, parting my soaked lips, and begins running the length of me. My thighs start to tense, my body trembles, and he wraps his other hand around my waist to hold me steady.

"Give me those beautiful fucking lips," he hisses.

I turn my head, glancing over my shoulder. My eyes meet his, which are no longer sparkling blue; they're nearly black as they focus on my lips. For a few moments, I feel like he's just gonna stare at them, and my mouth and throat go dry. I swallow hard and wet my lips with my tongue right before his crash against mine, capturing my mouth and my moan with his lips and groan. Then his finger slips inside of me, sliding up to meet my swollen clit. My body convulses at the first touch as he slips his fingers along that line again before he dips deep inside of me.

I cry out as my head flies back against his shoulder, my back arching, giving him more access. He smiles right before his lips glide down my neck, nipping at the skin as his fingers work inside of me, in and out slowly, a controlled pace, driving a little deeper as I writhe and moan under his touch. His other hand travels up my body between my breasts, fingers a semicircle around the base of my neck, and then sliding up my face to guide it toward him.

"Give me those lips again, Whit."

His hand tightens at the base of my throat, and I like it. I like the feel of him controlling my moves as he fucks me with his fingers, basically holding me up the entire time as our lips and tongues taste one another's.

When he breaks our kiss, I see a small smile curl on his lips. His hand descends again, sliding between my breasts and then back up, palming one tit, pulling me harder against him, allowing me to feel his hard length against my body as his fingers continue working their magic, moving slowly in and out of me. He squeezes my breast, plucks my nipple, and I see stars.

"Yes, yes, yes!"

My voice? I don't even recognize it. It's needy, throaty, and thick with desire for him to continue, knowing my orgasm is within reach, but then again, it always is. It's always right there, but what happens after is good, but not what I've always dreamed it would …

"Oh gosh, oh …" My eyes fly open as my heart pounds when they meet his. A knowing smile curls on his lips when he sees that I'm ready to fall apart.

"I got you, Whit, fucking always," he hisses as his fingers move inside me, deeper, a little faster. He hits a spot that's electric, and it causes stars to dance behind my eyes.

I'm right there. Right. There.

He stops and turns me to face him, pulling me in tight against his godlike body, palming my ass, and lifting me up.

Hands gripping his shoulders, I hang on tight as he turns and moves us into the suite's bedroom and then gently tosses me onto the bed. His eyes roam my body, and my face catches fire when I realize I'm spread out in front of him.

"Your pussy is more beautiful than I could have ever imagined." He licks his lips as he crawls up from the end of the bed. My knees immediately start to close, and he grabs one. "Let me see you."

Both hands now on my knees, he spreads my legs apart. "Move back a little, yeah?"

Every inch I go back, he moves forward until my back hits the headboard. Pope positions himself between my legs then moves one leg and then the other over his shoulders. His lips touch my thigh, and I immediately shiver as he moves further and further up.

He glances up at me as he settles between my legs. His dark irises flare as they hold mine, and then, without warning, his tongue darts out and connects with my center.

I grip the comforter as my eyes roll back. My head falls against the headboard as he licks me, dragging his tongue up and down my core. He pushes a finger inside of me, and that's when it happens …

All those stars explode, and I am blinded as pleasure rocks through my body.

It's all I can do to hold on and not scream his name so loud that people—our friends in the room next door—hear me.

He doesn't stop. He circles my clit, sucks, and licks, and kisses me as he eats me out like no one ever has before. I'm not sure what my ex did could even be considered eating me out because it was nothing like this. It was foreplay that led to sex and didn't come anywhere close to making me feel like this, let alone cause another onslaught of pleasure to be right there behind it, ready to ruin me.

His face is buried between my thighs, his hands gripping my legs and holding me to him as I try to wiggle away.

"Too much, *too* much."

He doesn't stop. He spreads me wider, keeping one hand on my thigh as his mouth continues to work me, along with his finger … one and then two, and then… he sucks my clit.

"Oh fuck!" I cry out, my body involuntarily trying to pull away until time freezes and I am stuck in … heaven.

Panting, he kisses up my body, moves beside me, and pulls me into his arms. Then, tight against him we both try to catch our breath.

His words finally break the not-so-silent silence, due to the fact my heart is beating so loud I can hear it. "Thank you, Whit."

I DON'T MOVE when he slides out of bed, and not because I don't want to, but I'm pretty sure I simply can't move.

When I hear the shower running, I turn my head to the side and can see his reflection in the mirror as he steps in. I watch as he stands under the stream of water, as he lays his hands against the marble wall, and as his head drops down, allowing the water to wash over him. He's gorgeous, and he's always known what he wants, so why am I overthinking this? Why do I allow myself to think that Pope would hurt me? Why am I keeping him at arm's length? Why am I letting him think he's alone in his feelings? Even our dreams for our future are the same.

I lie there, just watching him, until I realize the muscles that run from his neck to his shoulder on the left side are tensing and loosening, I force myself to sit up—okay, force is not quite accurate. I sit up because I wanna know if what I think what he's doing is actually what he is doing.

A groan escapes me as I bite my bottom lip when my suspicions are confirmed. He's not just taking a shower; he's taking care of the massive hard-on that I left him with.

Before I can talk myself out of it, which I could surely do, I slide out of bed and quietly make my way into the bathroom. I love that he doesn't see me, that I can take a moment to watch his hand work his thick, hard, veiny cock.

The walls of my pussy clench together, and I silently scold her for being so needy when it comes to the man who just got us off three times—once with his fingers and twice on his tongue.

I move quietly into the double shower behind him with a washcloth in my hand. I make sure to move so he can see me grabbing the soap.

When he slows his strokes, I shake my head. "Don't stop on my account."

He turns, facing me, and his lips twist up. His hand is on his cock, slowly stroking it as I take the wet washcloth and run it up his spectacular abs.

"You come to help me out, Whit?" He smirks.

"Yeah. Yeah, I did."

I run the washcloth down his left thigh, and I don't stop until I'm on my knees. Then I wrap my hand around his, and together, we stroke his long, thick shaft.

"You remember that time in the back of the old Bronco?"

We continue working his erection together.

"How could I forget?"

"There is a great possibility that if you don't get up off your knees, I'm going to beat my speed record."

"Is that so?" I can't help but laugh.

"Whitley, it truly is."

"That might be a good thing because I don't know how long I can keep my mouth open as wide as it seems it might need to be." I bat his hand away and lift to my knees.

His eyes widen as he bites his lower lip when my hand alone moves up and down his shaft. I press the tip of it against my tongue, pumping him once, twice, three times, before sucking his thick, fat crown into my mouth.

"Fuck," he sputters as one hand slaps against the shower wall and the other grips the back of my head.

I suck deeper, taking more of his length in, and watch as his eyes roll and his head fall back. He releases my hair, and I work him with my hands, both of them in sync with my mouth, rolling my tongue over the tip then sucking on it while stroking him. I'm learning his body, what he likes and what he loves. And there is not one move I make in which he doesn't react in a way that would make me believe he's not loving this. The most mind-blowing thing is, that he's not alone. I love the taste of his flesh in my mouth. I love licking the pre-cum from the broad tip and sucking all the way down as far as I can go. I even like the way I gag slightly when I take it deeper than I should have. I'm sure I'll be doing that again. It's empowering.

I take him out of my mouth and stroke him faster, and then my tongue traces down the bulging vein on the underside of his heavy cock and then back up.

"Fuck yes, fuck yes," he groans. "Fair warning: I'm gonna come so hard that I'm a little nervous about what it's going to do to you."

"I guess we'll have to find out together."

With him as deep as I can go, my palms resting on his thick, muscular thighs, I move back and forth faster now, harder, and without the use of my hands.

"Fuck yes, fuck yes, fuck yes!"

I feel the first hot burst of his cum hit the back of my throat and swallow it quickly. The second I'm not as prepared for, but I manage to swallow that down, too. It's the third that ends up dripping just a little out of my mouth. I look up, and before I can wipe it away, his thumb slides across my lips, and he holds it in front of me.

"I don't want you to miss a drop."

The thing that I find unbelievable is… neither do I.

After we wash each other's body, we kiss a lot. None of his kisses are the same; they all seem to have different meanings. I can't wait to figure them all out.

WITH ONE OF his shirts covering my body, I lie in bed as he's grabbing us some water in the other room when I get a text.

I roll over and grab my phone.

JOHN PAUL:

Good night, Whit.

ME:

Good night, John Paul.

I hear a laugh as he walks in the bedroom, two bottles of water in one hand and he gives me a thumbs-up. I lie back and cover my face, giggling.

POPE

16

Sunday

I didn't sleep for shit last night, but Whit did. She slept so hard that she was making a noise that somewhat resembled snoring, but in a way that was almost silent. Almost. It was adorable.

We got up, kissed, showered quickly again, and were in the lobby, meeting up with the others by three thirty in the morning in order to make it to church on time.

When we get to the airport in Texas, us men ride in Danny's truck and the women in York's, but before we part ways, I stop her.

Looking up at me, she gives me the *what's wrong* kind of look.

"I'm going to need to kiss you right here and right now to make sure I can do it in front of the congregation without ... well, you know." I wink.

Smiling, she shakes her head, but she doesn't say no. She fists the collar of my shirt, yanks me down, and kisses me—hard.

When we break apart, she asks, "You good?"

"I'd tell you to find out for yourself, but that would be counterproductive." I lean in and give her a quick kiss. "See you at church, Whitley Mae Belington."

We're driving separately so Whit and the girls can get ready with Nora, but also so that Marks and I can talk about the shit back home.

As soon as we get in the truck, Danny asks, "How was last night?"

"Good," I answer, not about to share any more. "How was it for you all?"

"Danny snores," Marks answers dryly.

"I do not. *You* snore," Danny retorts, throwing his truck in drive and pulling out as the girls drive by.

"You know who might snore?" Marks asks.

"I'll bite. Who?"

"Kris Krone, brother to Alice, who works at the women's center," Danny states.

I look from Danny to Marks. "You care to translate to a language I understa—"

"Oh, whatever, man," Danny huffs.

"Kris was the driver the other night when you took out the back window of Kal's car. He was also Kal's college roommate freshman and sophomore year. He dropped out his junior year but still lived in the house Kal and his frat bros rented off campus. Many of the D-bags still run in the same circle, and in the center of that is Kris. We're assuming Kris got into dealing, that he's still dealing. Alice, the sister, is the one who hands something off to Kal once a week."

"Any solid proof?" I ask.

"Nothing solid at all, but she rents a very nice apartment, and there's no way in hell she can afford it on what she makes."

"I'll make sure to work that into the meet with Seward."

"You know what you're after?"

"Yeah, for him to put a short leash on his son. I want to make sure he never gets close enough to my wife or daughter to even make out their form." I scrub a hand over my face.

"And there we have it. Shit got real last night." Danny chuckles.

"Let's leave last night alone and talk about what's coming up."

"You're marrying Whit."

"Damn right I am." I smile.

WALKING into The First Methodist Church of Walton, I see Nora sprinting at me in the little white dress that complements Whit's. I squat down and open up my arms in time to catch her.

She plants one hand on each side of my face and says, "Pretty soon, you're getting married, and you'll be my daddy, just like I knew you would when I saw you first."

"You see your mom's ring?" I ask.

"Uh-huh. It's *so* pretty. But she says it's scary 'cause of the 'surance if she ever lost it."

This kid is adorable.

"One day, when you're your mom's age, you'll get one just like it from some lucky young man." I set her on her feet and squat down as I reach into my jacket pocket and pull out a tiny little box. "The first time I met your mommy, I knew she was special, and within a couple of years, I knew I wanted to marry her one day."

She grins. "Today's one day."

"It is," I agree. "But I also knew I wanted to have a little girl. When we get your mom's name changed from Belington to Paul—because that's what you do when you get married—I'd love for you to have the same name, too."

"Yes!" She throws a fist in the air.

"And I'd love you to wear this." I open the box and pull out the little necklace with the sparkly baseball dangling from it.

She nods, and I spin her around.

"Pull your hair up so I can put it on you."

When it's on, she turns and looks at me. "I gotta go show my friends."

When I stand, I see the future Mrs. Paul walking toward me, looking beautiful in the white dress.

"Whitley Mae Belington, you just get prettier by the minute."

"I'd tell you that flattery would get you nowhere, but I'm not sure that's true."

I take her hand when the music begins to play. "Let's go get our girl."

After the opening hymn, we sit with Nora between us. Danny and Marks are beside me, and York and Chloe are on the other side of Whit.

"Back when Mildred and I moved here to become part of this church family, we had a calendar on the wall by the old rotary dial phone. There wasn't a month that went by that we didn't have a wedding or two booked to take place right here. As the years passed, they've become less and less. It's been five years since I've officiated a wedding here inside this church, and that's going to change today."

Gasps are heard around the sanctuary, and I look down at Nora, who looks to be seconds from jumping up and not giving the congregation the courtesy of announcing

"Spoiler alert," before stomping all over Pastor B's obviously well-prepared sermon.

"Today, we're going to celebrate the love shared between two people who the rest of us knew would one day not only exchange vows but also honor them. But before that happens, we have a slideshow to share with you all."

The lights dim, and the screen to the left of the pulpit lights up.

The first picture is of me as a baby with my parents, followed by several others of us at baseball games. The next few are Whitley as a child, a couple with her mom, and a few with her father at a batting cage, smiling from ear-to-ear.

"That's me, right?" Nora asks.

Whit smiles. "No, that's *me* when I was your age."

The next several are of Whit as a kid with her cousins and a ton with Nelly. When Whit's eyes get glassy, I stretch my arm out along the back of the pew, lightly grip the back of her neck, and run my thumb up and down her soft skin, hoping it soothes her.

The next group of pictures are of her and me, and then some with Whit, Danny, Marks, and me through the years. Mom was always there—*always*.

Pictures of Nelly and Whit are next, and Nora grins, waves at the screen, then looks at me. "That's my mommies right there. The one in the red shirt told me my daddy was a baseball player. My friends said I was making it up, but I wasn't."

"No, little slugger, you sure weren't."

"Popa B said I shouldn't goat, but I sure do wanna tell them all they were the ones wrong."

"Gloat," Whit whispers, correcting her, and I can't help but chuckle.

The next few pictures are of baby Nora.

"That's me!" She claps.

"It sure is." Whit sniffs.

I look over at her, and she nods toward the screen just as a picture of Mom appears, holding Nora, and there are several.

"That's my mom holding you when you were a baby. She's your grandma."

"And she's in heaven with my other mommy, right?"

"She sure is."

I smile at Whit and Nora, and my focus isn't on the slideshow until I hear a laugh that I haven't heard in far too long. As I turn to look at the screen, I feel Whit's hand lightly grip my wrist, and her thumb begins rubbing circles against my skin.

"Would you let me fix my wig, for crying out loud?" Mom laughs as whoever is holding the phone and recording sets it up so it's facing her.

"You look fine, B. Now, let's get through your little speech without tears this time."

"Nancy." I smile when I recognize the voice.

Then Mom comes into focus, wearing her favorite wig and a Syracuse Mets hat.

"I hope this doesn't make them feel uncomfortable," she tells Nan.

"Of course it won't ... unless you're wrong."

"I'm not wrong. I know what a Paul man looks like when he's in love." She looks at the screen. "Johnathon Gregory Paul, you are the greatest light in my light."

"Fuck," Danny mumbles from beside me then sniffs.

"And I'm not going to sit here, feeling sorry for myself that I am missing the day you pick the woman whom you will marry and love forever, because I'm sure I've had the pleasure of loving her like a daughter already."

"Hold it together, B," Nan says from wherever she's sitting.

Mom waves her off. "Whitley, my son—"

"What if it's not Whit?" Nan whispers.

"Then he's marrying the wrong one." Mom wipes away tears, but they're joyful ones.

I hear Nan sniff. "Dang it, B. Now we have to start over again."

"Leave it be, Nan." Mom shoos her away and looks at the screen. "He's going to love you so hard, and sometimes, it's going to be suffocating. The reason? He's just like his father, and there will be times he's away, so when he gets home, nothing else will matter but you and whatever children you two have. There will be times you two will drive each other crazy. I've already watched it happen, and you always work through it—don't ever stop doing that. Danny and Marks will be there to make sure you don't. Pastor and Mrs. B should be the people you seek advice from when you need guidance.

"Love deep and take care of each other. Love hard and support each other's dreams. Love forever, like I know you will. Johnathon and Whitley, Dad and I will be sitting in the bleachers in heaven, cheering you both on." She blows a kiss. "I love you, my boy, and I love you, Whitley."

Pictures of the proposal light up the screen as Pastor B calls to us, "Whitley, Johnathon, and Nora, could you join me and Mildred up here, please, to exchange your vows?"

As we stand, Pastor B tells the congregation, "This week has been one for the books. Both Whitley and John Paul have come to me separately from the other about this union that we are all going to be a part of. The one thing they each requested separately were traditional vows."

I give Mrs. B a hug, and she pulls Nora beside her as I take Whitley's hands.

"Let us begin. Repeat after me …"

I don't hear much else from that point on but my own promise to her and hers to me.

"I, Johnathon Gregory Paul, take you, Whitley Mae Belington, to be my wedded wife, to have and to hold from this day forward, for better, for worse, for richer, for poorer, in sickness and in health, to love and to cherish, till death do us part. According to God's Holy ordinance, and thereto I pledge you my faithfulness, always." I slide the platinum band onto her finger, one she bought in Vegas.

"I, Whitley Mae Belington, take you, Johnathon Gregory Paul, to be my wedded husband, to have and to hold from this day forward, for better, for worse, for richer, for poorer, in sickness and in health, to love and to cherish, till death do us part. According to God's Holy ordinance, and thereto I pledge you my faithfulness, always." She slides the ring onto my finger.

"Wait— I have one more thing," I say, feeling kind of like an idiot but also knowing this needs to be done. I hold up my pinkie. "Pinkie promise, Whit?"

"You're such a dork." Whit laughs through the tears streaming down her face and hooks her pinkie around mine. "I pinkie promise."

As the congregation erupts in laughter, Pastor B begins again. "These vows symbolize the lifelong commitment, love, and devotion that the couple promises to one another within the framework of their faith and also a pinkie promise."

When she wets her lips, I groan, and she tries but fails to hold back a grin, knowing damn well what she's doing to me. I love that she knows.

"Ladies and gentlemen, it is my honor and privilege to introduce to you for the very first time, Mr. and Mrs. Paul.

Taking First

You may now celebrate this joyous union as husband and wife. Go ahead, John Paul, and kiss your bride."

I have no idea why I didn't think that I'd feel this surge of emotions coursing through me. My heart races with excitement. My hands tremble slightly as I see her eyes sparkle with happiness, mirroring the love and anticipation I feel in this moment.

I feel the warmth of her hand in mine, and I lean in slowly, savoring every heartbeat leading up to right here and right now. I take her face in my hands as I pull her closer, and kiss her, my wife, gently, tenderly, reverently, yet still passionately. Then, knowing that not just me but both of us could get lost in this, I break the kiss, tilting her face up and kissing the tip of her nose and then her forehead.

"Hey, Whitley Mae Paul, I love you."

"You'd better."

ONCE PHOTOS ARE TAKEN and our family members head to the fellowship hall, *my wife* nods toward the white lilies.

I know exactly what she's thinking. "Yeah."

Hand in hand, we walk out of the church carrying two bouquets of flowers. We keep walking through the church yard to the cemetery saying nothing.

At my parents stone, Whit kisses her fingertips and places them on Moms name. "Miss and love you."

We replace the flowers currently there that are wilting, then I take her hands and turn her toward me.

"Hey Mom, Whitley and I got married today just like you knew we would. Dad, you should see my wife, she's stunning."

Her lower lip pouts out and quivers.

"I want to thank you both for teaching me what marriage should look like, how love should be given, and what it should feel like. We're going to make you proud."

She squeezes my hands as I lean in and give her a kiss.

Then we hear Nora yelling, "Hey, it's wedding party time, get back here!"

Laughing we turn and run —yes run— toward our Nora, who is running toward us.

AFTER A RECEPTION in the fellowship hall and at Nora's request to have my room, to which Whitley simply shrugs, the Vegas Six—Marks, Danny, York, Chloe, Whit, and I— begin moving Whit's and Nora's things to the house. I let Nora know that when I have to go to Florida, the contractors will be doing some more work, so she and Whit will probably go back to stay at Pastor and Mrs. B's house.

"Why can't we come with you to Florida?" she asks.

"Because you have school, and I have work." Whit tucks her into my old bed tighter.

Her little lip pops out. "I wanna go to school in Florida."

I was not prepared for that, but I wing it. "Your mommy would be lost without you."

Nora's nose scrunches up as she asks, "Aren't there sick people in Florida?"

Well, shit.

"There are, but we have Popa B and Gram here. They'd miss us very much, and we'd miss them, too."

"Aren't you gonna miss us very much too?" That question slays me.

"Of course I will." I look at Whit, showing her I'm drowning, and she looks amused. Fuck it. "We can—"

Taking First

"You two, we're going to ease our way into this, starting now, okay?" She leans down and peppers Nora's little face with kisses before sitting back and smiling at her. "We're married now, and that's a pretty big change. It means when John Paul's home, we'll be spending time with him."

I step in. "Lots of time. We'll wake up and see each other in the morning, and nights, we'll be together, like right now. We'll make a calendar so you'll know where I am, and we'll mark the days I'll be back here with you both."

Nora nods as she yawns ... Whit yawns ... and of course, I yawn.

"When you have school breaks and Mommy has time off from work, you can fly to see me and—"

Nora sits straight up. "We can fly?"

Whit closes her eyes and slowly shakes her head. "You've done it now."

"Yeah, little slugger. And when you have a school break and Mom has some time off, I'd love for you two to come watch a game and—"

"Watch a game?"

"Absolutely. I can't wait to know my girls are in the stands, cheering me on."

She sighs dramatically and flops back. "This is the best day ever."

"We're going to figure it all out, but not in one night. You need to get to sleep, and so do I."

"What about my new daddy?" Nora asks, squeezing one of her stuffies tight.

"Can you call me that, too?" I whisper to Whit and get an elbow to the stomach before addressing Nora. "Tomorrow night, you're gonna be with me until Mom gets out of work. We'll get started working on that calendar."

WHIT STAYS in with Nora until she falls asleep while I check all the doors and windows, making sure they're locked, and I get busy changing the sheets on our bed—mine and hers—in Mom's room, which is ours for now.

"You good?" Whit asks from behind me.

I look over my shoulder and toss the pillow on the bed. "Yeah, better now that you're here."

"I'm gonna use the bathroom and …" She nods to the next door over.

"I'm not going anywhere, Whit."

WHIT

17

Sunday

After a quick shower, I scrub all the makeup from my face with the environmentally friendly makeup removal washcloth that was in the gift basket of things Chloe and York gave me today, which they included Nora's name on.

Chloe's a true artist with makeup and hair, and she looks like she walked out of a magazine, even on her bad days. But I just can't imagine keeping up with that every single day. It took her an hour to do what she called the *"no-makeup makeup"* look and even longer to "soften" my natural waves. Don't get me wrong; it looked amazing, but I just don't see the point in doing it every day.

Manis and pedis once a month and waxing a few times a year? Count me in. Hair treatments once every couple months so that I can easily manage all this hair and therefore keep it long? I'll never stop. But full-glam makeup? Not possible.

I hold up the white silk nightie and choke back a laugh

because this is from Gram, and so was the matching robe. I walk into the bedroom with all the confidence I can muster while wearing this ridiculous thing.

He's lying on the bed, shirtless, his plump pecs and smooth skin covering all those muscles and valleys on full display. And that delicious V that disappears under the waistband of his black sweats, *all right there*. Even though they're not fitted, they cannot hide Pope's manhood. Quite simply, he's stunning *and hung*.

He thrusts his hips just a bit. "This work?"

"Did you forget boxers?" I ask, eyes following the outline of his massive shaft.

"I have baggy sweats on. They're not tight; they're covering everything, Whit."

He looks me over from head to toe as he curls up to sit, his ab muscles flexing as he does. It's ... disarming, although I'm not sure why I feel like I need to be armed.

"And here you are, looking stunning in white—again." His back is against the headboard of the queen-sized bed, a bed he fills near completely, but anything bigger would fill the room to the point that we'd be unable to open the closet.

"Before I get to unwrapping you"—he swings his legs over the side and stands—"I need to show you something." Two steps, and he has my hand, pulling me behind him.

"Who says you get to unwrap me?"

"That robe might as have a tag on it that says, *To Pope* ." He turns, eyes dancing, and looks me over before opening the back door and shoving his size thirteens into a pair of black-and-white athletic slides.

"I don't have shoes."

"Hop on." He squats down and looks back at me as I hesitate. "It's my back, not my dick, Whit."

My face turns red, and he chuckles.

"What has gotten into you?" I grumble but do as invited to, and I hop on.

When I hook my legs around his center, he stands. "Three of the goals I've had forever have been checked off my list. I'm happy, Whit, and in love. You're gonna feel the same when you allow yourself to lean all the way into this thing we got going on and stop pretending it's just a way to keep Nora, because it's also keeping us."

Us.

He turns and hits a button, and I hear a noise. "All the locks are now engaged, keyed in with a code. She's all tucked in, safe and asleep."

When he turns to the new back door of a garage that has more than doubled in size—much like Pope's already-big dick when it's hard—a light comes on.

"Motion lights at all entrances and some scattered around the perimeter, here and at your grandparents' house." At the door, he taps a code into the keypad, and that same sound—the lock moving—occurs, and he opens the door. More lights come on as we walk in, and he squats down so I can slide off.

He takes my hand and points left. "There are a couple of closets and a bathroom with a washer and dryer through there. Thought we can use them when the main part of the house gets renovated." He points to some steep, narrow stairs. "Those are temporary. A full set will lead into the house when we figure out how we want it laid out. We can talk about that later. But this …" He turns, biting his lush bottom lip but is still unable to hide his smile as he holds both my hands, walking backward. More lights come on, and that's when I see it—Pope's old ride, but it's had work done—a lot of work. "I'm gonna get my do-over in that thing." He stomps his foot like I did all those years ago, eyes smiling so much they sparkle.

Trying hard to not laugh, I say, "Honestly, I can't say I blame you for wanting to redeem yourself."

His smile deepens, and I drop his hands to get a closer look. He follows me around as I check it out.

"It's amazing."

He opens the door and pushes a latch, and the passenger seat folds forward. "You and Nora have a step to get up in here, and she's got her very own seat, so no more fussing with switching it from your ride every time we're together."

"She's going to love it."

And she will. Everything someone does for her makes her feel special, and the girl is as grateful as can be.

I follow him to the back, where he waves his foot under the chrome bumper and the hatch opens. He then opens the tailgate.

"I can put an air mattress back here next time you wanna—"

I smack his chest, and he laughs as he captures it beneath his own hand.

Both of us go still for a moment.

"Do you feel that? My heart, Whit, it's so damn full again."

Reflexively, my fingertips dig into his bare chest. "I hope you know I want to let mine feel that way too. I want to be able to say the words *I love you* without feeling that it's going to be a burden on you for the rest of your life. Because I do. I love you. These past two weeks …" I force a laugh. "Mostly the past week, I have felt like I did before Nelly's lie. And it hurts to say that because that lie … that lie is Nora. And she's not a lie. She's everything that's good in this world. Pope, these past couple of days have been so … big—so much bigger than I ever imagined life could be—but I am so afraid."

"You weren't afraid last night. You weren't afraid today in church when you said *I do*. You were happy, Whit, and I know it because I know what that looks like, what it feels like to be in the presence of your joy. It, too, is everything that's good in this world. We are going to get back to that. You, Nora, and me—we're going to have a good life, I promise you. I won't be without you again, Whit. I ached for you."

With the belt of the robe, Pope pulls me into him, catching me before we crash so hard into each other that the kiss would be bruising. This kiss, it's like a bridge, bringing us from then until now without all the hurt feelings and pain.

Both of us groan as our lips meld together with such precision that it causes heat to run all the way down to my toes. My heart beats harder, surging and swelling to the size it was always meant to be.

His hands run roughly up the length of me, a deep groan vibrating from his lips as he traces the curves of my body as if he's memorizing them. They finally make it to my face, and, God, I love how he holds my face in his firm grip. It makes me feel like I am beautiful.

My back hits the truck. My mouth opens to him, and his tongue slides in as his hands glides down, gripping my butt and lifting me up.

He sets me on the tailgate of his old truck, and we're still kissing. God, I love kissing. I could kick myself for not letting him kiss me that night we gave ourselves to each other. Then again, I can't imagine missing his kiss as much as I missed him all those years.

"I want you, Whit. Tell me you want me too."

"I want you, too."

His thick fingers reach down to untie the belt of my robe, and then he pushes it off my shoulder. "Absolutely beautiful." His eyes take in the thin, silky white material barely covering my body. "You're going to put your faith in me? Because I'm here with you right now, and even when I'm on the road, I'm still gonna be right here with you, yeah?"

"Yeah," I exhale as his lips press against my shoulder.

"You and I, we're unstoppable. And we're always going to be that way." He grips my knees and slides his hands up my legs to the hem of the nightgown. Then he drags it up my body until he pulls it over my head and drops it beside us. "I don't know where to start with you. Your tits are fucking spectacular." He cups them in his hands, swiping his thumbs over my nipples before he leans in and licks one and then the other. "Tastes so fucking good."

His hot, wet mouth surrounds my breast as his hands slide down my body until they're underneath my ass. Then he lifts me, moving me back into the Broncos flat bed. "Lie back, Whitley, so I can kiss your pretty little pussy."

Lying down in front of me, his chest bare, he slips one foot and then the other over his muscular shoulders until he is facing down, licking, tasting, and sucking me.

God, I love this, too. Foreplay is a gift to the women of the world. Even giving Pope head in the shower in Vegas was a complete turn-on. Yes, foreplay is a gift to women because sex is definitely for men.

John Paul's groans are guttural and increase my desire. I feel myself growing wetter with each long, lavish lick of his talented tongue. His hand runs up my torso and cups my breast, then he pinches my nipple, rolling it between his finger and thumb.

"Oh God, oh God, oh God, yes, yes, yes." I fall apart so quickly that I should be embarrassed, but I'm not, not one bit. What I am is determined to make him fall apart just as quickly.

I reach down, shoving my fingers in his silky waves, and grip it, pulling him up.

"Whitley, what are you doing? I wasn't done with you yet."

"I haven't even begun with you."

I push him to roll on his back and kiss down his chest. I shove his sweatpants down enough for his cock to spring free. Then I wrap my hand around his girthy shaft and begin to stroke him.

"Fuck yes, fuck yes," he hisses right before I wrap my lips around his fat tip, sucking the pre-cum from the slit of his cock. "That fucking drives me wild. You drive me wild. I can't wait to be inside that sweet pussy of yours."

His words, his praise, do something to me, and I move my body above him, my knees on each side of his hips. My hand is on the base of his cock, drawing it up and down the length of my soaked slit.

"Fuck me, Whitley. Are you trying to kill me?" He grabs my hips, his fingers and thumbs sinking into my flesh. "Your pussy is so hot, so wet."

I take him in just a little and realize just how big John Paul's cock truly is. He's massive, even more so when I'm trying to fit him inside of me.

"Whitley Mae, I know I taught you how to drive stick in this very truck. You can't sit there in neutral and expect me not to try to help you out." He thrusts upward, and I cry out his name, except it's not his name. It's something altogether different, a curse possibly. "This is kind of like starting you out at a stop sign on a hill and expecting you not to stall out."

He sits up, runs his hands down my back, and then rolls me, so I'm beneath him. He positions his cock at my entrance. "We're going to go slow to start, which is good because I do want to make love to my wife for the first time without tearing her apart or hurting her in any way."

His use of *"my wife"* has my insides quivering.

Why is that so hot?

Pressing into me, one hand on each side of my head, he holds the weight of his body above me as he kisses me, and those kisses almost make me forget that his dick is that big.

"That's it, Whitley. Take my cock just like that," he groans.

I start to circle my hips, hoping it helps speed up the process, because he's being far too nice—or maybe I'm being far too needy—but I want this. I want him inside me. I want to make him feel as good as he makes me feel.

Kissing, kneading my breasts, plucking my nipples, licking up my neck, bending to suck on my aching peaks, his hair tickling my skin, filling me ... so full of him, I am overwhelmed by all the pleasureful sensations he is giving to me all at once, and by the sounds he's making, I know I am not alone.

He grabs around my leg, hitching my knee up to rest on his hip, and he grinds into me.

"What—what—what ... Oh God, I think...I think—"

"You think you're gonna come, baby? You gonna fucking come on my dick? Your pussy is milking my cock so hard that I'm gonna come quickly again, but I won't do it until I get you there."

He begins thrusting deep inside of me, sliding out and filling me with one thrust. Then he stills, giving me a few moments to catch my breath. And then he moves. *God how he moves*. I feel his balls slap my ass over and over again. The feel, the sound ... *so sexy*.

Turned on like I have never been, I feel an orgasm begging to burst from deep inside of me. It's something I never knew happened—that intense build, the tension that causes my body to stiffen so much I know my muscles, as well as my vagina, are going to ache tomorrow, and then …

"I'm gonna come, I'm gonna come, I'm gonna come."

And I do. I come so hard that I swear I see stars.

"Fuck," he groans as my body shakes uncontrollably beneath him. "Fuck yes. Keep milking that cock. It's all yours, Whitley Mae Paul. All. Yours."

I had no idea it was possible, but somehow, he's driving into me deeper and faster, and my orgasm is just rocking my core.

"Fuck, Whit, you're on the pill, right?"

"No," I gasp, pushing him off of me.

"Son of a bitch." He grabs something and groans as his body releases his own orgasm.

"Oh my God, how did we not talk about this?"

Panting, he says, "We're good. But this sexy little number you bought to give me a show, I'm not sure it's gonna make it."

When he holds up the satin nightie, I can't help but laugh.

"What's so funny?" He smiles.

"I didn't buy it to give you a show. Gram did."

"No fucking way?"

He pulls me into his arms, and we both laugh.

"What's your name?" he asks, pressing a kiss to my head.

"Oh, please," I huff, knowing exactly what he's doing. He's asking because he said he'd temporarily make me forget my name.

"Come on. Tell me." He pulls me closer.

"It's Whitley Mae Belington." When his chest vibrates

in a silent chuckle, I push up off his chest and glare down at him. "You're good, but …"

I stop when his grin spreads, and he asks again, "What is your name?"

I narrow my eyes. "Not fair."

"All is fair in love and baseball." He winks as he grips my waist and pulls me up. "I love you, Whitley Mae Paul."

I playfully roll my eyes. "I know."

He sighs loudly.

I take his face in my hands, just like he does mine. "I love you."

"I know you do, but, Whit, I'm not sure I'll ever get sick of hearing it, so you keep saying it, yeah?"

I press my forehead to his. "I love you, John Gregory Paul."

Monday

"CAN we do Monday morning waffles every day?" Nora asks.

"You mean, every Monday?" Pope smiles down at her as she swings between us.

"Uh-huh." She grins. "They're my favorite. Fluffy waffles with banana, whipped cream, and a little bit of chocolate."

"When I'm home, we can do that. It's not as easy when it's just you and Mommy."

"How many more sleeps do we have until you gotta go to Florida?"

"We still have a couple of weeks," he says in such an assuring manner that she seems content with that answer, but a couple of weeks will go by just as quickly as the past two have, too quickly.

POPE HELPS Nora into her seat in my vehicle. We chose to drive mine so that she isn't bouncing off the walls at school today, talking about the wedding, her new house, *and* her new seat.

As I'm opening the passenger door, I hear a vehicle stop behind me and glance over my shoulder. It's Spud.

"Heard a rumor that you got married to a man other than your fiancé?" he snarls.

Before I even open my mouth, Pope is beside me. "Ex-fiancé. Now, move it along."

"You think you're the mayor of Walton, John Paul? You ain't shit, but one injury away from being a washed-up has-been, know-nothin', married to a money-grubbing wh—"

"John Paul," I yell as he reaches into Spud's truck, and all I can see are hands flying.

"You speak about my wife, my family, in any way, and you'll be hard to find."

I tug on John Paul's crewneck, attempting to stop him from getting himself into trouble. He steps back enough for me to witness Spud trying to pull down his sweatshirt, which John Paul somehow pulled up from the back and over his head.

He holds the door open for me. "Let's get a move on, Whitley Mae Paul. We've got things to do."

Sliding in, I look back at Nora, who's all wide-eyed, her lips rolled in like she's trying not to laugh.

"Nora!" I gasp.

"Mommy, he looked so funny!" She pulls her shirt up

by the collar and hides her face so all I see are her little pigtails as she waves her hands in the air. "Money-rubbing more."

Oh damn, I think because not only did Nora see what Pope did, but she also heard what Spud said that caused it.

I look from her to Pope as he looks between Nora and me, and then to Spud, who is still trying to straighten out his shirt, and the look in his eyes is not the John Paul I knew before he left Walton. He is major league pissed.

"John Paul, we need to go."

"Whit," he growls, "he's drunk."

I hold up my phone to show him I'm sending a text to York. "It's handled."

POPE

18

Monday

It's decided that Nora should stay home with me to do some "deprogramming" instead of going to school, hopped up on the happiness that our little family is official and the shitshow that went down on Main Street.

We drop Whit off at work then head into the city to grab the biggest calendar we can find so we can start on our little project.

While heading out of town, we pass Spud, who has been pulled over by the State boys, and something tells me he's gonna skate, as he tends to do when he's not in Walton. While in the stationery department, my suspicion is confirmed via text from Marks, who looked into his driving record, and all but the DUI that Marks had him on, which has not gone to court yet, are non-moving violations. And his lawyer? Kal fucking Seward.

As much as I'm trying to stay in the moment with Nora, my wheels get to spinning, and there's no doubt that

Kal, Kris, Alice, and more than likely Spud White are all connected in some way. We just need to connect it then see how that will play out in regards to keeping Nora where she's intended to be and also ensure Chloe's safety, as well.

After Nora is in bed, Chloe shows up with an old duffel bag and a suitcase. "Whit messaged me earlier and asked that I bring this over. It's all full of Nelly's things. Some of which we went through to get the photos of Bianca and Nora that were used in the slideshow."

I take the larger bag and open the door wider for her to roll the suitcase in.

"Whit must have gotten to thinking about the possibility of Nelly having something more in one of these since your wedding and the video your mom sent to Mrs. Nancy, which was so damn sweet, by the way." She smiles as she hefts it up onto the coffee table.

"It was something we'll cherish forever. Thank you for helping make Vegas and the wedding and all this special, Chloe. You're a good friend."

She waves me off like it's no big deal, but it is. In my eyes, it's huge.

"Well, anyway, she got to thinking there could be something on her old phone or a notebook."

"It's worth a look." I agree, placing the duffel next to the suitcase and unzipping it.

"You want some help?" she asks.

"Sure," I say, pulling out a bunch of notebooks.

She sits beside me and picks one up.

"Found out today that Spud's lawyer is Kal."

She glances over at me. "I didn't get up into many of Spud's dubious affairs. Him being connected to someone like Kal, who looks down on everyone, makes little sense, but their common friend, Kris"—she taps the side of her nose

—"was someone I hated to see comin' around. Whenever Spud got into the nose candy, things did not go well for me. When I called the fool on it, he'd beat me down mentally, and if I didn't seem to be breaking, he'd do so physically."

"I mean no disrespect, nor can I pretend to know what your life has been like, but it is glaringly obvious that you're out of his league. What kept you there?"

When she looks down, I feel like an asshole.

"Please, forgive me for—"

"No, it's actually good to talk about it. Helps me in a way. At first, he was sweet and treated me better than any man had ever treated me. He convinced me I should live with him, told me I'd be able to help my little sister with the things she needed that financial aid and a work study at school wouldn't pay for. I wanted her to succeed where I failed, and he seemed to understand that need … until he was drunk or getting into the coke."

"What's your sister going to school for?"

She lights up. "Cecilia's going to be a veterinarian one day."

"That's wonderful."

"I'm very proud of her."

"And you, Chloe, what's your next step?"

"I'm taking my steps one at a time. Walking from the Pastor and Mrs. B's house without feeling like he was going to come after me the other night and again tonight, those were big steps."

I hate to piss on her pumps, but after today's run-in with Spud, it's unavoidable. "No woman should ever feel like they have to look over their shoulder. It's no fun, playing defense all the time, but after what happened this morning and until Spud's not feeling like he has the right to accost people on the street, I really want you to let someone know where you're going, even if it's a simple walk from there to here."

Her lips curve into a frown.

"It won't be forever. He'll get his, Chloe. I promise you he will."

"What happened this morning?"

I feel like I've just stepped in shit. I'm sure York and Whit didn't tell her for a reason. There's no turning back now, though. I either stand here in shit or wipe it off. So I tell her everything, and when I get to the part of Nora's reaction, she looks mortified … until I give her a reenactment.

After that, we get busy going through the bags, and when we find an old dead phone, we scramble to locate a charger that will work. When we can't, I order one online and send a message to our group chat, asking if anyone has one. I get a response from Danny immediately.

DANNY:

> Think I might. I'll get back at ya in a bit.

ME:

> Bring it over if you have one. No stress though. I have one coming in tomorrow.

We dive back into the massive amounts of pictures Nelly had, and Chloe starts sorting them based on dates on the printed photos.

When Danny arrives with a cord, we plug in Nelly's phone. I send a text to Pastor B that Danny and Chloe are here and that he doesn't have to come over when I go to get Whit from work. Neither of us wants Chloe to be alone.

A MILE from the med center, lights flash in my rearview mirror. I pull over to the side of the road, allowing an ambulance, and then another, as well as a Walton PD car, Marks's truck, and a state patrol vehicle following behind to go by.

My phone rings. It's Marks, and I hit *Accept*.

"What the hell's going on, man?"

"Cocaine Kris was shot. He's bleeding out pretty fast. Massive accident on the interstate—it's all backed up. They called our bus out and decided to bring them to our Med Center."

"Them?"

"His sister, Alice, Pope. This happened outside the women's shelter."

"Fuck."

"Yeah, well, they're trying to stop Kris's bleeding until a helicopter can get here and take him to Dallas. Pope, Whit's gonna wanna stick around and help, but this isn't sitting well with me. I think you should get her home."

I park as far away from the action as I can and jog to the emergency entrance, where I see Whit relieve the EMT doing chest compressions on who I know is Kris. I'm not getting her out of here; she's right where she thinks she needs to be. Having never seen her in action before now, I wouldn't argue that fact. She's doing good. She's helping people, even ones who wouldn't do the same for her.

They're unloading the second ambulance. They have Alice in a seated position on the stretcher; her foot bandaged up an bleeding through.

Marks hurries to her and walks beside the stretcher as they enter the emergency department. "Need your help finding the shooter, Alice."

"I ... I ... Is he going to be okay? Is Kris going to be—"

"They're doing everything they can, and we need to make sure we do too. Did you see the shooter? Do you know—"

"She's asked for her lawyer," one of the state boys cuts Marks off.

"Why did I ask for a lawyer?" she asks the officer, clearly confused.

"Alice, shut your mouth," he sneers.

"Nah, that's not how this shit works, Berk," Marks sneers back at him.

"This situation is out of your jurisdiction." The officer, Berk, glares at him.

Marks boxes him out. "Alice, I want to make sure everyone in Walton is safe. If you know who did this—"

"That's enough. My client needs medical attention. Step aside, Officer Marks."

Motherfucker, I groan inwardly.

When Kal is beside her, she looks at him and starts crying. "It was—"

"Self-defense." He quickly interrupts her. "I know. But right now, we need to make sure you're okay."

"What?" She shakes her head clearly confused. "I—"

"Alice, not here." Speaking over her, Kal firmly states.

"Alice," I call to her, and they both look back. When Kal sees me, his lips curl in disgust. "Do not take the fall for someone else."

Kal's cool and callous demeanor changes, and he allows his arrogant mask to fall briefly. The look he gives me is murderous. "This is none of your business."

I step close enough that I don't need to raise my voice and direct my eyes at Alice. "He's never been anything but a punk-ass bully. He'll never be anything else, Alice, but you can do the right thing."

"Get him the hell out of here!" Kal roars.

"Not in my ER, Seward!" Whit's friend and co-worker, Laurie, yells.

"She's my client. I'm not leaving her side."

"Like hell you aren't."

"She's not to speak to the cops without me," he spits then points at Alice. "Not a damn word."

Officer Burk takes him by the elbow. "Let's wait outside."

Laurie looks me over. "I'm guessing you can behave."

"You'd be guessing correctly, Mrs. Laurie."

She waves me off and turns, saying, "You could charm the panties off a nun, John Paul, but you'd better be ready for a fight if you think about taking Whit from us."

Standing in the hall with our backs against the wall, trying to stay out of the way and keep our mouths shut so Laurie doesn't kick our asses out, too, I look at Marks without saying a word.

He nods. "He's trying to get her to take the fall."

"He could be the shooter."

"Can't see him getting his hands dirty." He scrubs a hand over his face. "What a fucking night."

"You think Kris is gonna make it?"

"Not sure, but if he doesn't, Alice might be going to prison for murder."

"She'll talk. She wanted to talk," I say, believing that wholly. "He's covering for someone who would do his dirty work. Right now, Whit is going to worry about the women at the shelter. You think York could find out what's going on with the residents?"

"She saw me in the parking lot, pulled a U-turn, and called. She's on her way there now."

"She gonna look at the footage?"

He nods. "The ones the board know about and the one

in the back she had fixed and has running on a separate feed that they don't know about."

"Smart woman."

He winks. "Your wife's idea."

"Genius woman."

My phone vibrates in my pocket, and I pull it out and look at the screen. It's a message from Chloe in the group message chain.

> CHLOE:
> Spud is here. Danny went out. He needs help!

"Fuck!" Marks and I say at the same time.

"Gentlemen, do not—"

Whit comes running down the hall. "Laurie, stay with Alice. Do not let anyone in there, except you and Doc." She looks at me. "It's Spud. Spud's the shooter, and he's—"

"Let's go."

Marks, Whit, and I run out through the automatic doors.

As we pass by Burk, he yells, "Where are you going?"

"Ask him, you worthless sorry excuse for a cop!" Whit screams.

"This way." I grab her hand, and we run to the vehicle.

Sliding in, she pants, "Alice ... Alice said it was Spud. They park in the back parking lot. Spud gives Kris drugs; he gives Spud money. Spud wouldn't give him the coke unless Alice gave him Chloe's new address. Kris called her out to his vehicle, and she tried to explain she didn't have Chloe's information. Spud pulled a gun. Kris, he told Spud he knew where she was, and he shot him, anyway. He shot him, and Alice ran. He—"

"Whit"—I throw my arm in front of her as I take a

corner, going a good sixty miles per hour over the speed limit—"they're going to be okay."

"She said that it's Kal's operation, and"—she sobs into her hands—"she said Nelly knew. That Nelly used to do runs to make money when she was here, visiting. Alice thinks he was trying to get rid of Kris, like he did Nelly."

As farfetched as this seems, it would connect a whole lot of dots.

"Whit—"

"Nora was in the car accident that killed Nelly. If he could do that, he's—"

"We're going to take this one step at a time, but I can promise you, if that man comes near her, I'll end his life."

"You can't say that. You can't be—"

"I'm one year in the pros, was prepared to do ten before I came back and bent down on one knee, told you how much I love you, begged you to marry me. I'd make it look like self-defense and be out before—"

"Stop, just stop." She bats away her tears.

I throw a hand out again as I take another corner. This time, the speedometer is buried.

At the stop on the corner by our house, we see the yard where we play ball is lit up with the motion lights I installed, and headlights coming from Spud's jacked-up S-10.

I follow Marks as he drives across the field toward a man swinging a bat—Spud. There are two people on the ground.

Danny throws himself in front of Chloe, taking the swing to the arm.

"No, no, no!" Whit screams and tries to open the damn door.

I grab her arm and throw the vehicle in park. "Go check on Nora!"

"Oh my God, oh my—"

I run as fast as I can to get to him before he swings again. Marks is right by my side, and we tackle him from behind.

"Talk to me, Chloe! Danny, talk to me!" Marks yells.

"If this doesn't get me laid, I'm giving—"

"Wake up, Aiken!" Chloe sobs.

"You whore!" Spud screams as Marks wrenches his arms back and gets him in cuffs. "You filthy fucking whore."

I slam the back of his head down, pressing his face in the dirt.

"Call 911!" Chloe cries as she looks at her hands covered in blood. "Call 911!"

A shot rings out from somewhere, and we all hit the ground.

"I told you, not in my neighborhood."

I look up and see Pastor B holding a shotgun, still aimed toward the sky.

"Pastor B, call 911. Danny's been shot," Chloe sobs.

AFTER CHECKING ON NORA–WHO, thank God, slept through all of this—Whitley sets the alarm to the house and runs right back out. She's on her knees beside Danny, who was shot in the side. The bullet went straight through.

"When he pulled the gun, Danny dived on him." Chloe, who seems unaware of her own injuries, sits with her back against Pastor B's legs, shaking. "I had to help him. I set the alarm. Nora was safe. I promise Nora was—"

"She's safe," Whit says calmly as she keeps pressure on Danny's wound.

"You did good, Chloe. You did really good," I assure her.

"I grabbed the bat. I got two really good swings in—home-run swings—and he-he grabbed it and threw me down and—" She stops. "I think my arm is broken. Maybe my face? Am I broken, Whit? Did he break me again?"

"No, Chloe, you beat him this time. You and Danny are going to heal, and he's going to jail."

"Promise?" She leans down and kisses Danny's cheek. "I'm so sorry, Danny Aiken."

One ambulance arrives, and Whit passes what information she has then looks at me. "The other one won't be here until—"

"You think Chloe and you can ride with Danny in this one? I'll follow Marks with this steaming pile of shit in the back seat, and your grandparents have got Nora."

"He has a gun," she says, shocked.

She's not alone.

"Yeah, I guess he does."

"You two get along now. Nora, Millie, and I will be just fine. My friend, Remington, is here, too, if needs be. Get Danny and Chloe fixed up. I expect them in church on Sunday."

WHIT MADE the decision that Danny was going to need more care than the med center could give him. She was confident she'd done everything they would have been able to at the med center, and the extra time driving some back roads to avoid the traffic jam would be no less than waiting for another helicopter to bring Danny to receive the best care he could get.

Marks continued to the med center so he could keep

Spud under his jurisdiction. He was making calls to get state boys whom he trusted up here and on the case.

York was doing what she needed to, and then she would be going straight to our place.

I called Danny's father and let him know what happened and which route to take to get to Dallas.

19

Tuesday

Curled up on Pope's lap in the chair between Chloe's and Danny's beds, I whisper my fear. "He's going to get away with this."

"As much of a piece of shit as her brother is, he is still her brother. Alice will talk. Spud is going to go one of two ways—he'll talk, or he won't—but he won't get away with any of it."

He pulls his phone out of his pocket and hits an app. "This is our security system."

The screen lights up several different rectangle boxes, and he hits the one for the front door then turns the volume all the way down. We both tense when we see the flash of the gun going off and Danny slumping over. It shows Spud pulling him down the stairs by his hair, forcing him to his knees and pointing the gun to the back of his head. Tears spill down my face because there is nothing that could ever prepare anyone to see someone they love like a brother in that situation.

And then Chloe appears, swinging once and knocking Spud to his knees, kicking the gun away before swinging again and hitting him across the back. The third time she swings, he grabs the end and shoves the other end into her stomach. Danny somehow kicks him in the face and pulls Chloe to him, and the other camera picks up as they both crawl across the yard.

Spud comes into view again, and Danny sees the moment the bat is about to come down on the back of Chloe's head. With a bullet having just gone through him, he finds the strength to push up enough to cover her body with his, taking the blow across the back. Spud then kicks both of them repeatedly—her in the face, him in the side. He stomps on her arm and her…

"I can't watch any more of this." I sniff and look up at him. His eyes are fire and fury. "Stop, please just—"

"After I send it to York and Marks," —he strokes a few keys then clears his throat— "Kal will be connected, and he'll do time, as well."

Just like that, we're back to the conversation.

"Alice might be afraid of them. They have enough pull to make me resign a volunteer position from a place I helped start."

"York's gathering the information from the center. I hear that was your idea."

I shake my head. "It was a collaborative idea."

He lifts my chin with his thumb. "Seeing you in action at the ER and then with Danny, I know you can take care of yourself and Nora and half the fucking town, Whit, but when this all comes to a head, it's gonna suck, not being able to take care of you. I want you to seriously consider going to Florida with me. I'll rent a house on the beach. Your grandparents can come. Nora's in school, yeah, but it's preschool, and she's no doubt smarter than all of them anyway. She won't have to hear whatever shit kids talk when their parents say too much in front of them, and I won't have to say *fuck ball* after one damn night away."

"My job."

"Nora asked if there were sick people in Florida. I'm guessing there are, but we could bring Danny and Chloe while they recuperate. Neither is going to be able to work."

A gargled, "In," comes from beside us.

Danny.

Danny's awake.

"*Shh,* … you have a tube to help you breathe." I stand up and walk over to him and hit the call button.

"Ow," he says and starts to lift his arm.

"And you have a broken arm and shoulder."

A nurse comes in and checks his vitals.

"They're good," I assure her.

"*Mmhmm,*" she says, no doubt not liking me telling her how to do her job. "Daniel, we're going to remove this, and it's not gonna feel all that good."

As soon as it comes out, he asks, "Does my dick still work?"

"Why would that be the first thing that comes out of your mouth after you almost died?" I scold him.

"Because it's the only part of my body that doesn't hurt." He turns his head and looks at Chloe. "How's my little hero?"

"She's got a few broken ribs, and she had to have surgery to fix the breaks in her arm."

"I'm going to kill that bastard."

"No, you're gonna let the state of Texas do that, if they see fit."

"They aren't gonna do shit 'cause we made it, even though it wasn't his intention."

"Before he came to Walton, he went to the center. He shot and killed Kris Krone and shot Alice as well."

"What?"

Pope gives him the information. "He wasn't going to do their drug deal until Alice gave him Chloe's whereabouts. She wouldn't get him the information, but Kris did, and he still killed him. Texas is gonna give him life or end his. Either way, he's done."

"After what he did to her, I want one fucking hour with him. Just one," Danny says, void of emotion.

"You damn fool, he did worse to you." Chloe opens her eyes and looks over. "He hurt you to get to me."

"You'll make it up to me."

She turns away, brows furrowed.

"Hey, Chloe Shaw, when we get out of here, we're going to relax on a beach, and then get Nora amped up about Disney World." He smiles like he does when he's trying to make others do the same thing. It usually works, but right now, it's not working on Chloe.

WHEN I SEE Kevin Seward's name, and remember today is the day they're supposed to meet, I feel sick to my stomach and whisper, "Tell him no."

After all that's happened, I'm shocked that after all that had happened, he'd have the balls to message him again.

I watch as Pope replies:

> A little busy this morning, I'll see you a noon.

Shaking my head, I tell him, "No."

"Whit, I wanna know what hand this fool thinks he has to play."

"No!"

"He's not wrong, Whit," Danny grumbles.

"I can't lose him again." I push his chest with both hands. "I won't lose you again!"

He grabs my shoulders and hauls me into him, wrapping me up in his arms. "I'm never gonna let that happen."

I glare up at him. "But you are. Right now, you're—"

"Participating in a collaboration." He kisses my forehead. "Marks has guys he trusts down here. He's not gonna be far, and neither are they. I'm going to make sure Seward shows his hand, and then I'm going to take every card he thinks he has to play and shove them down his fucking throat."

I INSISTED that both Danny and Chloe take their pain meds, knowing they both need them, but they refused so they could keep me what? Entertained? That's ridiculous. They're now out like a light, and I'm sitting here between them, swiping between the cameras at home, checking to make sure they're all safe, and Pope's location. Marks shared his location with me as well, which I know is to put me at ease, seeing that he is in fact close to the hotel downtown, where Pope changed the meeting to last minute.

When my screen lights up and I see Gram's number, I hit *Accept* to the FaceTime request.

Nora's face lights up the screen.

"Mommy, are you still at work?"

"I'm not working, little slugger, but I am at the hospital."

She smacks her forehead. "That's right. Miss Chloe

and Uncle Danny gots in an accident, and you had to go help them at a different hospital."

I'll never teach her that lying is okay, but this kind of lie is necessary to allow her to be a kid.

"And they didn't go to heaven, like my other mommy."

I swallow back the Nora-sized lump in my throat. "They're going to be okay, but they did get pretty banged up."

"Like me when I was little?"

"But they weren't in super-safe seats like you were."

"Can I talk to them? I wanna tell them *get well soon*, and we're making them snickerdoodle's, and I won't even try to eat them all."

"That's very sweet, Nora. They'll love the cookies."

"Well, can I talk to them?"

"They're sleeping, but they should be able to come home tomorrow. Chloe will be staying with us so we can help her."

"What about Uncle Danny?"

"Well, he might want to stay with his family, but if he wants, he can come over."

"His workers are making lots of noise in the garage rooms."

Shit, I didn't even think about that.

"We will figure it out."

"Where's my daddy?" She grins.

"He went to get us something to eat."

"Is he coming home soon? 'Cause we only have a few sleeps, and he missed one already."

"I promise we'll be back as soon as we can."

She pouts out her bottom lip. "Okay."

"I love you, Nora."

"I love you, and Daddy, and Uncle Danny, and Miss Chloe."

"What about me?" I hear York ask.

"Miss Gwen, too."

"You should hand Gram the phone so I can talk to her and go get Miss Gwen a cookie so she knows just how much you love her."

"Okay, Mommy!"

Gram holds the phone up so that I can see her and Popa B. "How you holding up, Whitley Mae?"

"Oh, you know." I shrug.

"You'll get through this whatever way you need to."

I nod. "John Paul offered something I never thought I'd consider, but there's bound to be a lot of talk in town, and I want to shield Nora from whatever we can."

"You going with your husband to Florida and then New York?" Gram smiles.

"I don't know. I just don't know if—"

"You do know, Whitley, or you wouldn't be having this conversation with us right now."

"I don't want to leave you two, and Nora has school and—"

"You're right." Popa B cuts me off. "Gossip has a way of making its way around Walton, and the story seems to have a way of changing from person to person. It's best for Nora and you to let things settle down. We'll miss you, but we'll be all right as long as you three are."

I wipe away a tear. "I feel like you're kicking me out."

Gram smiles softly. "You moved down the street a couple of days ago of your own accord. This is just a few more steps away."

"He didn't ask us to come to New York. He asked—"

"Whitley Mae, that man would put you and Nora in his pocket and take you wherever he went if you'd allow it."

"He said Chloe and Danny should come to Florida, too, so they can heal."

"Chloe could use a bit of time away from here."

"We'll probably have to go to court."

Popa B chuckles. "I reckon we'll all be there."

"Um, yeah, when did you get a gun?"

"Had once since I was about fifteen."

"I've never seen one."

"That's because a responsible gun owner only brings it out when necessary."

I want to ask him what Jesus would think, but I don't.

"You need any more reason to go with John Paul other than he's your husband? It's best for Nora not to hear the gossip, and he wants you and Nora, and Danny and Chloe, who by the grace of God are alive, there. We've had news vans around our little neighborhood all day. Been able to keep Nora busy, but if they come knocking on the door, it won't be easy."

I nod and tell them, "I love you both so much. I hope you know that."

"Whitley Mae, you've never given us a reason to question the depth in which you love us or anyone else."

"This will all blow over soon enough, and you all can come home whenever you want. We're always going to be here." Popa B winks. "Always."

I end the call and flip through screens as I head to the bathroom to fix my face and pull myself together before Danny and Chloe wake up and also to call Laurie and try not to start crying all over again.

POPE

20

Tuesday

Last night, when York went to the house, she spent hours going through Nelly's phone.

Today, Marks, and one of the state boys, and their tech geek ran the numbers. Nelly never erased, messages, or her call history. Most of the numbers she called were no longer in use, all prepaid numbers connected to ... no one. None of the numbers ever called or messaged were to Whitley or Pastor and Mrs. B. The phone was clearly a burner, just like the ones she'd contacted through it. The phone was last used the morning of the accident that took her life.

Pictures still remained, as well. Pictures of locations, like street signs, or "*Now Entering*" signs and many of public parks. She also took photos of her dashboard, showing dates and times. On the morning of her accident, she took the only selfie on the device—it was of her and Nora. It was the only way to prove the phone was, in fact, hers, aside from fingerprints. The team York and Marks put together were looking into those locations, hoping to find surveillance cameras that still had footage dating back that far.

They pulled up the accident report, which claimed she was at fault. With only one vehicle involved, it would be hard to prove otherwise, but not impossible, thanks to the evidence on the phone.

I didn't like the fact that I was lying to Whit about the location change of the meeting, but I dislike her worrying even more. Marks booked a room at the hotel, where he and the state boys, as well as a federal agent, prepared me with a wire for the meeting. I left my phone there, as well, swapping it out for one that had a tracking device in case shit went sideways.

It's not going to.

Stepping off the elevator that opens up to Kevin Seward's offices on the top floor, I expected to step into a bustling hive of volunteers buzzing about. But there isn't. There's not even a receptionist at the desk. Beyond reception are desks covered in flags, banners, and posters, emblazoned with the Seward name and slogan. One corner looks like a war room with maps and graphs of polling data, no doubt where they plot the campaign's next move, like generals on a battlefield. Giant whiteboards and cork-boards are covered in sticky notes, charts, mapping out precincts, fundraising goals, and messaging strategies.

Another corner is a cobbed-up press area with cameras, lights, and microphone stands, ready to capture false promises.

"Come on back, John Paul."

I turn toward the doorway Kevin Seward is standing in.

"They're all out for the next of couple hours, which will give us plenty of time to hash this out like men."

I walk in as he sits in a large leather chair across a mahogany table. I unbutton the sport coat I'm wearing and pull the phone out of my pocket, making a show of scrolling through messages that are not there, and then powering it off.

"I'd prefer no interruptions." I set the phone, screen up, on the desk.

He chuckles. "I leave my cell with my receptionist at eight o'clock and don't pick it up until I leave the office. Just surprised to see you doing that with all the happenings in Walton. I heard some Spud character attacked a friend of yours and one of Whitley's just last night."

I feel my jaw tense and want to slap that fake-as-hell look of concern off his face.

"Also heard you married Whitley."

"I was always going to marry Whitley," I grind out.

"Yes, so I heard, and that has been a problem for Kalvin. He was in love with that girl."

"He wasn't in love with her; he wanted something he knew was mine."

"John Paul, that's an arrogant way of thinking."

I un-ball my fists and flex them a bit before leaning back in the leather chair. "My first day at Walton, your son, who was years ahead of me, shoved me in a locker."

"Oh, Jesus, that was years ago."

"He continued bullying me that entire year and didn't stop until I hit a growth sport over the summer, and then I took his place on the varsity team."

"It was never his intention to become a sports celebrity," he says with a fucking condescending smile, trying to diminish my accomplishment.

"It's called a professional athlete," I say, trying to remain calm, but this motherfucker is pushing every button he can.

"Right." He sits back and steeples his fingers. "He was always better at golf. Could have been a *professional* athlete in that sport."

"Golf a sport?" I shrug. "I consider it part of my training regimen during the offseason. Might take it up *professionally* when I'm an older man."

He glares at me. I glare back.

"You know, I came here with some expectations that are not being met. Maybe an apology to my wife and a promise to put your son on a leash. I planned to offer to write you a check for his rear window and expected you to be a man and refuse it since his actions caused my reaction."

"My son is his own man."

"A man?" I laugh. "A man doesn't tear a phone away from a woman and step on her hand, injuring her when it drops on the ground because he sent messages to her phone when he was coked up. A man doesn't donate money to a women's shelter and ensure certain people in his organization are employed so he can use it as a place to exchange drugs for money and has the board, which is in his pocket and on the take, force the woman who had helped build that place and volunteered at it to resign."

"From what I understand, that's all fabricated."

"It's all caught on surveillance cameras. Just like the murder of your son's right-hand man, Kris Krone, by the man who delivers his drugs, Spud—"

"His sister, Alice—"

"Is innocent. She was shot too. But something you might want to know… right in front of me and Officer Marks, your son tried to get her to take the fall for that."

"What do you want?"

"Your son in prison and you to stop bullshitting the public that you have their best interest at heart."

He narrows his eyes at me. "You do know that's not going to happen."

"I can assure you, one day, it will. Until then, you can pull the funding for the shelter your son exchanged a victim's whereabouts to her abusers in order to manipulate him."

"I'm sure my money will be appreciated elsewhere. I assure you, my son did not have anything to do with what went down last night. He's a defense attorney and represents those men. That's the only connection."

He's clearly not caving. I need to bring this back to where I'm getting answers I need, that Whit needs.

"You expect others to believe that, but I'm not eating the shit you're shoveling. You might even be able to stomach it yourself because it's easier than figuring out how the hell you can be his father and not see who he truly is. As a father myself, I will not watch my kid go down the wrong path and not jack her up and put her back on the right one."

He says nothing. Doesn't even react.

He fucking knows.

I push forward.

"I'm telling you, there's evidence piling up against your son, and you'd better hope none of those stones being turned over exposes your involvement."

"I can assure you, I have nothing hidden."

I stand and grab my phone. "This meeting went a little off the rails."

He stands. "The car has been fixed. I don't want a check."

"Good, 'cause I wasn't gonna give you one," I grumble.

"And what should Kalvin expect from Whitley?"

"If he, or any of his lackeys, comes near her, or our

daughter, or anyone we love, he should expect a fucking war."

"They were together for quite some time. What if the child asks about him?"

And here we go, I think.

"Trust me; she won't."

"All right then. I'll see you out."

"No need."

CLIMBING into Whit's vehicle with plenty of time on the parking meter, I peel away from the curb as I power up the dummy phone.

Within a minute, I'm pulling up to the hotel and heading up to get these wires off.

Walking into the room, I look at the less-than-enthusiastic state and federal officers. "I pushed buttons. It will get back to his son, and that will lead to something more than we've already handed you."

"Pope, we're on the same team," Marks says as he pulls the suit jacket off that has the voice recorder wired into it.

"Who's on Alice's team? Whether Kevin is involved or not, she's not safe, and neither is the information no one but her is motivated to give."

"She was taken into protective custody last night. She's safe," one of the two detectives informs.

"Spud talking?" I ask.

"Asking for his lawyer every five minutes. We're taking our time fulfilling that request."

"What are your plans?" Marks asks me.

"Trying to convince my wife to take off with me, bring Danny and Chloe to recuperate. You and York get some time off and come hang with us."

"You're witnesses," one of them states sternly.

"You'll have to subpoena me if needed."

He narrows his eyes at me.

Marks chuckles. "You know how the girls used to get a period pass to get out of gym?"

I look at him like he's crazy.

"Pope needs one so he doesn't get in trouble for missing a game."

"Shit, right, he plays baseball."

I don't know if I should be bent out of shape that they didn't remember who I was or elated because they were focused on the task at hand. I go for the latter.

"Whit and I will do whatever we can, but, yeah, I'm gonna need a *period pass* if it's during training or regular season."

"We're going to be building this case brick by brick so they can't huff and puff and blow our case down. It's gonna take some time to do that and some time to get it on a docket and in front of a judge who isn't connected with Kalvin or his father." Marks winks. "He's going away."

HOLDING WHIT'S HAND, I pull out of the hospital parking garage and head toward Walton. Dany's parents and Marks are staying with Danny and Chloe for a night so that Whit and I can go see our girl and hopefully be packing bags and finding a house to rent.

"Are you going to tell me what happened?"

"Yeah, Whit, of course. I think he knows everything but turns a blind eye. In regard to Nora, I'm sure he has suspicions, but I don't think he has any intention of trying to get any sort of visitation." I continue by telling her verbatim what he said.

After that, she doesn't look any more or any less stressed.

"I'd like to discuss Nora, your grandparents, Danny and—"

"My grandparents will never leave." She turns and looks out the window. "Texas is their home, and work and life."

I pull her hand up and run my fingers across her knuckles.

"They think we should go."

"And what do you think?"

She turns and looks at me. "I've only ever been to Arizona, and now Nevada, and I'm scared. But it's best for Nora."

"I don't just want you two in Florida. I want you in New York, and if I get traded, I want you there with me, too." I swear my eyes are burning.

"And if things go bad, you're still open to Japan?" Tears fill her eyes.

"Whit, I'd take us to the moon."

She leans over and kisses my cheek. "I love you, John Paul."

"I love you."

"When should we leave?"

"With all the shit that's going on, I say the sooner, the better. I can book flights—"

"Danny can't fly after abdominal surgery for at least a week."

I chuckle. "I guess we rent something and drive then."

Smiling and, dare I say, a little excited, she pulls out her phone. "Clover Park, right?"

"Yeah, it's in Port St. Lucie."

"Louisiana, Mississippi, Alabama, Georgia—oops, nope, that's Florida. Three new states."

"If Georgia's just an oops away, we can hit that too if you want."

She shakes her head. "You've been to all these places."

"Not with you I haven't, and not with Nora."

She smiles big and real. "She's going to be so excited. Like off-the-hook excited."

"Yeah, she is." I laugh. "Admit it, Whit, so are we."

"And Danny and Chloe?" She covers her face. "They're gonna be so annoyed with us."

"We can drug them so they sleep through it."

"It's seventeen hours. That's crazy. It'll be like twenty hours with bathroom stops."

"Three hours of bathroom stops?" I laugh. "Might as well rent a big old RV with a bathroom."

"Can we?" She grins hugely. "Danny and Chloe can sleep the whole way and—"

"Jesus, Whit. Right now, you look just like Nora—or rather, she looks just like you. Oh, and, hell yes, let's rent an RV. We'll get an atlas, and you and Nora can mark off states. By the time she's in kindergarten, she'll have been to almost all of them."

"Wait—what?"

"I learned more while traveling with my parents than sitting in front of the TV. Until Nora has to be enrolled in school, travel with me. She'll love it, and so will you, Whit."

"I have to make money and pay our way. I can't just travel all over the country an—"

"Whit, your husband's making a mil a year, and that's just for the next two years. It'll be much more. We can afford to do cool shit with Nora before she starts kindergarten. Consider it our honeymoon."

She frowns. "I don't care about that kind of money."

"With all the shit going on, we're going to make the most of every dollar and every good moment we get."

WHIT

21

Us

Pope wanted me to tell Nora we were going, but I didn't want to. I wanted to watch the way she reacted to him telling her the news. Pope told her that the doctor said Danny and Chloe would heal better if they were around smiles and extra love. She, of course, volunteered. When he told her the doctor said that Florida was the best place to heal, but they needed another nurse, her stunning brown-and-gold-flecked eyes grew huge as she looked at me.

I didn't make her wait. I couldn't. I needed to bask in all the love she was, especially right then.

She dived on us, hugged us, kissed us. Then, she stood up, threw her hands in the air, and asked the most important question to her at that moment. "How many stuffies can I take?"

Spoiler alert: she brought them all.

Popa B and Gram brought us to get the RV, which was about ten minutes from the hospital. Nora completely freaked out as we loaded it up with the things we knew we'd need for us and Chloe.

Danny's parents, who had come the night he'd been shot, brought a bag for him. Gram and Popa B promised they'd stay safe and told us that they were planning to come to New York for the season opener. To that, Nora freaked out because she was jut finding out we were going to New York.

The house Pope rented had an enclosed pool, and Nora was in it more than half the day. I would have felt awful for Danny and Chloe being unable to use it, but they were enjoying getting to know one another. And when she told him that she wasn't going to be in any kind of relationship, even if it was just physical, until she could love herself first. Danny must have clearly changed after almost dying, because he didn't even make sexual jokes anymore.

The days we went to Clover Park, Nora was in her glory. I honestly believe she loved watching her daddy play ball more than she would enjoy Disney. We did do two days at Disney, and each day, she asked when we could go back to the house and swim ... after she got another stuffie, of course. Chloe loved it, and Danny loved that she did.

We received updates on the cases. Spud was charged with murder and is awaiting trial. He's still yet to talk. Alice decided she no longer wanted to be in witness protection. She retracted most of what she told the officers and investigators and basically said she had been under duress. She and Kal have been spotted meeting up.

Our last weekend in Florida, Marks and York visited for a couple of days and drove the RV back for us, with plans to take Danny and Chloe with them. She told me that they thought Kal and Alice were fucking. It made me sick to think of what a disgusting human being I allowed in my and Nora's life and in my bed and even more that there were brief moments when I wondered if I could deal with it to keep her safe.

The night before they were to leave, Pope asked me if I thought Chloe, who was amazing with Nora, would consider working with me on the charity he wanted me to start, thinking it would help her heal, and also as a nanny for us so we could go on dates on occasion. I fell harder for my husband.

When she said yes to our offer, she was even more excited because her sister, Cecilia, went to vet school in New York, and she hadn't seen her since she'd left for school last fall.

I knew it hurt Danny a little, but I also think that Pope was doing this for him, too, so that she could grow and heal like she'd said she wanted to, and then, one day, she would realize he loved her in a way no man ever had—the right way.

We have now been in his New Jersey house—or, I guess, *our* New Jersey house—for three days. Nora describes it as our "fancy, tall house" because, yes, it is fancy when compared to the house in Walton and even more so than the rental in Florida. and there's a twelve-foot ceiling, so it certainly seems tall.

On day one, we found out his tenant will be moving out in a month. Pope asked if we should rent it out or keep it for guests. I asked him why he would ask a question he already answered himself. When we offered it to Chloe, she looked a little scared, and I told her I'd rather she be here with us, anyway.

To that, she exhaled, "Thank you."

For years, I've been on a roller coaster of emotions, and even though there's no exit in sight, right now, I'm finally enjoying the ride.

TONIGHT, we're going out to dinner, just the two of us, alone for the first time.

L'Angolo d'Amore is a small family-owned restaurant with outdoor seating that we can see our front porch from.

Hand in hand, we walk down the street, looking at the New York skyline across the river.

"Be honest, do you like it here?"

"I do. It's completely different from home, but your neighborhood is much quieter than I expected."

"We'll check out the options for schools in our neighborhood tomorrow."

Ours.

"Chloe is making a list," I tell him. "She's going to be a great teacher."

"Or cosmetologist." He chuckles, as it's become an inside joke for all three of us.

"She's leaning more into teaching. It's more stable. She said she could still teach with a broken—"

He turns me to face him, cups my cheeks, and leans down to take my lips. One hand moves down my neck, gripping the base, and he uses his thumb to press the underside of my chin, causing me to lean back and open more fully to him.

He licks and sucks along the skin of my jaw, my neck, across my collarbone. He moves to claim my mouth again, his tongue swiping up and down mine, tasting me, groaning as he breaks our kiss.

"I just couldn't go another minute without kissing those beautiful lips of yours, *wife*."

"You don't hear me complaining, *husband*." And it's a good thing he doesn't hear my body buzzing or my insides softening as my core heats up.

"I should probably be the gentleman that Mom taught me to be and take my wife to dinner instead of ravishing her on a sidewalk."

Somehow, I manage to keep my thoughts about that to myself and attempt to be a lady. It's not easy though because, I love the way Pope ravishes me.

He moves to my side—closest to the road, of course—and takes my hand as we head to the crosswalk.

As we get closer, I swear I can smell the scent of garlic, tomatoes, and herbs in the air.

"This isn't just an Italian restaurant; it's a hidden gem."

"So, you've been here before?"

"I've never brought a woman here, Whitley, but I've had my share of takeout. You're going to love it."

We hurry across the road, still hand in hand, and he opens the door for me. "After you."

"Right this way, Mr. and Mrs. Paul," the hostess says, and I can't help but grin up at him.

He places his hand on the small of my back and guides me through rustic wooden tables, all topped with a candle, casting a spell of intimacy inside of this adorable little place.

I notice the black-and-white photographs on the wall are all people standing in front of rolling hills and a quaint village. It's quite stunning.

The sound of quiet conversation fills the air, as do the occasional clink of glasses and gentle instrumental music playing softly in the background. The ambiance is truly romantic. And I am so glad it is.

We're seated at a corner table for two, giving us a bit of privacy.

John Paul pulls my chair out for me, and I say, "Thank you." He then bends down and kisses the top of my head before walking around the table to take the seat beside me.

The hostess hands us a menu. It's handwritten in elegant script, almost like a love letter. I'm going to have to trust him on what to order, being that the only thing I recognize is chicken parmesan.

I don't even have to tell him that I want him to order; he just does. He also orders a bottle of red wine and a shared antipasto platter to start.

"Does that sound okay to you?" he asks.

I simply nod and wait for the hostess to pour still water into the glasses before she leaves us.

Staring up at him, I watch as he searches my face curiously.

"Tell me what you're thinking." He tucks a strand of hair behind my ear.

"I'm thinking that we've never really talked about what we want our family to look like."

"I wasn't joking when I said I wanted a lot of kids, but if that's not something you want, I understand. It is your body, after all, and it's gorgeous. I love your body."

"Let's say I wanted to give Nora a sibling sooner than later. How would you feel about that?"

He lifts my hand to his lips, brushing them across my knuckles. "I think, as a nurse, you know that it doesn't matter how strong a man's pull-out game is—it's not one hundred percent. I'm ready whenever you are, Whitley Mae Paul."

"How do you feel about a holiday baby?"

I watch as a smile begins to form on his stunning face. His beautiful blue eyes sparkle in the candlelight as he leans in and rubs his nose gently across mine. "Are you telling me you're pregnant?"

"I'm telling you that it's been over a month since my last cycle. Right before Vegas, actually. The fact that you did not fall out of your chair, in shock, I'm guessing you were aware of that already."

"A man can hope, and he can pray, and I'm not too proud to say I've done both. Tell me you're happy. Tell me you're as excited as I am."

"I am, and the timing couldn't be more perfect, it'll be the offseason. I'd be lying if I said I wasn't a little nervous, too, but that's to be expected."

"Nora's going to lose her mind."

I love the fact that he's beaming at the thought of telling her.

Laughing, I agree, "She certainly is. I think we should wait to tell her until the end of the first trimester."

"And I'm guessing you're not going to share the bottle of wine I ordered?"

"You're guessing right. And if there's any soft cheese on that appetizer platter, or processed meat, it is not going in my mouth."

He bends in and brushes his lips against mine. "I am so happy. Thank you. I love you, Whitley."

"I love you."

Dinner is delicious. For the main course, he ordered a plate of al dente pasta, swathed in a rich marinara sauce, and topped with plump, juicy meatballs. He knows me so well that he ordered something basic. I'm a sauce snob, and if it's not good, I'll never eat it again. It is amazing. Between Pope and me, we eat every bite, and then we share his favorite dessert, which is something I've never had—tiramisu.

"Espresso-soaked ladyfingers and creamy mascarpone. It's going to melt in your mouth, Whit."

And it does.

We sit and talk about Nora and then the season opener against the Yanks. He changes the subject to the charity and asks me what I envision. I'm honest. Women want to feel safe and strong, and I want to help them build that confidence. We also talk about how much I miss York and my work friends.

"I've seen you in action, Whit. You're amazing, and you love what you do. If you want to work, we'll figure it out."

"I do think I need to get my feet underneath me here first."

"And here, all I can think about is getting you home and off your feet." He winks.

And to that, we both know it's time to pay the check, grab the takeout order we placed to bring back to Chloe, and get home.

AT HOME, Pope double-checks that Nora didn't sneak in our room while I bring Chloe dinner.

"Thank you. Now go have some fun." She shoos me away.

As soon as I walk into the bedroom and shut the door, Pope locks it behind me. His mouth is on mine, his hands on my waist, and he's pulling me against him as he walks backward toward the massive California king—or as Nora and I call it, the Pope-sized bed.

After unbuttoning his shirt, my fingers inch up the hard, defined ridges and valleys of his torso. I break our kiss as he pulls my shirt over my head. As soon as it hits the floor, I'm back to exploring his abs, his chest, his shoulder muscles, and holding on there as he wraps an arm around me and lifts me before depositing me on the center of the bed.

"Love you so much, Whit."

The deep, raspy tone of his voice hits hard at my core and causes my nipples to pebble to painful points.

He quickly rids me of the skirt I wore to dinner and licks his lips as he hooks his thumbs under the strings at my hips and pulls my thong down my legs with a swiftness. Then he grips my ankles firmly before slowly running them up my legs. Pushing them apart, he settles between them.

"I can't wait to taste you."

A moan rips through me as his hands hook at the top of my thighs, yanking me closer to him. He grins up at me before burying his face between my legs. I feel the first flick of his tongue like a bolt of lightning hitting me straight at my core.

I pull on the duvet cover and arch my back as he does the same thing again, this time harder. I want to see him, watch how he licks me, how he sucks me, so I push up on my elbows just as he swirls his tongue around my clit.

"Oh, yes, yes, yes," I cry, hoping that I'm not too loud but unable to truly give a damn as I let my head fall back so I can soak up every ounce of this feeling as he continues sucking, licking, and fucking me with his tongue.

"Fucking tastes amazing," he groans, causing a vibration between my legs.

It's insane how good he is at this. An expert, I think.

His tongue runs flat, up and down the length of me before he inserts two fingers, stretching me open, and I attempt to muffle my cry.

He continues circling his tongue as he curls his fingers inside of me., pumping them in and out once, twice, three times, and then curls his fingers in a come-hither motion, like he's calling for my orgasm.

My legs begin to shake, and my back arches as my body responds to his request, his demand, him.

I come apart as he kisses up my body, holding himself

up with the one hand beside my head. He slicks his cock against my soaked center, and I curl up so that I can watch his beautiful cock fill me, inch by glorious inch, stretching uncomfortably at first, but I know—oh God, how I know—that feeling will turn into pleasure soon.

"I can't wait to fucking come inside of you, fill you up until you're overflowing."

My pussy contracts at his words, causing him to groan.

"You're fucking perfect everywhere. Beautiful, sexy, and sweet. You're everything I always knew you would be and so much more."

He slowly buries himself inside of me, so deep that it steals my breath. Then he rolls his hips as one of his massive arms pushes underneath me, holding me up so he can take my mouth again.

"See how good you taste? So fucking good."

He gently lowers me, grinding his hips once again as his tongue swirls with mine. His hand now cups my breast and rolls my nipple between his thumb and index finger.

"I love your tits." He leans down and sucks the other in his mouth, swirling his tongue around my tight peak.

My hips thrust forward, and he groans against me.

"You wanna come, don't you? You wanna coat my cock with your orgasm."

"Yes," I moan with the first thrust he delivers, so deep, so hard that his muscles flex.

I wrap my legs around him and grind against him, needing friction. "So good."

"You feel amazing. So fucking good." He continues thrusting deep and slow. Too slow.

"Faster," I whimper as my legs tighten around him.

And he does. He moves faster, harder, unleashing like he never has.

I grip his back, trying desperately not to sink my nails into the muscles working together beneath them.

"If this is too much, tell me." He sputters curses. "Tried to hold back, worried if I got you pregnant too soon, it would put too much pressure on you." He thrusts deep again. "Might have forgotten for a minute how strong you are."

"Don't you dare treat me like I'm going to break," I say before meeting him thrust for thrust.

This time, when I come, I do it into his chest, trying to muffle the cry from the strongest orgasm I have yet to feel. John Paul follows less than a minute later, his cock twitching, the hot liquid filling me, just as he said.

Hands on my face, he kisses me softly over and over again until his breathing, and mine, start to even out. "You're fucking amazing."

Eyes closed, I smile. "No, you are."

Epilogue

Seven Years Later

A year after we left Walton, Spud was doing life. And after gathering strong evidence that Kal was involved, the case against him was finally going to trial. It never did because Kal was killed in an accident. Karma? Maybe.

Whit was angry, so angry, and I couldn't blame her. There was enough evidence to convict him on several charges, and if they got the right jury, he could have been charged with Nelly's murder, as well. But, as it worked out, Nora would be sheltered from all that shit for a long time, maybe even forever.

When my contract was up with the Mets, and I declined their offer of a four-year, forty-million-dollar contract. Instead, I signed a three-year, twenty-million-dollar contract with Houston. The baseball world speculated that I was having a mental breakdown or that Whit and I were getting a divorce. The reality was, that Whit was pregnant with twins and with Nora and Baby B—

which is what Nora calls her little sister, Bianca Mildred Paul—and with Pastor and Mrs. B getting older and being asked to retire, we wanted to settle near them. So, we bought the field beside our house and built a bigger home for our family, giving them the house I grew up in. We also fund their ministry so they can continue spreading the Word at the jails and rehab centers nearby.

Danny and Chloe got married that summer, and they continue to work with us. Danny is always fixing something on one of the shelter properties or our homes, and Chloe flies with him to check in with the ladies. The program they've all put together is based on empowerment, and there are more success stories than not. When they're home, they're at the lake or with us. During the season, Chloe or York, who co-owns a PI firm with Marks, travels with Whit when she can make it. Two kids are doable. Four? That's a beautiful kind of chaos I don't think we were prepared for.

After Houston, Whit and I decided we were ready for a change again. After meeting the owner of the Jersey Jags and seeing that his team was run a hell of a lot different than any I'd played for, in a way that was like a family, I was interested. He had Leland Locke, who was playing for them, reach out to me. He'd never steered me wrong. He said the team might not win a lot of games, but it didn't feel like you were selling out to them. Chuck Turner was also playing for the Jags. He'd been a damn good friend when I'd played with him my first three years with the Mets.

We needed to make sure Danny and Chloe, who were expecting their first child, were willing to make the move. Chloe's sister had graduated veterinary school and happened to be working in Trenton and buying an animal clinic from a vet retiring. Chloe wanted to help her out.

So, I signed a four-year, fifty-million-dollar contract, and we moved.

The younger three had no memory of anywhere but Walton, so the change was big. Nora and Bianca loved it from day one. The boys, Gregory and Grant, took a week or so, but now, they all have dozens of friends and are involved in activities after school.

With the charities running themselves mostly, Whit sprang on me that she wanted to go back to work part-time, and she acted nervous. That was crazy to me. I told her that she should do whatever makes her happy, so my wife took on two shifts a week at Mercy West in the ER. She did that until she found out she was pregnant with baby number five. Chase is a year old now.

TODAY, after practice, we found out that our newest player, who is one of the best I've seen in years, our designated hitter's, Amias Steel, family is buying the team from the current owners.

To say it's a shock is an understatement, but we should have seen it coming. The stadium is shit compared to others, the ticket sales are way down, and I'm guessing the owners wanted to retire with some money and not broke.

I have zero idea what I want to do, which is why I'm not doing a damn thing until I talk to Whit, and then we'll talk to the kids and, of course, Danny and Chloe.

When I walk out to the parking lot, I see Amias is surrounded by a bunch of his people, and he doesn't look all that happy.

When I get to my vehicle parked next to his, I ask, "You good?"

"Fuck no, I'm not good," he huffs.

"Something I can help you with?" I ask, not wanting to leave him in a bad spot.

"Stop being a big-ass baby," one of the girls says to him.

"Stop getting all up in my business," he snaps back at her.

The girl, Tris, turns around. "I'm the youngest of us three, but he's the baby."

"Tris, that's one of my teammates, and you're—"

"One of the new owners of this dumpster fire of a team that we're going to make number one," she cuts him off.

I can't help but chuckle.

"You think I'm kidding?" she asks me.

"I think that's a good goal to set, but don't be too disappointed if it doesn't happen."

"Oh, it's gonna happen, and you're gonna help take us there. Which means you need to sign a new contract and stay with us."

"T, I'm not sure that's how negotiations work." The biggest one crosses his arms.

"Why don't you have an agent?" she asks.

"Never needed one," I answer, completely amused.

Another girl walks over and holds her hand up. "You're about here." She lowers her hand. "We need you at about here."

"She's Amias's older sister." T rolls her eyes. "And she's one of the new owners."

"Nice to meet you."

"Brisa. My name's Brisa." She holds out her hand, and I shake it.

The big kid starts walking over. "You remember me?"

"Sorry, I'm not sure I do."

"You have a wolf, wings, and—"

"Yeah, yeah, yeah. You did my tattoo." I reach out my hand, and he shakes it. "You still an artist?"

"I hit the city once in a while and work at one of our cousins Bella and her husband, Tag's, shops, or the one our grandmother, Momma Joe, owned. Our fathers all are pretty damn good with a pen. Justice Steel."

"JT." I nod. "I'd love to add to my piece. I have five kids that need representation."

"Anytime."

"Small world," I say, hitting the *unlock* button.

"It sure is. Look, we love this game. We pooled our money and bought this team when we heard Buck was thinking of selling. You're one of the best on here. We really want you to stay on."

"The rest of the team?" I ask.

"Lot of them are beat to hell." He's not wrong. "But we're not looking to pocket a bunch of money or fuck anyone over. We all have our own things going on. Tris, the mouthy one, is a little pop star. Brisa's a social media wiz. Kiki's husband is Brand Falcon—"

"Country singer?" I ask.

"Yeah."

"Um, hello? Pop star right here," Tris calls to us, and Amias drags her away.

I can't help but laugh.

"We're going to make this stadium a place people want to be. And we want you to do that with us."

"I need to talk to the boss. If we stay in, at least it'll be entertaining around here."

"Family man. Can't choose 'em, but never wanna lose 'em, you know?" He nods to them. "Forever Steel."

Taking First

LYING in bed with Chase on my chest, I look up and see Whit taking a picture.

"Next time, give me a heads-up, and I'll flex."

She laughs as she sits down and leans against the headboard, running her fingers through my hair. "What was it that JT kid said?"

"Family man. Can't choose 'em, but never wanna lose 'em?"

"No, I get that part, but then—"

"Forever Steel. Guessing it has something to do with their last name being Steel."

"Weird, right?" She looks up. "I googled the others. Tris was, in fact, the lead singer of a band called Four Play, and Brand Falcon is still topping charts."

"Yeah." I rub my lips across Chase's hair.

"So, what do *you* want to do?" she asks.

"Make about five more of these."

"When you can start carrying them, we'll talk. One day, my body's not going to bounce back."

"Your body's perfect," I tell her, because it damn sure is.

"Well, one day, I'll be on the trampoline with the kids and pissing my pants."

"One day?" I laugh, and she flicks my ear. "Hey."

"In my defense, I didn't piss my pants. My water broke, which was the intention. Chase would have never come out otherwise. Now, answer the question."

"Whit, I wanna do *you* for the rest of my life."

She bends down and kisses ... Chase.

"Not cool."

She leans in again and kisses my cheek.

"Better."

"Focus. Do you wanna keep playing?"

"I'm thirty-two with no injuries and making stupid

money that helps us do good things, but I'm also tired of being away from you all."

"And?"

I can't help but laugh. "It will be entertaining."

"Three years?"

"Yeah."

She nods. "If they promise to give you number 22, then yeah."

There is much more to come.

Read Amias's story now
Smashed Steel

Preorder
Stealing Second

Stealing Second

What's Next?

ROME

Even before Hudson received the request to join the virtual draft, I knew he was going to be a top pick. He's one of the best wide receivers out there. This past season—his senior year in college—he was the number one receiver in the nation. He says his game was elevated due to the connection he and the quarterback had. Still, he deserve this. He's worked for it and has the talent.

Am I saying this because I'm his brother? Hell no. I'm the first to give him a kick in the ass when he dogs on the field or messes up a play. Why does he take it? The same reason that, in every damn interview he's asked, "Who's your favorite player?". He still answers with my name, Roman Hart. It sure as hell wasn't our father who tossed a ball with him.

In high school, I was the number one player in both football and baseball. I received an MLB offer my senior year as well as scholarship offers for both sports to D1 schools. I chose football even though I love baseball, too.

Growing up, our mom pounded it in to our heads that friends, girlfriend—hell, even spouses—come and go, but the one thing we will always have is each other.

I once wrote a paper in school about the Aaron brothers, and another about the Alou brothers. At one time, all three of them, Felipe, Matty, and Jesús Alou, played for the San Fransisco Giants. There was one game all batted in the same inning. The next game, the three were in the outfield together. It blew my mind. I later learned that there were over four hundred sets of brothers playing a game they no doubt grew up playing together, in the majors. I wanted Hudson and I to be one of them.

Hud was good at baseball, but it was crystal clear football was his love.

When Hud got the call, he told me that he wouldn't ask me to be there if it would hurt me. Can't blame him. I'm pretty sure the one of two times I've ever cried was watching the draft and waiting for the phone to ring. It didn't.

I told him that there was no way I'd miss seeing his dumb-ass smile when he was picked. I also reminded him we were all stuck here under the same roof, so I'd be here regardless of whether he wanted me to be or not.

Grandma Hart's in her recliner with her dog, Zoey, on her lap, asleep. Mom and Jillian are beside me. And, as planned, I hit *accept* when Hudson gets the invitation to join a Zoom and mirror it on the TV that we dragged out of my room for the occasion so he and two other teammates, who were also invited to be available live, could be together. The three deduced that at least one of them was gonna get picked, and if the rest didn't, it would make for good TV.

"Nobody cries man, nobody," one of his teammates says right away.

The hot brunette with the QB and coach palms her face and groans then sighs, "We've been through this. Every one of you is to be as excited for any of you who gets picked. Owners want team players. This draft isn't the end all be all. You could still get an offer. So yeah Hunt, no crying."

The brunette, that Hud mentioned before, said she was an agent they all agreed to sign with when the time came. I tried not to overstep but told him to make sure he's careful. He told me she was already working on sponsorship deals and would be taking less of a cut than the other agents who'd contacted them. Apparently, she's a friend from college whose already signed some of their hockey friends and they're making bank. Mom confirmed, but yeah, I still looked into it. Seems solid.

As they're chatting I give Mom's hand a squeeze to grab her attention, then nod toward the main TV where they've been airing highlights when one of Hudson's biggest play, a Hail Mary that helped them cinch a bowl game is being aired. She tries to hide her excitement, but I'm not having it.

"So help me God, Linda, if you give me another look like that, I'm gonna quit my job and join the military."

Our sister Jillian, giggles.

"First of all, it's Mom. Second, I would kneecap you and—"

I pop a kiss to the top of her head. "Today is all about Hud's shot, yeah?"

"Yeah."

A few minutes later, they cut to a commercial, and Hudson mutes the call he's on. He turns and looks at me, "If it wasn't for you all, this wouldn't—"

"You worked for this. This is your moment. Shine."

He nods once but still looks miserable.

"Bro, fix your face and take this in. You are going to kill it in the pros, but not if you keep carrying around extra baggage."

His jaw sets.

"Come on man; this is a win for us all. Am I right!"

"I may not—"

"Am I fucking right!" I cut him off.

Jillian snorts.

"Rome!" Mom scolds.

Hud laughs. "Yeah, you are."

I nod toward the TV. "It's go time bro."

"Is it time?" Gram wakes and starts sitting up in her chair, and Jillian goes to help her.

Zoey hops off her lap and trots over to my feet. I pat my lap, and she tries, she really wants to, but she can't jump up anymore. So, I bend down and scoop her up.

The commissioner begins with the normal shit about unprecedented times, and I'm zoning out already. I hate this shit. I don't see why people can't just stay the fuck away from each other if they're not needed to assist those who need help.

Mom and Hud give me shit about the fact not everyone is as antisocial as I am. It's not that I'm antisocial. I like people enough, unless they're assholes.

Taking First

The first draft pick usually goes to the team with the worst record from the previous season. This gives them the chance to snag the top talent that college football has to offer. Helps to even the playing field so to speak. It's like being handed the key to unlock a treasure trove of potential. That key goes to the New York Knights being they're dead last.

"'Ladies and gentlemen, tonight marks a pivotal moment in the journey for the new New York Knights." The camera spans out, showing bones of a stadium being built. "I'm one of the owners Lucas Links, and this is our coach Trucker Cohen. We've both been where you are, waiting to be picked by a team to bring us on, make us part of the family. As we stand before you, we're filled with an overwhelming sense of pride and excitement for what lies ahead for the Knights."

Cohen steps up. "But before we delve into the future, we want to take a moment to express our deepest gratitude to the passionate supporters who've stood by us through thick and thin. Your unwavering dedication fuels our drive for excellence, and it's with your support that we embark on this exciting new chapter."

Links takes over, "Now, onto the reason we're all gathered here tonight – the NFL draft. With our pick, we have evaluated the talent, weighed our options, and deliberated tirelessly to ensure that we make the best decision for our team's future."

Cohen smiles. "And so, it is with great enthusiasm that we announce our selection. With the 1st pick in the NFL draft, the New York Knights proudly selects Cody Warren from Lincoln. Cody embodies the values and spirit of our organization, and we believe wholeheartedly in his ability to make an immediate impact on our quest for greatness."

Hudson flies out of his seat, throwing both arms in the

air cheering for his teammate and so does the other kid, Hunt. Cody is visually shocked, the chick with him is beaming.

When Links holds up the black and gold jersey with his name on the back, they finally quiet down and laugh as they watch their reactions being shown to the entire country.

Links smiles as he watches the monitors. "Welcome to the Knights' family, kid. You are now a part of something that's going to grow even bigger than any of us. Together, we'll chase our collective dreams with unwavering determination. We're going to build a legacy."

Cohen speaks again, "To our fans, I urge you to join us in embracing this exciting new chapter as we bring this team to a class it's never known. Together, let's rally behind our new players, and the entire New York Knights roster."

Links chuckles. "And to those who aren't willing to embrace the change," —he holds up two fingers—, "deuce's."

Cody graciously thanks them with his words measured and deliberate.

After the first round is done, they go to break and Hudson and the guys all go absolutely nuts. I love this for him. He's worked hard for it.

Before they start the second round, Hudson looks at me, and I know that look— he's freaking out but doing a good job hiding it.

"Wide receivers are typically rounds three though six, strap in."

He runs a hand through his hair and nods. "Thanks, man."

The commissioner introduces the Knights again, and this time, three people walk out.

"Good evening, I'm Logan Links, and this is my wife,

London. We're also part-owners of the New York Knights."

London steps up, smiling, "We were told to be on better behavior than my father-in-law." She grins, holds up two fingers and laughs. "We're not going anywhere."

Logan rolls his eyes, and she looks at the other girl and they both snickering.

Is this odd? Little bit, yeah.

"I'm Riley Brooks." The other girl quickly flashes two fingers with a little smirk then continues, "There are things that should always go together, like Logan and London here, peanut butter and jelly, and ham and pineapple on pizza." London makes a face at Riley, who grins, then she continues. She doesn't have to, though, because I know exactly where this is going on. One glance, at the screen and it's obvious that his teammates and coach do, as well. "We may not all agree with the last example, but the owners and staff of the New York Knights all agree that there are few players in this year's draft who have a kind of obvious chemistry that Hudson Hart and Cody Warren share." My brother looks back at me in total shock as she continues,"The Knights are excited to announce our second-round pick for this NFL draft is also from Lincoln. Hudson Hart, welcome to the family."

After all the cheering, hugs, and congratulations are shared, Hudson sits back down in his seat.

"I have no idea what to say, other than thank you. Thank you to my family for all their support. My brother, Roman." He pounds a fist to his chest and points to me. "To my coaches through the years, especially this one." He points to his college coach who is wiping away tears, again. "And a huge thank you to the new New York Knights. Cody and I will not let you down." He holds up two fingers and we all bust up. "And we won't let the faithful fans of the Knights down either. Hell we'll bring a few more to join you."

×

WE WATCH the whole damn draft, and during commercials, the agent, Drew Daniels, has reporters all lined up, and adding them to different chats for interviews. It isn't until the draft was over that the owners of the Knights pop on and offer Hunt a place on the team, too.

Not gonna lie, I knew what he was feeling before that. I'm almost as happy for him as I am Hudson… almost.

As they all say their goodbyes for the night, I stand to start cleaning up so Mom doesn't have to before we all go to bed for the night, because tomorrow is going to be a long day with virtual contract negotiations.

Before I retire for the night, I make damn sure Hudson knows how proud I am of him.

He tears up. "Bro, the sky's the limit now. Take a year off, go back and get your Master's so you can make more. Hell, get a whole new degree so you can stop teaching and coaching at the center. I can handle the bills now, man. It's my turn to support this family."

"The truth is I love teaching and coaching. Maybe not this virtual shit, but I'm happy. I'm good. Just make sure you get Mom, Jillian, Granny, and I tickets to every damn game, including the super bowl."

"I'm gonna buy us a huge house in New York. You can teach there."

"I'm so fucking proud of you."

×

"ROME," Hudson says, shaking me.

I slowly open my eyes and see it's still dark. "Bro, I'm stoked for you but the sun has yet to rise."

"You have an interview request."

I roll over, giving him my back. "Tell that hot ass agent to schedule shit after the damn sun comes up."

I hear deep laughter. It's not from Hud, and it's certainly not Mom.

"Hudson, if you have me on IG or one of your social media channels that's a real bad idea and there will be consequences," I warn.

"Roman Hart, we just have a couple questions, and then we'll let you get back to your beauty sleep."

Fucking annoyed, I roll over and shoot daggers out of my eyes at Hud as I sit up and take the phone that he's all but shoving in my face.

Looking at the screen I see four men in maybe their forties —fuck, I don't know. I suck at guessing ages— sitting in a conference room and then I see the damn time. Six thirty in the damn morning!

"He's got good hair." One says.

"Nice shoulders too," Another says.

Nuh uh, nope, this shit is not happening.

"Look, gentleman, it's six thirty in the morning and as you can imagine, we were up pretty late last night, celebrating my brother's accomplishment."

"Nice voice, too." One of them chuckles.

"All right, this is a bit odd, so if you want an interview, you might want to start asking questions, yeah? And you might want to hurry up because I'm getting feet pic vibes, and I'm not down with that."

One grins as he smacks his hands together and rubs them. "Yep, I want him."

"Okay, hitting end." .

Finger hovering above the screen, one asks, "Tell us, how does it feel to have your kid brother going pro."

I arch a brow, waiting for one of them to say some stupid shit.

"Bro, answer," Hudson whispers.

I glare at him then look back at the screen. "He's earned it. Best wide receiver in the draft yesterday. He—"

"You think he's better than you?" One of them asks.

What the fuck?

"He was drafted so, obviously, he *is* better."

"Heard that you were offered MLB and turned it down. Why the hell would you do that?" one of them asks.

My jaw muscles tighten as I hold back the obscenities I wanna throw at these assholes.

"Be honest kid. We want to know."

Fuckers.

"Football was more of a challenge for me. But more than that, I thought it would be cool to play in the same league, maybe even on the same team, as my brother one day."

One of them leans forward. "Kid, I'm gonna be honest with you; you dodged a bullet with that one." He throw his thumb over his shoulder. "I work with all three of my brothers and it's not all its cracked up to be."

"Truth," One agrees.

Another asks, "You may have liked the challenge of football, but baseball was the better choice for you, don't you think?"

I scrub a hand over my messy- as -fuck hair. "You know, sometimes you make choices in life, and it may not pan out the way you'd thought it would. You move on, you find another thing you love, and you celebrate the hell out of your brother's victory. So let's get back on track now, yeah?"

"We'd rather talk about you and baseball. It's a better sport."

What the fuck is wrong with these fools.

Another one nods his agreement. "Intelligent sport."

"And no pads, so if your ass looks good in the pants, you simply have a good ass." One chuckles.

"Makes baseball a less deceptive sport, too." One of them leans forward and jots something down on a legal pad.

I glance at Hudson, and his shoulders and palms rise while he mouths, "*I have no idea what the hell this is.*"

"How far is the drive to Bumble-fuck-Valley, New York, to Trenton, New Jersey?" One asks me.

"Not sure, but I'm guessing Google would let you know," I answer dryly.

The one who looks like he stares in the mirror while he's fucking leans in and steeples his fingers. "Look, kid, you passed on major league baseball, which was a major fuck up on your part because why?" he asks, looking at the others.

They all answer in unison, "Because baseball loved Roman Hart more than Roman Hart loved baseball."

I'm ready to light into them when Steepled Fingers says, "You know, I did some dumb shit when I was your age, too. Took getting into a relationship to realize that life does give second chances."

"Speaking of relationships." One holds up the legal pad, and it says:

Roman Hart,
Do you love me?
Yes

Or
No
Circle one.
XOXO
Baseball

"LOOK, I've played nice, but you four need the kind of help that only Jesus, your momma or a good shrink can give you. I'm not any of them."

The fools crack up.

Then one of them holds up another legal pad, and I can't see it, nor am I gonna look to hard because I think it would encourage them.

"You have a nice—"

"All right, you four, go back home and let us do this." Someone snags the phone off the stand and shakes his head. "You can't pick family, but you can pick baseball. Even though those four are far less mature than their kids." He flashes the camera around the room, and I see it's full.

"Don't piss on *our find*," one of the older men growls.

"Show him the notepad. It's fucking brilliant," another chimes in.

"You four need to find a hobbies," a female huffs, standing in front of the camera and holding the pad up again. This time, I can read it.

My heart pounds out of my chest as Hudson sits behind me reading it, too.

Swear to God, I can't breathe.

The phone is set back where it originally was, and now half a dozen people, all about my age are standing behind the men, all of them smiling.

"Hey, kid, I'm Zandor Steel. You may not know me, but I'm Amias Steel's father."

"Holy shit," Hud whispers.

Steepled Fingers, aka Zandor, continues, "When the world opens back up, we'd like you to join the Jersey Jags in Florida for spring training." He holds up the notepad again.

Roman Hart,
Would you like to join the Jersey Jags for spring training and a second chance?
Circle
Yes
Or
No

The Steel Family

"WE WANT to take a chance on you; how about you take a chance on us?" One of the older men smiles.

"Hell yes, he will." Hudson dives on me.

"I have a job, kids who depend on me—"

Hudson covers my mouth with his big paw. "Circle *yes*, you idiot."

"We're hearing end of June, beginning of July, before training camps opening back up."

I push Hudson off me, and we both look at the screen again. They're all smiling.

Zandor chuckles. "Give us a couple weeks and nothing less than a hundred ten percent, and we'll give you either a contract or a handshake."

"Bro"—Hudson throws his hands in the air—"what are you even doing? This isn't just my time now; it's *our* time. Say hell yes!"

I catch Mom and Jillian out of the corner of my eyes as Mom wipes a tear away while holding her phone up, no doubt recording this.

I can't help but laugh and make a circle with my finger. "Yes. Hell yeah. Let's do this."

Roman's story releases April 18th
Stealing Second

Hudson's story is coming in July
Title TBD

Thank You

To the reader of this book

Hey you, the person who picked up **Taking First** and took a chance on it, **THANK YOU** .
Your support means everything to me! Seriously, seeing you dive into the world of the characters that keep me awake at night, and feel all the feels alongside them is incredible.
I hope you enjoy Pope and Whit's story as much as I enjoyed writing it.
Your enthusiasm keeps me going.
I'm so grateful and blessed to have you on this journey with me.
Forever Steel,
MJ

Books by MJ Fields
MJ FIELDS

Rounding The Bases
Baseball Romance
Taking First
Steeling Second
Coming soon
Force at Third
Catching Feels

Taking The Shot
(Recommended reading order)
Hockey Romance
Long Shot
Snap Shot
Hot Shot
Flip Shot
The Holiday Hat Trick

THE STEEL WORLDS
(Recommended reading order)
The Men of Steel Series

Taking First
Jase
Cyrus
Zandor
Xavier
Forever Family
Raising Steel
Or get the
Men Of Steel complete box set

The Ties of Steel Series
Abe
Dominic
Eroe
Sabato
Or get the
Ties of Steel complete box set

The Rockers of Steel Series
Memphis Black
Finn Beckett
River James
Billy Jeffers
or get the
Rockers of Steel complete box set

The Match Duet
Match This!
ImPerfectly Matched!
or get the
complete duet

The Steel Country Series
Hammered
Destroyed
Wasted

or get the
Steel Country complete box set

Tied in Steel series
Valentina
Paige
Gia
or get the
Tied in Steel complete box set

Steel Crew
(Generation 2)
Tagged Steel
Branded Steel
Laced Steel
Justified Steel
Tricked Steel
Busted Steel
Smashed Steel
Marked Steel
Maxed Steel

Mercy West
No Mercy

THE LEGACY SERIES FAMILY OF BOOKS
(Recommended reading order)
The Blue Valley series
Football Romance
Blue Love
New Love
Sad Love
True Love

Taking First

Blue Valley series spin offs

The Way We Fell
The Way The Wildflowers Grow
Coming soon
The Way The Heart Breaks

The Brody Hines series
Rockstar Romance
Wrapped In Silk
Wrapped In Armor
Wrapped In Us

The Burning Souls
Rockstar Romance
Stained
Forged
Merged

Love You Anyway

The Truth About Love Duet
27 Truths
27 Lies

The Firsts series
Football Romance
Her First Kiss
His First Crush
Their First fall
27 Truths About Their First Goodbye
Their First Time

The Norfolk Series

Irons
Shadows
Titan

Timeless Love series
Unraveled
Deserving Me
Hearts So Big
Couture Love

The Caldwell Brothers Series
(co-written w/ Chelsea Camaron)
Hendrix
Morrison
Jagger
Visibly Broken
Use Me

Standalones
Basketball romance
Offensive Rebound

The Holiday Springs series
(co-written w/ Jessica Ruben)
Broody Brit
Irresistible Irishman

About the Author

MJ Fields is a **USA Today bestselling** author of contemporary and new adult romance novels. She lives in New York with her daughter, smoochie faced Newfie, Theo, and diva/terror Ellie
When she's not locked away in the cave, she enjoys spending time with her family, watching sports, listening to live music, taking in a show, singing off key, dancing to her own beat, listening to audio books, and reading— of course.
Forever Steel!
Join MJ's mailing list:
http://bit.ly/MJFNews

Follow MJ on BookBub:
bookbub.com/authors/mj-fields

Check out MJ's website
www.mjfieldsbooks.com

Made in the USA
Columbia, SC
07 June 2024